Catered All the Way

AN MM HOLIDAY ROMANCE

ANNABETH ALBERT

Catered All the Way

Copyright © 2023 by Annabeth Albert

All rights reserved.

No part of this book may be reproduced in any form or by any electronic or mechanical means, including information storage and retrieval systems, without written permission from the author, except for the use of brief quotations in a book review.

Cover Illustration: Lauren Dombrowski
Photo Design: Reese Dante
Edited by: Abbie Nicole

 Created with Vellum

Catered All the Way

Tis the season for a hopeless crush on my older brother's best friend…

This year will be different. I'm all grown up, my gaming channel is a huge success, and I finally have the confidence to make my move on Atlas Orion, the hottest chief in the navy.

However, I don't intend for my smooth move to be covering Atlas in cranberry sauce. Not at all how I want to reintroduce myself to my new roomie and coworker. Atlas is in town to help save Seasons, my family's historic holiday gift shop and event space. Seasons is booked solid with catered parties, so we need to avoid any more disasters.

Like my malfunctioning air mattress. We're down to one bed, two dudes, and a whole lot of holiday-fling temptation. Atlas has never been with a guy, but I don't have to do much persuading. And what better way to explore than a secret romp? No strings, and no one has to know.

The problem? With every passing week, I fall harder for Atlas, who's far more than his drool-worthy muscles and heroic job. He's kind, funny, makes me breakfast in bed, and each midnight snowball fight brings us that much closer to heartbreak.

Atlas can't stay in Kringle's Crossing forever, and I can't

imagine leaving the only place I've called home. Our feelings run deep, but is it a holiday illusion? Can we find our way to a lasting future?

Catered All the Way *is a brand-new, full-length holiday romance from the beloved author of* **The Geek Who Saved Christmas.** *Lovers of stand-alone swoon-worthy Christmas stories will fall for this geek + military pairing. Full of spicy first times, bisexual awakening, quirky small-town residents, and guest appearances from some fan-favorite characters, this only one bed, brother's best friend romance is sure to find a place under many trees! Dual POV and the happiest of endings guaranteed.*

Author's Note/Content Advisory

CATERED ALL THE WAY is a lighthearted holiday romp, but it does touch very gently on issues of grief, loss, and neglectful parenting, all in the past. Like all my military romances, the realities of military service are briefly mentioned. A happy ending is guaranteed!

Kringle's Crossing is a made-up small town somewhere west of the Philadelphia metro area. CATERED ALL THE WAY takes place in the same universe as THE GEEK WHO SAVED CHRISTMAS and my other novels, but it is entirely a stand-alone. Longtime readers will enjoy the Easter egg hunt! Any resemblance to real towns, persons, places, businesses, and situations are entirely coincidental.

*To Abbie Nicole.
I always say I couldn't do it without you, but this one truly wouldn't be here without you.*

One

ZEB

THANKSGIVING DAY: 30 SHOPPING DAYS UNTIL CHRISTMAS

"What do you mean Atlas isn't coming?" I glared at my older brother, who always managed to bring out my grumpy side, especially this early on Thanksgiving. Not that it was the crack of dawn, but I was dragging because I'd streamed late into the night on an important collaboration with some popular Australian gamers. However, I didn't dare mention my tiredness to Gabe. I'd already been scolded for being ten minutes late to help prep for the annual Thanksgiving dinner hosted at Seasons, our family-run gift shop and event space.

"There was some sort of delay again with his flight back to the States from wherever he's been deployed." Gabe sighed, the same world-weary sound he made whenever Atlas, his longtime best friend, had to cancel plans because the navy wanted to whisk him away. It was the same heavy exhale Gabe did when I disappointed him too. A natural manager, Gabe had been born precisely on time

1

with high expectations for the rest of the world. "It's okay. We can make do with a limited crew as long as no one else calls out."

"And you wanted to lecture me about my reliability earlier?" I continued my work setting up the cold section of the buffet, which would house various salads and condiments, before leading into the dessert section full of pie slices. We'd expected Atlas to arrive two days ago, and I should have known better than to count on that timeline. "How many times over the years has Atlas let you down, Gabriel? Shouldn't a freaking SEAL assistant be more reliable?"

"I don't know, *Zebediah*." Gabe matched my deliberate use of his hated first name. "He's out there saving the world. More important things to do than play bartender for Seasons, that's for sure." For all Gabe's good qualities, and he did have them, irony wasn't his strong suit. "And the technical term is SEAL support, which is possibly even more mission-critical."

"So what you're saying is you're fine with not being a priority." I plopped a large green salad into the refrigerated buffet table. I wasn't truly upset with Gabe. Or Atlas, for that matter. Gabe liked to paint him as some sort of superhero, which wasn't that far off the mark. Atlas wasn't a flake. All the times he'd had to cancel, he'd had world-hanging-in-the-balance emergencies. Couldn't argue with that. And we could manage fine without Atlas's help for the upcoming holiday season. But even so, I felt deflated, like an off-balance parade balloon sagging too low.

I'd had *plans* for his month-long leave, damn it. For the first time, I was ready for Atlas to see me as something other than Gabe's pesky little brother. I wanted to impress him. I had no idea if he was into guys, but I was more than willing to find out. And all my plans required Atlas in the flesh, so yes, I was a little cranky.

And reckless. My unintended force made the salad contents dance around inside the clear bowl.

"Watch what you're doing." Gabe's voice was as sharp as if I'd scattered greens everywhere, yet all the contents were perfectly safe under a layer of plastic wrap. "You're going to drop something."

"You think I don't know how to set a buffet table by now?" I rolled my eyes because I, like Gabe, had grown up in this place. I could prep Thanksgiving dinner in my sleep. Speaking of which, I stifled another yawn.

"I don't know, Mr. Priorities," Gabe shot back. "You missed the Bauman's annual Halloween party because of your gamer friends—"

"I was at a con." I was exhausted by his constant minimization of my chosen career. And yes, I'd missed a couple of fall bookings, but I'd had good reason. "It was one of the largest gaming conventions, and I was on a panel—"

"Uh-huh." Gabe sounded distracted, which was his permanent condition these days. And it wasn't like I didn't sympathize—the business was struggling, expenses were up, and he and Paige were expecting twins. Impending parenthood or not, I had a hard time keeping my cool when he started rearranging the items I'd laid out.

"What are you doing? The buffet looks fine."

"The bowls weren't spaced evenly, and they'll look better grouped by size."

"Whatever. Suit yourself." I tried to let Gabe's pickiness go, but he kept huffing as he moved items around. And every micro-adjustment served to remind me he hadn't heard a word I'd said earlier. "Why do you keep acting like I'm still some couch-surfing slacker?"

"Because you're too old to be working here part-time. Being a gamer is not a viable profession." His big-brother-knows-best voice had grated even before our parents died in a car crash a decade ago, and now I chafed whenever Gabe went all paternalistic on me.

"It's hardly like the small-business life is super stable." The ongoing cash flow issue here at Seasons was a low blow, but he was the one who kept treating me like I was still seventeen, living on corn chips and energy drinks and playing games with other broke teens all night. However, I was reformed and on a mission to get the world, especially Gabe, to finally take me seriously. "And I'm making money now."

"I know you are." Gabe might as well go ahead and ruffle my hair. "But hospitality is evergreen. Just like Seasons." He did love to tout the long history of Seasons. For all he worried about money, he also tended to ignore how trends changed and fewer people rented small-town event halls now. Proving my point, he thrust a giant crystal bowl of cranberry sauce at me. "Hold this."

"WTF? The cranberry sauce was fine in the middle where it always goes."

"Your placement wasn't the middle."

"Why do you have to be such a perfectionist about everything?" I used to wish I could be more like Gabe. Perhaps then we would get along better. Maybe if I developed a love of ironing, early mornings, and precise details, we wouldn't fight so much. But these days, I liked who I was. I simply wished Gabe didn't always manage to bring out my inner whiny kid.

"I don't know, Zeb." Instead of taking the cranberry sauce back, Gabe moved three other smaller bowls fractions of an inch this way and that. "Why do you have to be lackadaisical?"

"That's right. Go for the ten-dollar word." Trying to tamp down my ire, I managed half a chuckle. Gabe did love Scrabble and every other word game that came his way, having inherited our grandfather's love of crosswords.

"Atlas." Gabe's eyes widened, and his gaze drifted over my left shoulder.

"Good one, bro," I groaned. When Gabe wasn't micromanaging the business, we had a long history of minor pranks on each other. Every now and then, the dude managed to find his sense of humor. "Act like he's right behind me and could hear me ranting about him no-showing mere hours before—"

"Hey, Gabe." That distinctive, deep, dark, and delicious voice could only belong to one person.

"Atlas." I, on the other hand, squeaked like a freaking gerbil as I whirled around. The cranberries came with me, a tidal wave of cold red sauce that was no match for the thin plastic wrap over the top of the bowl. And oh my fucking God, Atlas Freaking Orion was right there, like mere inches behind me, and I crashed into him, sloshing berries everywhere, including all over the one guy I wanted to impress this holiday season.

"Zeb." Gabe went straight for scolding me. "What did you do?"

"I told you the sauce was fine where it was." I glared at Gabe because anger was far more practical than embarrassment. I'd had plans, and this unmitigated disaster was not in any of them.

"Uh, guys?" Atlas glanced between Gabe and me. "Some help?"

Oh, right. While Gabe and I were trying to score points off each other, Atlas was wearing gallons of sauce. Atlas was every bit as tall as I remembered and quite possibly broader. Paige and Gabe had visited him in Virginia a couple of times, but pictures hadn't done the man justice. Ripped like an action star, he'd trimmed his black hair super short. The look was hot as hell on him, especially with his Mediterranean coloring and dark eyes. He had on the sort of everyday BDUs all the navy guys seemed to wear on duty unless it was a formal occasion. Sadly, the uniform was soaked and probably done for.

"Sorry—" I started, only to be cut off by Gabe.

"Sorry, Atlas. You probably remember my little brother, Zebediah. Always causing mayhem. But it's good to see you." He grabbed an entirely inadequate bar towel from the cart I'd used to bring in the salads and handed it to Atlas before clapping him on the one clean spot on his meaty shoulder. "Thought you weren't going to make it."

"Me too. I caught the last transport out of DC right before my phone ran out of power, then lucked into a ride heading this direction." He sponged off his face before turning his attention to me. "And this is little Zeb? I remember you being a kid in high school—"

"I'm twenty-eight now," I brightly informed him. My tone was too crisp, tinged by my irritation at Gabe. "Neither little nor a kid, despite what my elder statesman of a brother thinks. Time flies."

"Huh. I guess it has been a while since I've been back." Atlas rubbed his stubbled jaw. Probably hadn't shaved or slept in a couple of days, given his tired red eyes, and I immediately felt bad for the dig at his lengthy absence. My shoulders slumped, and my gaze dropped to the messy floor.

"Let's get you cleaned up," Gabe said to Atlas before

turning back to me. "You work on this mess, and I'll help Atlas find a spare server's uniform."

"Guess I would have needed to change anyway." Atlas was far more good-natured than either of us deserved. "But I might need hosing down first."

"There's a shower," Gabe steered him toward the double black doors that led to the kitchen area. "I'll show you."

"I remember." Atlas chuckled fondly. Why, oh why, did every damn thing on the man, including his laugh, have to be so sexy?

"Oh, that's right." Gabe joined in Atlas's laughter. "Didn't my dad catch you and Marla Kleinsdorf in there senior year?"

"She needed help getting glitter out of her hair after her birthday party." Atlas sounded more factual than bragging, but my back still tensed. Maybe his perpetual bachelor status wasn't the sort of clue to his sexuality that I'd hoped for.

"Sure, buddy, sure. She still lives in the area, you know." The way my luck was running, Gabe would have Atlas and Marla, who owned a flower shop, engaged before December. Pausing at the kitchen door, Gabe turned back to me as I attempted to scrub the worst of the sauce from the carpet. "And, Zeb, don't try to salvage the table linens. Fresh set. Our guests have high expectations of a Seasons' Thanksgiving dinner."

"I'm aware." My voice was crouton dry, not that either of them would notice.

"And for God's sake, smile." Gabe gave me the widest, fakest grin ever. "It's the happiest time of year."

Uh-huh. More like about to be the longest month of my life.

Two

ATLAS

I took my time in the shower in the corner of the employee changing room. It had been a while since I'd had unlimited hot water at my disposal. No one waiting for either the shower or my attention was a nice luxury to boot. Enjoying the relative privacy, I put an upbeat playlist on low on my phone while it charged. A power nap would probably serve me better, but without that on offer, some music might make me forget how long it had been since I'd seen a bed.

A cough sounded from behind me as I toweled off with the old but clean beach towel Gabe had found.

"Gabe?" I didn't bother turning around or covering up. Fifteen years of navy locker rooms and tight quarters had taken what little modesty I had, and Gabe had seen it all on various camping trips when we were kids anyway.

"I…uh…" Definitely not Gabe. Way too uncertain. Wrapping the towel around my waist, I turned to find Zeb standing near the door, face as red as the cranberry sauce had been. He clutched a white dress shirt on a hanger to his chest like he was the naked one. "Gabe said he couldn't find you a dress shirt wide…errr…big enough, but I found this in a different supply closet when I went to get one for myself."

Zeb's wide green eyes were riveted to my chest. Probably taking note of my tats.

"It's supposed to be a phoenix." I shut off my phone music to spare Zeb the musical taste one of my SEAL buddies had called "aggressively over-hyped club shit." Luckily, I didn't much worry about others' opinions. Give me an upbeat tune and driving bass line any day.

"Pardon?" Zeb wrinkled his nose as he handed over the shirt.

"My tat." I pointed at my left pec, where the flames and stylized feathers leaped toward my shoulder. "Thought you were trying to figure out my tattoos."

"Oh. Yeah." He nodded a little too enthusiastically. Surprisingly, he made no move to leave as I shrugged into my last clean T-shirt and then buttoned the borrowed shirt. I didn't stress. Zeb would tell me his real purpose eventually. But I also wasn't one to wait around, so I dropped the towel and pulled on a pair of boxer briefs.

"Gonna have to do laundry." I bent over the nearby bench to pick up the black uniform pants Gabe had located for me. Zeb inhaled sharply, but when I turned to ask him what the deal was, his expression was blank and his gaze was on the row of ancient metal lockers behind me.

"Are you supposed to show me the ropes or something?" I didn't mind his presence, but I wasn't into guessing games. "It's been a while, but I learned plenty from helping out when Gabe and I were in high school. Of course, you probably don't remember me. You were little—"

"I remember you." He quirked his lips. "And I was

nineteen when Paige and Gabe finally got married. You came back for the wedding."

"Oh, that's right." I vaguely recalled a short, skinny kid with big glasses dancing like he didn't care who was watching. The sort of terrible-but-joyful movements that were hard not to appreciate. Present-day Zeb was still short, or at least shorter than me, but he'd bulked up, broader shoulders, trimmer waist. Hint of a belly, which was strangely endearing. No glasses, and he'd added a well-trimmed beard that matched his light auburn hair. "Thought you were younger at the wedding, but I guess I forgot. Makes sense because the wedding was after your parents passed."

"The accident was why they got married." Zeb's tone was matter-of-fact, but the flash of pain in his eyes hit me low in the gut. The jack-knifed semi accident that had taken Zeb and Gabe's parents had devastated this small community. I'd never admit it to either brother, but their parents' absence had played a role in why I hadn't visited more. I missed the pair who had seemed right-out-of-sitcom perfect—adoring each other and their boys as well. And I had no idea what to do with that emotion other than give it a wide berth. I carefully swallowed as Zeb continued, "Paige said life was too short to keep playing games with Gabe for years and years."

"She can be quite persuasive." I chuckled. Gabe was married to my cousin Paige, and the three of us had all been friends in high school. Gabe and Paige had had an epic will-they-or-won't-they romance going that had lasted close to a decade.

"Gotta love Paige," Zeb agreed. "And yes, the wedding wasn't that long after the accident. Gabe leaned on her a lot the first few years as they both figured out how to run this place."

"I'm glad they have each other." When people pressed, which was more every year, I usually said my work kept me far too busy for relationships. And I was okay with that, mostly. But there were moments like at Paige and Gabe's wedding when I wondered if I simply hadn't met the right one yet. I'd dated a few women, but nothing seemed to stick, and I had far less experience than any other straight guy I knew. None of my SEAL team buddies seemed to have my issue of being hopeless at dating, so my single status was one more thing I tried not to dwell on. "I can't wait to see Paige. She's coming by later, right?"

"That's the plan. And wait till you see her." Zeb grinned, eyes crinkling. He had a way more approachable smile than his brother, wide and impish. "She's been tired but otherwise doing great. Gabe's had his work cut out for him, making her rest."

Ordinarily, Paige would be in the thick of Thanksgiving meal prep, but after years of trying, she and Gabe were expecting miracle twins, and she was under doctor's orders to cut back on work until after the delivery, which would likely be sometime before New Year's.

"Twins. Man, I can't believe it." I shook my head. "Hope they get here before I have to report back."

I had a shit ton of leave banked, and the higher-ups had finally convinced me to take six weeks. I'd missed so much in Paige and Gabe's life that agreeing to spend my leave helping Gabe through the holiday rush had been a no-brainer. I'd finished my duties with one crew, and when I returned, I'd be in a new role with a fast track to senior chief status. Much as I was happy to be here, I couldn't wait.

"I'm excited to meet the babies too. Paige says you're going to be Uncle Atlas whether you like it or not." Zeb's smile took on a more mischievous edge as if daring me to object.

"Guess that makes you Uncle Zeb." I offered him a fist bump, which he awkwardly returned before glancing at the door. Heck. I'd lost track of time. We were getting closer to the first seating. "We'd better get out there."

"Wait." He held up a hand. "First, I want to apologize."

Ah. I'd known Zeb had a motive for sticking around. I figured his objective involved the cranberry sauce incident.

"No need." I gentled my voice the way I would with a green recruit who'd screwed up. Zeb was already beating himself up plenty. He didn't need my piling on. "Accidents happen. I know it wasn't on purpose."

"Of course, it was an accident." Mouth twisting, Zeb bristled. "I meant more what I said when I was ranting about you no-showing. That was rude."

"It's okay. You had a point." I shrugged. I'd learned the hard way that there was little reward in arguing with the truth. I'd been back for the wedding, my uncle's funeral, and a few other sporadic visits, yet I'd also canceled far more often than I'd shown up due to emergency deployments and such. Uncertainty over how to deal with grief for those I missed, like my uncle, Zeb's parents, and others, played a role, but the reality of working a demanding military job was the main factor. "I've missed a lot over the years."

"Yeah, but you've had good reasons." Zeb nodded firmly as if trying to convince himself as much as me. "And you're here now."

"Yep." Our eyes met, and I was unprepared for both the intensity of Zeb's gaze and his empathy. The green of his irises reminded me of a turtle I'd tried to make a pet of once, a friendly collection of mottled shades, but the unexpected depth there had me peering closer. Warmth gathered in my belly as Zeb held my gaze. No trace of the scattered kid he'd once been. He nodded subtly like he knew a thing or two about letting people down.

I should have said something, acknowledged the connection, but before I could figure out what, Zeb gestured at the door. "Gabe's probably looking for us both."

And sure enough, as soon as we left the changing room and made our way back toward the main event space, Gabe cornered us near the kitchen. The meaty scent of roasted turkey wafted out of the kitchen.

"Oh good, Zeb came through with a shirt." Gabe gave my attire a cursory once-over. Funny how different Zeb's gaze in the changing room had felt from Gabe's out here. "We've got a lot to do before the doors open for the first seating."

"Put me to work, boss," I said right as a person with shockingly white hair adorned with magenta tips emerged from the kitchen. Thin but muscular like a rock climber, they had matching eyeliner, looking more ready to highlight one of my playlists than any culinary endeavors. This had to be Nix, who had starred in several breezy email updates from Paige.

"Gabe!" Nix shook a gloved hand in Gabe's direction. "What am I supposed to do when—not if—*when* we run out of cranberry sauce for the second seating?"

Next to me, Zeb slumped against the wall. "I'm so sorry, Nix. Just tell people the truth. I dropped the bowl."

Seeing Zeb so sad made something twist in my chest. He'd apologized enough for one day.

"Can't you get more?" I asked Gabe. As far as I knew,

cranberry sauce came in two forms, both canned and trotted out for this one meal each year. I liked it, but I couldn't say I'd ever craved the stuff.

"It's homemade." Gabe made the same sour face he had when faced with a pop quiz back in the day. He'd always hated being unprepared. "Grandma Seasons had a secret recipe."

"Cranberry sauce needs to be made the day before," Nix added while Zeb continued to look miserable. "It needs time to chill."

"What makes it different from canned?" I asked Nix, not giving up on my quest to save Zeb from taking all the blame. "Would guests really know the difference?"

"Yes," Gabe insisted at the same time Zeb said, "Probably not."

"The secret is citrus." Nix rolled their eyes at the feuding brothers. "Orange zest and some juice, along with a few other ingredients. We could probably doctor up some canned stuff to pass, but good luck finding an open grocery store around here today."

"Some stores have Thanksgiving hours." I'd shopped at base commissaries so long I wasn't entirely sure what chains northeastern Pennsylvania featured these days, but surely a case of cranberry sauce and some oranges weren't that big an ask.

"Welcome to the sticks." Zeb groaned, the same tone used by generations of Kringle's Crossing high schoolers desperate to escape this little town, which sat at the intersection of rural and Philadelphia suburb. The city was too far for easy daily commuting but close enough for temptation. And grocery stores.

"Philly?" I asked.

"Too far." Gabe huffed a defeated breath. No way was

this the same guy who'd once driven two hours with me in his old junker Civic searching for a rare Whoopie Pie flavor. There was a time after high school when his drive and determination had far exceeded mine. However, this version of Gabe was already ready to give up. "There's no time to make it there and back, and we've had two servers call out. We're going to be spread thin as it is."

Gabe pulled an honest-to-God cotton handkerchief from his pocket to mop at his thinning hairline. Damn. Thirty-five was apparently the new eighty. I guessed we really had gone and gotten old.

"This isn't an insurmountable problem." I already had my phone out and was scrolling contacts. "What you have here is a logistics problem. Supply chain issue. Let me make some calls."

"I appreciate the offer, but this is cranberry sauce, not national security." Add grumpy to the other new things about Gabe. Probably stress. Dude needed to learn how to delegate, and lucky for him, he had me to help.

"Exactly." I might suck at taking time off, but I lived for problem-solving, and the idea of saving what could be a rather trivial disaster was catnip to my soul. "Ten minutes with a decent cell signal, and I'll have a solution."

I didn't give him a chance to protest, leaving the other three workers standing in the hallway as I paced back and forth to work my magic. The fourth call was the charm, and I hightailed it back to Gabe, who was straightening silverware on the tables. Zeb was working nearby on setting other tables.

"Any chance of three extra seats for the second sitting? I've got a lead on some sauce and oranges from a supply specialist I sat near on the transport flight. He's in Philly and returned from DC to surprise his girl for Thanksgiving. He's willing to drive to bring us the goods if I can guarantee him dinner. His girlfriend and her mother hadn't planned on cooking today."

"We've been sold out of reservations for weeks." Gabe looked around the room as if willing an extra table to appear.

"We can make it happen." Zeb was surprisingly decisive. I liked that quality in a person. "Tell your new friend to come hungry. Dinner is on Seasons."

"Excellent." I clapped him on the shoulder, the same as I might Gabe. But Zeb's shoulder felt nothing like Gabe's slim frame. Where Gabe was tall, thin to the point of scrawny from all the worrying and forgetting to eat he did, and clean-shaven, Zeb was sturdy. A sparkplug, my Uncle Joe would have called him. And Zeb smelled good, like cinnamon cookies. Couldn't say I'd ever noticed Gabe's scent before. Before I could move my hand, my palm went warm and itchy, a weird sort of energy arcing between us. "That's the spirit."

The holiday spirit wasn't something I'd ever thought much about, but if I was stuck in town, working at Seasons this winter, I supposed I better learn quickly.

Three

ZEB

No more disasters. It had been my mantra all day. After all, it would take a pretty big calamity to top covering my brother's best friend, the guy I'd had a crush on for a decade now, in cranberry sauce. Atlas waving away my attempt at an apology and all but patting my head and calling me *kid* again was the garnish on top. I'd like to think we bonded over rearranging Gabe's careful seating chart, but in reality, Atlas was likely only being nice.

Yet another nice, super hot, super unattainable crush to add to my collection. Living in the sticks meant more than the grocery stores closing early. There were slim pickings for a nerdy gay guy with little interest in apps.

Oh well. At least Atlas was likely here for a solid month. Maybe I'd get another shot at impressing him. And if nothing else, at least I got to watch him work. He'd spent most of the evening behind the bar, handling drinks with the efficiency of a longtime server. Apparently, SEALs and those who worked with them truly were good at everything.

"After-dinner coffee or tea?" I asked one of the last tables. Most of our patrons had already headed off into the chilly November night. Many of our guests were families who made letting Seasons cook an annual tradition, grandparents and sleepy kids included, and they tended to make an early night of it. But groups of Friendsgiving adults like this chatty group of widows were likely to linger. And linger. "Something before you hit the road?"

I tried hard not to show my exhaustion, keeping my tone chipper and smile bright, but Gabe still frowned from across the room.

"Or more pie." Laughing, all four older ladies at the table made their way back to the buffet. And to my credit, I didn't so much as groan as I refilled their water glasses and braced for yet more waiting until we could clear the last of the food.

"Zeb." Gabe hurried over, dropping his voice to a stern whisper. "Quit trying to hurry people out the door."

"Lighten up, boss. And hydrate with something other than black coffee." Handing Gabe a glass of water, Atlas got away with the sort of teasing I never could. "And we're slow enough that you should go sit with your lovely wife and mother-in-law." He gestured at the small table by one of the windows where Paige and her mother, Aunt Lucy, sat. Technically, Aunt Lucy was only Atlas's biological aunt, but as a former elementary teacher, she seemed to be an honorary aunt to half the town, me included. Once upon a time, our joint families had required one of our largest tables, but we seemed to keep shrinking. Yet another reason the twins would be a very welcome addition. Atlas deftly maneuvered Gabe closer to the dessert table. "Eat some pie yourself."

"Thank you, Atlas," Paige chirped brightly as we neared their table. "So glad you're here to boss Gabe around. He won't listen to any of us."

"I'll make sure you both rest." When a dazed Gabe simply stood in front of the selection of pies, Atlas plucked up a piece of our famous pumpkin pie and steered Gabe into the empty chair next to Paige.

"Your brother is an ulcer waiting to happen," Atlas said as we left the others to their desserts. He strode back to the bar, and after a quick glance to make sure the Friendsgiving group didn't need me, I followed. "I've never seen Gabe so uptight."

"I know." Groaning, I started organizing newly washed glassware that one of the teen bussers had returned from the dishwasher. "And he's not usually this bad. Paige's pregnancy has him on edge, and business was down all summer. Fewer weddings and fewer fall parties, so we really need a successful holiday run."

"That's why I'm here to help."

"Thanks." I had no idea why Atlas's affable statement made my back tense. Perhaps because he so easily accomplished what I couldn't, joking around with Gabe and caretaking for him to boot. I should be glad at least someone got Gabe to take care of himself more. "You're off to a great start. Fantastic rescue with the cranberry sauce."

"No problem. And our unexpected guests had a great night. Bet Petty Officer Warren proposes to his girl by the end of the weekend." Atlas chuckled as he wiped down the bar top. "Doubt anyone even noticed the difference in the sauces between the first and second seatings."

"Hopefully not. Grandma would be proud." My dad's mom had been short like me, with similar flyaway hair and the sort of plucky spirit that would have appreciated Atlas's ingenuity.

"I remember her from one of my early visits." Prior to spending his senior year here in Kringle's Crossing, Atlas and his jet-setting parents had been semi-regular, if highly unpredictable, visitors. "And then later, your grandpa was still around when we were in school. He was a card."

"Yeah." I glanced around the room, all the tables for six, eight, and even ten. Atlas made it hard to avoid thinking about who wasn't here.

"At least you and Gabe have carried on here, keeping the traditions going." Atlas had the same tone that out-of-towners often adopted, idealizing small businesses and minimizing how much pressure those same traditions could exert.

"It's mainly Gabe." I had to give credit where credit was due because, for all Gabe could be a pain, he was also the driving force that kept Seasons going. Through a complicated will dated prior to my unexpected birth, Gabe had inherited all the responsibility that went along with owning and running a fourth-generation family business. Finishing with the glasses, I turned to start rolling flatware but misjudged and crashed into Atlas. Again. "Whoops."

No dripping sauce this time, so I could better appreciate how damn solid he was, especially his firm grip on my arm.

"Better watch your step." He smiled as he delivered the warning. He had one of those naturally devilish smiles aided by the cleft in his defined chin, the type that made him always look like he was thinking something dirty, even when he likely wasn't. And it was ridiculously easy to get lost in those brown eyes. Almost a decade ago, he'd grinned at me at Gabe and Paige's wedding with the same kind and bemused expression, launching years of fantasies and longing. The memory alone had me wobbling as he righted me.

"I'm not usually this clumsy." I suppressed a sigh as he released my arm.

"You're probably just tired." He shrugged, all humble like he couldn't pull four of these shifts back-to-back. "Been a long day for you, Gabe, and the crew."

"Says the guy who did how many international flights?"

"True that." He gave a weary chuckle. "Can't wait to get to Gabe's and crash."

"About that—"

"Night, Zeb." The last table was finally leaving, the women donning their wool coats in a cloud of expensive perfume amid hugs and promises to call. Petunia, who'd made the reservation, waved jauntily at me. "Don't let that brother of yours work too hard."

"I won't. See?" I gestured over to where Gabe was helping Paige into her coat. "We even made him eat pie."

"Good boy." Petunia patted my cheek. And this was why I had such a love-hate relationship with Kringle's Crossing. I couldn't imagine calling another zip code home. However, whether I was twenty-eight or eighty, I would always be a kid here.

That sour thought clung to my brain cells as we made it through the rest of the cleaning. Paige and her mother had long since departed, followed by the teen servers and bussers we employed for special events like this, and finally, Nix and the kitchen crew headed out, leaving only Atlas, Gabe, and me.

"Wow. Thank goodness. We did it." Gabe slumped into a nearby chair as I wound up the vacuum cord. The dining area was so clean one would never guess at the earlier chaos. "Only a few minor hiccups."

"Everyone seemed happy." In a bid to avoid Gabe listing all the things that could have gone smoother, I forced a smile. "That's the important thing. A number of people mentioned coming back for small business Saturday to shop, so here's to hoping business stays good."

"Yup." Gabe actually returned my smile. "Oh, we got a last-minute booking for a holiday wedding rehearsal dinner."

"Noooo." I groaned as I stowed the vacuum in the nearby cleaning closet. "I mean, great."

"Not a fan of weddings?" Atlas asked. His boundless energy finally seemed to be flagging as he sat next to Gabe.

"Zeb? He's a hopeless romantic." Gabe laughed before I could give him a brotherly poke. "It's the bridezillas he doesn't like."

"And the bridesmaid-zillas."

"One wedding, Zeb. One wedding." Gabe laughed, traces of his old humor appearing. Turning to Atlas, he explained, "These college girls went a bit overboard with the demands. And one kept hitting on everyone, Zeb included."

"Sounds miserable." Unlike most dudes who might crack a crude joke, Atlas sounded genuinely sympathetic.

"Eh." Case in point, Gabe waved a hand like earning uncomfortable flirting was a badge of honor. "Probably happens to you all the time, am I right?"

"Eh." Atlas echoed Gabe's own noncommittal tone. "So, are we ready to lock up? I'm gonna need to swipe some toothpicks to hold my eyelids open if I don't get some shut eye soon."

CATERED ALL THE WAY

"Yeah, we're about out of here." Stretching to pop his back, Gabe stood as Atlas did the same.

"Good." Atlas yawned. When he smiled, he was undeniably appealing, but sleepy, he was a different sort of attractive. Vulnerable. A weary warrior I couldn't help but want to tuck in. "Hope we don't wake Paige coming in. I'll be quiet."

"Oh crap. I forgot to tell you." Gabe groaned. "You're with Zeb."

"I'm what?" Atlas rubbed his upper neck and ear like he'd misheard something. But he hadn't. I'd suspected the mixup earlier, and now, instead of the convenient arrangement I'd been hoping for, I would have to deal with a confused and disappointed Atlas.

"You're bunking with Zeb," Gabe said breezily. "Ever since your Aunt Lucy moved in, space has been at a premium." He wasn't kidding. The farmhouse we'd grown up in hadn't been huge to start with, but like with the business, no way did either of us want to see the property sold. "The old guest room is about to be a twin nursery. And I know you said you'd be fine on the couch, but then Zeb volunteered."

"I did?" I blinked because that wasn't how it had gone down at all. More like Gabe had reluctantly asked after other options had fallen through, handing me a stack of reminders to clean and prep like I didn't know the basics of hosting someone. But Atlas didn't need any more of our brotherly squabbling. "I mean, yeah, I did. I've got more room at my place than Gabe and Paige right now."

"It's my old apartment. You'll feel right at home." Gabe clapped him on the shoulder, and Atlas released a weary groan.

"Honestly, I'm so tired I could sleep on a cactus."

"Zeb's place is a step up from cacti. A small step." Gabe laughed. I didn't.

"Let's go." This had all the makings of an epic fail. I had little hope of resurrecting my original plan to impress Atlas, but at least maybe I could spare myself further embarrassment.

Four

ATLAS

"My old bones aren't used to the cold," I joked with Zeb on the walk to his place. I hefted my duffel bag from one shoulder to the other. I'd rather stay with Gabe. I barely knew Zeb, but he'd apparently offered, and I didn't want to offend his hospitality by being grumpy at the change in plans.

"It's not that cold. Wait another few weeks." Zeb shoved his gloved hands deeper into his coat pockets. Unlike me, he was prepared with a thick black coat, a colorful scarf that was likely an Aunt Lucy original knit, and gloves. "It hasn't snowed yet this season, but I bet it will soon."

A bitter wind whipped through the night, leaving our breath hanging in the air and me wishing for a thicker jacket. I'd forgotten the harshness of a Pennsylvania winter. Zeb lived in Gabe's old apartment, which was only a block or two down Main Street, located behind the hardware store in a seventies-era fourplex that showed every decade of its age. But it was familiar, in the same way as a tattered pair of sneakers.

"At least we didn't have far to go." I followed Zeb up the stairs to his apartment, waiting as he unlocked the door. "And Gabe was right. I've spent tons of nights on the couch here. I'll be fine."

"Ah. Yeah." Zeb made a vague noise as he flipped on the entryway and living space lights. "There's no couch."

"No…" I started to protest because Gabe had had a giant, lumpy leather sofa for years. But I trailed off as I gazed around the transformed space. No giant couch. No ancient TV or chipped coffee table. No Formica dining set either. Instead, the space was dominated by a U-shaped desk with three surfaces, multiple monitors, speakers, lights, and a green screen behind an office chair that looked like it could double as a captain's chair on any sci-fi show. Some monitors appeared to raise and lower, while another desk seemed solely for racing games with a steering wheel and joystick controller. Hardly the setup I'd expect from a broke part-time server. "Damn, Zeb, did you rob an electronics store?"

"I'm a gaming streamer." He gave me a withering look as if I should have known this fact. "Professional gaming vlogger and streamer. I make money recording gaming content, so this equipment is how I do my job."

"Job." I chewed on that word for a second. I didn't know anyone who made a living playing video games, and I'd always thought that was something of an urban legend —put up enough free content and watch the money pour in. Seemed too good to be true, but Zeb appeared plenty serious, stony stare and all. "Sorry, I thought Gabe said you bounced between gigs and worked part-time at Seasons. Didn't realize you had a whole side hustle going."

"It's more than a side hustle. It's my full-time job. Not that Gabe believes that, but it is." He sounded unnecessarily defensive. "I put in way more than forty hours a week. I had to prerecord a bunch of content to get me through the holidays. I'll still have to do some live streams, but I cleared enough space to help out."

"I get no one taking you seriously." Gentling my voice, I tried to banish my earlier skepticism. "Early on in my military career, I had to do a ton of justifying to people who expected a way different career choice for me."

I wouldn't say my parents were disappointed in my career choice, but they certainly weren't supportive, and it hardly fit with their elite friend group and one-percenter entourage lifestyle. And conversely, military folks were surprised I hadn't gone for a more status-oriented career in keeping with my privileged upbringing.

"Yeah. Everyone's got opinions. Including that gaming isn't a 'real' job. But it is."

"Has Gabe seen your setup?" I gestured at all the blinking monitors and other equipment. "I'd believe you were running a NASA mission from here."

That earned me a laugh, a real one, musical and genuine, and the sound did something warm and strange to my insides. "Thanks."

"But where am I going to sleep?" Short of crawling under one of the desks, I wasn't sure where I'd fit.

"My room. I'll sleep out here." Zeb sounded decisive, but I groaned and shook my head.

"Aw, man, I can't take your bed."

"It wouldn't be the first time I've slept in my gaming chair, but I planned ahead." Moving around me, he dragged a large box out from under the closest desk. "I ordered an air mattress."

The box promised "royal comfort," but it looked like

every other twin-size camping mattress I'd seen. However, I'd certainly slept on way worse.

"I'll take that." I reached for the box, but Zeb batted my hand away. Entirely unused to my orders being ignored, I tried again and was again denied.

"Told you. I have a plan. My bed's undoubtedly more comfortable, and I already put clean sheets on for you earlier. And I don't want to keep you awake by checking my messages and work stuff in here."

He'd *planned*. My chest pinched with an unfamiliar twinge. I couldn't say anyone had changed bedding for me in recent memory. It would be rude of me to continue to fight Zeb when he was trying to be a decent host.

"At least let me help you set it up."

"Okay." He shrugged off his coat, putting it on a hook near the door, and I followed suit.

Kneeling on the thin rug near the computer desks, we worked together to unpack the air mattress. I'd set up enough of these that I didn't need instructions, so I tossed that paper aside and helped Zeb unroll the mattress. Turning, he plugged in the built-in electric air pump.

The movement made his black pants stretch across his ass. Couldn't say I was in the habit of noticing asses on anyone, but Zeb's seemed unusually plump and…*there*. I looked away and waited for the mattress to start inflating.

And waited.

The pump hummed to life, a croaky sound that wasn't particularly hopeful, but no matter how hard the pump whirred, the mattress didn't budge.

"It's not working." Zeb frowned at the mattress like it had personally offended him.

"Flat as a pancake," I agreed and reached for the

instructions. "There must be some trick to it. Let me take a look."

Holding the instructions, I bent closer to examine the pump. *Huh.* Somehow, Zeb smelled even *more* like cinnamon after the long shift at Seasons and a walk in the cold. But I had no business sniffing anyone. I had no idea why I kept…*responding* to Zeb, a weird thrum to my pulse and awareness of him. It had to be jet lag because this wasn't like me at all.

I busied myself with examining the plastic box that housed the pump. I checked around the casing for obvious defects and verified the intake and outtake air valves were turned in the correct direction.

"Let's try again." Zeb flipped the power button. The pump started churning again, fan huffing, but a metallic smell filled the air and the mattress didn't inflate even a millimeter.

Disaster. "It's working too hard doing nothing." I flipped the pump back off. "The last thing we need is the motor to burn out."

"Yeah." Zeb's voice was faint and hopeless. "What do we do now?"

Crap. He needed me to have an answer. I shouldn't have been surprised. Everyone always looked to me to have the solution, and usually I did. And I wished I could get an easy win here, like earlier with the cranberries. Not that I was trying to impress Zeb, but it would be nice to see him less down, maybe see a hint of that freewheeling dancer from Gabe and Paige's wedding.

"We can check for leaks." I didn't really expect my close inspection to work, but examining the mattress bought me time to think of a better plan. "Okay, no leaks.

And it's getting late. Just give me a pillow and a blanket. It's not like I haven't bedded down on the floor before."

"Absolutely not." He sounded horrified. "It's *cold*. This place has iffy heat to begin with, and the hardwood floors seem to hold a chill. You'll freeze."

"I've been cold before."

"If anyone is taking the floor, it's me," he said firmly. I couldn't remember anyone else showing this level of concern over where I slept and whether I was warm enough. Earlier in the night, I'd hugged Paige and Aunt Lucy. Hugging was another thing I didn't do very often, but Zeb's caretaking felt like a hug.

"Then you'll be cold," I pointed out reasonably, only for him to make a frustrated noise.

"Better me than you."

"I disagree." I sighed because I was way, way too exhausted for this argument. Screw it. "How about we share?"

"The floor?" He glanced at the flat and useless air mattress.

"No, your bed." Hefting myself off the floor, I strode toward Gabe's old bedroom, praying Zeb didn't have a twin-size bed. And thank God, he didn't, but he did have the smallest-looking double I'd ever seen, pressed against one wall to make room for yet more electronic equipment, including a TV and a couple of gaming consoles. "You game in bed?"

"Sometimes. Space is at a premium." He stood in the doorway, gaze locked on his bed as if willing it to transform into a king. "Speaking of, no way are we both going to fit in my bed."

"Sure, we will." I clapped him on the shoulder before venturing more into the room. The bed was nicely made, covered by a thick blue comforter and a patchwork quilt I recognized as one of my Aunt Lucy's. Familiar. Maybe this wouldn't be terrible. But Zeb still hung back in the doorway, wide-eyed and radiating discomfort. "Come on, you've never shared with a buddy camping or on a road trip?"

"That's different," he gritted out.

"How?"

"Ugh." Zeb made a loud, rude noise but didn't address my question. "Fine. Suit yourself." He finally entered the room, crossing to his dresser. "Do you need pajamas?"

"Pajamas?" I blinked. I didn't usually wear more than boxers, but that might horrify Zeb further. I supposed I could find a pair of sweats or something in my bag. "Oh. Uh. No. I should probably shower again though."

"Okay, you first, then me." Zeb sounded resigned to death by a thousand fire ants.

"It's a bed, not a torture chamber." I headed for the bathroom, hoping the alone time while I was in the shower would mellow his attitude some. Unlike earlier in the day, I was too tired to linger. Zeb had helpfully hung clean towels on the rack in the bathroom. That soft place in my chest pinged again. He was a good host.

After drying off, I dug through my bag, finding a serviceable pair of sweatpants, but no such luck on a shirt. Oh well. We were both dudes, and Zeb had seen more than my chest earlier.

"Okay, your turn," I said as I walked back into the bedroom from the hall bath. Zeb was perched on the edge of the bed, fiddling with a game controller. "I didn't have a clean T-shirt, sorry."

"Oh." Zeb made a startled noise, flying off the bed. "I have one you can borrow." And okay, he was *way* more modest than me. I accepted his offering of a shirt from a convention for the *Odyssey* card game franchise a lot of my buddies played in their downtime. I pulled it on. As I'd figured, it was a size too small, tight in the neck, arms, and chest, and a little short to boot, but I wasn't going to complain, especially with Zeb waving a hand and making distressed noises. "Ah. Um."

"It's fine." Not giving him a chance to protest further, I crawled onto the far side of the bed, against the wall. "Thanks. You go shower now."

Zeb took what felt like an entire decade in the shower, and I drifted in and out of sleep, the sound of the water running soothing. Awkward bed arrangement or not, it was nice to not be alone.

When the shower shut off, I pressed myself against the wall, trying to create maximum space for Zeb, who crept into bed like he was performing a stealth perimeter check.

"Good night, Zeb." I yawned and pulled my pillow closer.

"Night."

I should have dropped right into a deeper sleep as soon as he flipped off the light, but I couldn't. Zeb held himself so stiffly the bed vibrated from his efforts, and if I wasn't mistaken, he was clinging to the side of the mattress. This wasn't going to work.

"Are you going to be able to sleep?" I asked, resigned to leaving the cozy bed in favor of the floor so the guy could sleep. "You sound kind of…tense?"

"I'm fine." Zeb exhaled as if forcing himself to breathe. I didn't buy the *I'm fine* act for a second, but I also didn't particularly want to abandon the bed. If he wanted to be a martyr, so be it.

"Okay. Hopefully, *fine* lets you sleep soon."

"Go back to sleep, Atlas," Zeb ordered in a voice that would have made many a senior chief proud but only irritated me further. I gave orders, and I didn't much like taking them from a dude who seemed hell-bent on making himself miserable.

Worse, I was now wide awake, sleep eluding me. Instead of sheep, I counted off mission supplies, then made my way through standard procedures for common tasks, mentally reviewing rules I knew by heart. Nope. No sleep.

I was acutely aware of Zeb's nearness, his warmth, the way he managed to still smell like cinnamon, his little huffs of breath, and the moment when he finally surrendered to sleep. Good. At least one of us had finally relaxed. I had slept next to tons of buddies through the years: camping, missions, and more. Heck, I'd slept next to Gabe more than once, but Zeb was proving to be nothing like his brother, a fact that was starting to worry me.

Five

ZEB

BLACK FRIDAY: 29 SHOPPING DAYS UNTIL CHRISTMAS

I dreamed I was buried under a mountain of warm mashed potatoes, the sort of post-holiday stress dream I hated, disaster after disaster that felt increasingly like I really was sweltering under a heavy, immovable load.

And then light teased the edges of my consciousness. I blinked, testing my alertness. Weirdly, I was still hot and sweaty and pinned to the mattress by...

Atlas. The previous night came back to me in a rush. I'd been so scared that I'd be the one to accidentally sleep-cuddle that I'd legit fallen asleep clutching the rolled edge of the mattress. I hadn't remotely contemplated a world where Atlas ended up migrating from his spot by the wall, sprawling across the entire bed, me very much included.

Apparently, his sleeping self had decided to make me his personal body pillow, head smashed up next to mine, one big hand pinning my shoulder to the bed, the other wrapped around me, holding me close.

Painfully close.

Atlas radiated heat despite both sets of covers having ended up on the floor. Yet it wasn't the heat that was the issue. Rather, it was *him*. His every muscle pressed against me, including a very insistent erection riding my hip. It was morning, after all. I couldn't take it personally. Happened to the best of us. I needed to roll him to the side and wiggle loose before he realized and became embarrassed.

Yes. That was it. I needed to escape.

But Atlas felt so damn *good*. He smelled spicier than my usual soap, and I wasted precious seconds trying to decide what brand he used. Finally, I tried moving him. I might as well have saved my strength because he budged not at all. Wiggling was also a no-go as he clutched me that much tighter.

And now I had an erection situation of my own to contend with. One that was becoming more *pressing* with each passing moment.

"Uh, Atlas?" I whispered, soft but urgent.

"Moof?" Atlas sighed into my hair, which sent a shiver down my back and made my heels dig into the soft mattress. I drank in his last sleepy inhale, already cursing myself for trying to wake him. What if this chance never came again?

"Ooof." Atlas's next exhale was a cross between a groan and alarm. And just like that, he was gone, the luxury of his warm weight removed as he rolled back against the wall. "Sorry."

Cheeks flushed a bright magenta, he very carefully rearranged the covers. Yup. He was embarrassed.

"It's okay." It wasn't, but that was the polite thing to say rather than beg him to treat me as his personal cuddle pet every night.

"Thanks." Hefting onto his side, he squinted at me before brushing a hand across my forehead. I shuddered again, another electric sensation racing down my spine.

"What was that for?"

"Your hair was in your face."

"It does that." I matched his matter-of-fact tone.

"I see." He nodded like we were discussing state secrets and not the condition of my unruly hair. "We better get up. Gabe will have our hides if we're late."

Ugh. I didn't want to think about my brother right then or how Atlas was only here as a favor to him. *Nothing personal.*

"You hungry?" I asked as we exited the bed. We'd eaten late last night, sneaking bites between cleaning up, but we'd need our strength for the next two days of Black Friday and Small Business Saturday shoppers.

"Always." Atlas grinned at me, cheek and chin dimples on full display, and the boyish enthusiasm had me reconsidering my plan to offer him my impressive assortment of cereal choices.

"How about eggs?"

"Sounds good. Love a hot breakfast." The sparkle in his eyes made my skin heat and made me glad I'd changed from the cereal plan. Atlas frowned at his duffel bag, which he'd set in the corner of my room. "Any chance of me running a quick load of laundry before breakfast?"

"Yeah. The washing machine and dryer are in the basement of the building." I grabbed a jar of change off my dresser. "You'll need quarters."

"Seriously?" Atlas tilted his head. Most laundry facilities seemed to have transitioned to cards, but this creaky building had laundry facilities that hadn't been updated in decades.

"Yep. Old school all the way." As I passed him a handful of quarters, our fingers brushed. His hands, like the rest of him, were big and strong. Wide palms, warm skin, long fingers. I wanted them everywhere, and it would be fine with me if Atlas never did laundry again. Reluctantly, I released him to point at the door at the end of my short hallway that led to the basement. "It's cold down there, so take your coat."

"I'll be fine." Atlas scoffed in the way macho dudes always did, and I wasn't surprised when he reappeared shivering a few minutes later as I was working on breakfast.

"Okay, you weren't lying." Standing beside me at the stove, he rubbed his hands together and stamped his bare feet. He stood way too close and wasn't likely to get much warmth off the gas stove, but who was I to turn down a chance to bask in Atlas's nearness. "Cold as fuck down there."

"I have coffee." I brushed by him, working double time to not happy sigh from the contact. Retrieving a cup, I pointed at the just-brewed pot.

Atlas made a pleasured moan that was likely illegal in ten states. "My kind of man."

I wish. I wasn't sure Atlas had a type of man, but if he did, short and stout gamer guys were unlikely to be on the list.

"There's toast and sausages too." I plated the eggs next to the toast and the turkey sausages I'd found in my freezer.

"I feel spoiled." Atlas took a seat opposite me at my way-too-small dining table. Since I needed as much space as possible for electronics equipment, I'd opted for a teeny wooden table and chair set. It wasn't like I had that many guests. Or any guests. But I hadn't considered my knees brushing Atlas's legs or our hands almost touching as we ate.

"You deserve it," I said without thinking, the fond tone better suited to mornings after and not strictly platonic friends of my brother's. *Oops.* I took a quick swig of coffee before backtracking. "Because of all you do in the navy. You're always helping…"

"I got your meaning." Atlas smiled at me over his coffee cup. He was so effortlessly easygoing that his affable nature made it impossible for things to stay awkward, even given the close quarters of the tiny dining area.

After breakfast, Atlas quickly rotated his laundry, this time opting to wear his jacket plus my over-stretched T-shirt.

"What's the dress code today?" he asked as he returned to stand behind my desk, where I was sneaking a quick check of my email. Once again, he was too close, and once again, I was hardly going to complain. He rested a hand on the back of my chair, and it took most of my self-restraint to not stretch toward his fingers. "Please tell me it's not another penguin suit day?"

"Nope." I chortled along with Atlas because I also hated the standard food service attire of a white dress shirt and black pants. "Today is jeans or whatever you want on bottom. And then, on top, Paige ordered these elf T-shirts for us to wear when working in the gift shop. I think she sent over the right size for you." I fetched the shirts from a bag in my hall closet. I changed in my room while Atlas took his shirt to the bathroom.

It didn't matter what size shirt Atlas wore. He looked edible in everything from camo to my old shirt to this silly green cotton T-shirt, which looked like an elf's costume from the front while the back proclaimed: *Have a Holly Jolly*

Holiday at Seasons. He'd paired the red-and-green shirt with black tactical pants, which should have looked ridiculous but instead made me want to climb his North Pole right then and there.

"I feel silly." Forehead wrinkling, he looked down at the shirt. He must have taken a moment to shave because his jaw was smooth. I wanted to touch so badly that my fingers kept clenching.

"Nah. You look good," I assured him. Crap. Maybe that was too much? I swallowed. "Fine, I mean fine. Let's go."

I grabbed my coat before I could hand out any other unintended compliments, then frowned as he did the same.

"You need a warmer coat."

"Maybe." He zipped the jacket up and buried his hands in the pockets. "Not going to be here that long though."

I didn't like the reminder that he wasn't staying, wouldn't ever stay in Kringle's Crossing, any more than I liked him getting cold. Digging around in my hall closet, I came up with a pair of stretchy fleece gloves that were too big for me and one of my many scarves from Paige and her mother.

"Here. Don't want you to freeze."

A strange look crossed Atlas's face as I draped the scarf around his neck.

"Thanks," he said softly. "Can't say as I'm used to people worrying about my comfort. It's…nice."

"Good. Get used to it." I had the ridiculous urge to spoil the man silly. If he thought a simple breakfast and the loan of a scarf were nice, I could do so much better. Assuming he'd let me. But for the first time, I was emboldened to try. Atlas deserved all the caretaking.

Six

ZEB

"Put your finger here," I ordered Atlas, keeping my tone confident. This might be new to him, but I knew exactly what we were doing. "Firmer." I made a happy noise when he complied. "That's it. You'll be an expert in no time."

"Wrapping presents is harder than it looks." Atlas scrunched up his face as he tried to duplicate my technique. I'd been gift wrapping for years as part of our annual ornament and gift sale, and never once had I found the process a turn-on.

But that was before I'd tried teaching Atlas.

We were standing side-by-side at the wrapping station near the registers, and I was acutely aware of his proximity. And my every word suddenly seemed to have a double meaning. I had sex on the brain, and I needed to cut it out because we'd be opening to customers soon. I couldn't be having tie-me-up-and-put-a-bow-on-me fantasies in the middle of one of our busiest days of the year.

"You'll get used to it," I said breezily as Atlas bungled my fold-fold-press-tape technique. It was honestly nice to be better than him at something, especially considering how many clumsy mistakes I'd made the day before. "However, if you want, I can handle the wrapping requests."

"Nah, I need to get good at it." Atlas tried again, this time with perfect creases on the first time. Naturally, my time as the wrapping expert was short-lived. "Wrapping is probably better than helping people pick gifts."

"Helping pick is the best part of Seasons." In addition to the event space we rented out and used to host special events like the Thanksgiving dinner, Seasons also featured a large year-round gift shop of seasonal decor. Tourists, in particular, loved selecting handmade ornaments during their summer vacations. We did nods to Valentine's, Easter, and other holidays, but winter was far and away our biggest business. Many families annually drove an hour or more to select a one-of-a-kind ornament for their collection. Figuring out which items would appeal to which shoppers kept me from getting too bored while working in the retail area when we didn't have a catered event. But Atlas didn't seem moved by the magic of Seasons. "You don't like to shop?"

"Not really. If I need something, I get it." Stretching, he straightened the wrapping station, paper rolls perfectly aligned and scissors back in their holder. "Buying for others is difficult. Expectations, you know? And growing up, we were never in one place long enough to keep gifts around, so exchanging presents started to seem pointless."

I had vague memories of Atlas's parents visiting, especially the year or so he'd lived in Kringle's Crossing for high school. His mom was Paige's father's younger sister, who had skipped out on an Ivy League scholarship to travel the world with a trust-fund guy. Somewhere along the line, they'd had Atlas and had simply continued traveling with occasional pit stops in Kringle's Crossing.

"Your parents didn't keep stuff you gave them?" I shouldn't have been surprised since Gabe and Paige complained all the time about Atlas's entitled parents.

"Nah." Atlas carefully rewrapped a spool of ribbon. "It was mainly silly stuff. Drawings. Craft items from school the years we landed somewhere long enough to do embassy school or whatnot."

"Atlas, you're breaking my heart here." I lightly touched his arm, then thought better of it and quickly dropped my hand. "My mom kept all those sorts of things from Gabe and me. It's what moms do."

"Not mine." He said it so simply that I wanted to personally track down the woman and shake her.

"I'm sorry."

"It's okay." Liar. He sounded exactly as fake as I had earlier. "Not like they keep in touch these days anyway."

"Gabe said they lost their cool when you joined the navy, but that's been what, fifteen years?" I moved on to straightening nearby racks of Victorian-style paper ornaments—delicate things that tended to get tangled. Each corner of the shop represented themes and holidays like Pride, Hanukkah, Kwanza, Solstice, and more.

"It's complicated." Atlas joined me, big fingers surprisingly deft at sorting the fragile ornaments. "At first, after high school, I didn't have much purpose. Bounced around. Tried a little college, but it wasn't until my folks went broke that Uncle Joe sat me down and talked about how the navy gave him structure and how I needed to get my act together."

"Wait. Your folks went broke?" I turned to stare him

down. "I thought your dad was some sort of trust-fund baby."

"Emphasis on was." Atlas kept right on working, not glancing my way. "They roared through the whole thing. Bad investments, too much traveling, too much spending. There wasn't enough left for me. That much was made clear. Now they're basically professional upper-class couch surfers who can't see beyond the next house party and don't bother to call. So I don't either."

"Wow." I whistled low because that was a lot. And a lot that Atlas had triumphed over. "I'm proud of you."

"For what?" He met my gaze, at last, peering closely down at me. My skin heated.

"For choosing yourself. During my own time as a professional couch surfer and perpetual college student, I met a lot of people trying to make toxic, dysfunctional situations work." I spoke slowly, choosing my words carefully. I knew a thing or two about trying to please everyone but oneself. "You could have ended up like your parents or trying to make them happy, but you've built your own life. And from what Gabe says, you're really good at the SEAL support thing."

"I like to think I am. Get them in, get them out, get everyone home safely." Placing a hand on my shoulder, he squeezed lightly. "And thank you. That means a lot, you not trying to tell me what a bad person I am for not keeping contact with my parents."

"I was blessed with great parents. But I've also muddled along the last decade without them. Family is great, and I love mine, but life is too short to be miserable simply because you're related to someone."

"You're really wise." Atlas's gaze turned warm and soft, eyes widening slightly.

Taking a huge risk, I leaned into his touch. He didn't pull away, even when I turned more toward him. Instead, and most confoundingly, Atlas used his other hand to smooth my hair again. I held myself still, held my breath, hell, held my thoughts. I couldn't so much as *think* because there was no way on earth Atlas was about to kiss—

"Everyone ready?" Gabe called out cheerily as he entered our section of the store. "We're opening the doors!"

Atlas dropped his hand and stepped away, taking whatever moment that had been with him.

But it had been a moment. I was sure of it. Gabe opened the big glass double doors to admit a crowd of early Black Friday shoppers. The shop swirled with noise and happy chaos, but I took a last look at Atlas. Cheeks pink. Gaze anywhere but my direction. Could it be that he'd felt it too? A true holiday miracle if so, and I was determined to test that theory again as soon as possible.

Seven

ATLAS

"You're a wrapping machine." Zeb's tone was warm and genuine from behind me. In my work, praise could be rare as time was at a premium and competence was simply assumed as the minimum standard. All day, despite the constant stream of customers, Zeb had found reason to praise me, and his words landed far differently from those of a superior officer. Made my stomach go soft and gushy and my skin feel a size too small, like my body and brain disagreed over how much to enjoy the compliments.

"I think I have new callouses from the scissors." I quirked my mouth as I turned toward him. Victory: brain. I couldn't get too used to praise for little tasks.

"Poor baby." Zeb patted my stiff shoulder, a fleeting touch that seared me nonetheless. No longer jet-lagged, I'd had more than sufficient sleep, food, and hydration. I was running out of reasons why my senses kept insisting on taking notice of Zeb.

Hell, I'd woken up on top of the dude, painfully aroused and embarrassed both. I'd slept in all manner of strange locations without ever once migrating in my sleep.

No one in their right mind would ever accuse me of being cuddly. Yet I kept having these strange urges to touch Zeb, even while awake. And those last few seconds before I'd fully woken up had been bliss, my arms full of Zeb and my body as relaxed as I could remember.

"That was the last customer." Gabe came bustling in, a welcome break from my thoughts. "We're finally done and ready to do it all again tomorrow. Then, Sunday, we have the crafters' dinner."

"Not much time to breathe." I smiled at him, trying to send calming vibes. Gabe had always tended to the anxious side, but ever since I arrived, he'd been a ball of stress. The extra people with the crafters and customers filling Seasons hadn't helped either.

The same event space that had hosted Thanksgiving had been transformed into a craft bazaar for Black Friday and Small Business Saturday, special additions to the usual stock of ornaments and gifts in the shop. On Sunday evening, the artisans and fellow small business owners would gather to celebrate a hopefully successful and profitable weekend.

Buzz. Buzz.

"Heck." Gabe pulled out his phone, which was vibrating incessantly.

"At least we get chow now." I stretched. Retail work was surprisingly physical. Earlier in the day, Gabe had promised pizza at his house. Thank God. Not that I had anything against Zeb, but I wasn't ready to be alone with him again, at least not until I figured out my bizarre reaction to the dude.

"Change of plans." Looking up from his phone, Gabe frowned, deepening the worry lines around his eyes. "Paige isn't feeling well after the late night yesterday. Lucy wants her to rest."

"Probably a good idea." Fifteen years of playing poker with special forces operators allowed me to school my expression and voice to not reveal any disappointment.

"If it's okay, I'm going to leave you guys on your own for dinner and go check on Paige. Sorry." Gabe pulled some cash out of his worn black leather wallet. "I'll buy your pizza to make it up to you."

"I don't need your money." Zeb held up his hands, but Gabe merely turned and handed the money to me instead.

"Order the Mafia Meat Trio and think of me."

"Done." Unlike Zeb, I knew when to drop an argument. I'd simply return the cash when Gabe wasn't looking.

Back at the apartment, Zeb used an app on his phone to order pizza from the same place my crowd had frequented in high school.

"Pizza should be here in thirty minutes." He set his phone down on his desk. We both stood awkwardly in front of the one chair in the room. As I shifted my weight from side to side, my foot brushed the malfunctioning air mattress box.

Saved. Dropping to one knee, I examined the box, looking for any parts or clues we'd missed last night. "A half hour is enough time to solve this air mattress issue."

"Good idea," Zeb said way too brightly. He knelt next to me, and I glanced over at his locked front door. I never backed down from a challenge, but hell if I wasn't looking for an escape. We were alone, a whole evening stretching in front of us, a fact I was way, way too aware of.

Alone with only one viable bed.

Unacceptable. I couldn't spend another night mauling

Zeb in his sleep or staying awake trying to figure out why the scent of cinnamon was now my biggest turn-on. Nope. I needed rest and sanity.

Never had I scoured directions or packing materials so closely. As carefully as a surgeon performing open-heart surgery, I fiddled with the valves, swapping one for a spare in the box. Pressing the On switch, I held my breath.

"It's working!" Zeb crowed. Funny how enthusiasm totally transformed the guy. Earlier, when he'd been talking about the pleasure of helping customers find the perfect ornament, he'd been appealing in a way I really couldn't describe. All I knew was that watching him work all day had been a pleasure I really shouldn't have indulged in. And even more reason to pray the mattress stayed inflated. But so far, so good as air slowly filled the bed. "Go you!"

After I flipped the switch off, Zeb turned toward me, hand outstretched to slap mine.

"Go us." I accepted Zeb's high five, but a weird jolt of electricity shot down my arm. I held fast to his hand, trying to figure out why a simple gesture, one I'd done thousands of times, had my skin tingling and abs quivering. For his part, Zeb didn't flinch away. To the contrary, he locked eyes with me, gaze steady and sure as he closed his fingers over mine.

Now we were holding hands in midair, but hell if I could move. Breathing was challenging enough, let alone pulling away. My heart revved like a chopper about to lift off, my stomach doing the same swoopy thing it did every helicopter ride. Zeb's eyes were so pretty. How had I ever thought they looked like a turtle? No, the shade was closer to jade, the mottled beauty of natural stone, the sort that invited closer examination.

My other hand slid forward on some unauthorized

mission my brain wasn't a part of. It skimmed across Zeb's sturdy shoulder. *Reconnaissance.* He'd hung both our coats in his front closet, and despite the cool air of the apartment, his skin was so warm through the thin T-shirt. My fingers flexed, testing the muscle, enjoying the contrast to his soft palm.

"Atlas," Zeb whispered, drawing my name out with a breathy sigh. Had my name ever sounded so good? His mouth parted, pink tongue darting out to lick at his full lower lip.

And I lost my damn mind.

I closed the gap between us, mouth hovering over his. Never before had I experienced this overwhelming need to kiss someone. I'd been kissed before, but I couldn't remember being the one to move first. But I definitely was here. I couldn't blame Zeb for the way I lunged at him, the way my chest pounded with need.

"Please." Another ghost of a word across those mesmerizing lips. My ears rang with the heady novelty of the polite request—something rare in both my work and personal life.

I kissed him.

I couldn't not, and it wasn't simply the *please.* Rather, it was some sort of biological imperative, a need I couldn't quantify but had little hope of controlling. Further, Zeb's *please* was the sort of implicit consent that made pumping the brakes that much harder. Not to mention the enthusiastic way he met my mouth.

Also hard? My dick throbbed in my pants. Did I think Zeb was merely *attractive* when he was excited about something? No. He was intoxicating, a hundred-proof blend of joy and eagerness. Watching him enjoy himself had been fun, but kissing him was all-consuming.

His lips were impossibly soft, and he smelled even more like cinnamon this close. *Closer. Closer.* Whatever the distance between us, it was too much. I crushed him to me, and he made the sweetest sound of surrender, clinging to my shoulders, body radiating potent energy against mine. That devious tongue of his darted out, making contact with mine, and I nearly levitated, leaving the earth behind. All I wanted was more of this kiss.

Living dangerously, I mimicked his motion and was rewarded with a low moan. His beard was bristly against my skin, but I welcomed the added sensation. There was no mistaking I was kissing a guy, which should have been weird but somehow wasn't.

Or at least it wasn't weird enough to slow me down. Putting a hand behind his head, I tumbled him gently onto the air mattress next to us. And whoa, that was even better, him underneath me—

Knock. Knock. "Pizza."

"Oh fuck." Reality shoved its way back to the present, making me leap away from Zeb. Zeb, the guy I'd been kissing. Zeb, Gabe's little brother. Zeb, my roommate of sorts for the next month. "What did we do?"

"You kissed me." Zeb sounded all kinds of dazed, which only made him that much sexier. "First time a high five has ever turned into a kiss for me."

"Probably should have stuck with a fist bump." I groaned, flopping back down next to him. The bed was alarmingly squishy, but that was the least of my worries right then.

"Oh. You didn't like it." Zeb's expression went from passionate glow to crushed in zero point five seconds.

"Pizza!" The door rattled again.

"I better get the door." He clambered off the bed as if

I'd shoved him, and I might as well have for how dejected he looked as he fetched the pizza and brought it to his too-small dining table. "We'll need plates. And forks? Do you use a fork? Some people do. I'm not sure who, but—"

"Zeb. Chill." Putting a hand on his shoulder, I stopped him in front of the cabinet that held his collection of assorted plates. "We should talk."

"It's okay," he said far, far too brightly as he pulled away from me. "We don't need to."

"I hurt your feelings, and I didn't mean to." Might as well get that out there. I was nothing if not direct.

"But you also didn't mean to kiss me." He exhaled, the weight of my rejection hanging heavy between us.

"Can't say as I did." I rubbed my jaw.

"So not helping." He shook his head and retrieved two mismatched plates, handing me one. "Plate?"

"Wait. That didn't come out right." I trailed behind him to the table, where he plopped two slices of pizza on each of our plates. "I've never kissed a guy before."

"Never?" Zeb wrinkled his nose as he took a seat. He sounded decidedly skeptical. "Never even been tempted?"

"Not particularly." I waved a hand helplessly. "It's just…never come up."

"Well, something came up just now." He looked so pointedly at my groin that I couldn't sit down fast enough.

"Yeah, and trust me, no one is more surprised than me."

"How do you go thirty-five years and not know you might dig kissing guys?" Zeb scrutinized me like I might have the answer written on my forehead in invisible ink.

"No clue." I searched the deep recesses of my brain, the places I seldom went. Nope. Couldn't recall ever having the urge before. Never considered the possibility. I'd shared locker rooms with other guys for as long as I could remember—swimming pools, sports, military barracks, and more. Always kept my eyes to myself, thoughts carefully blank. I'd no more consider kissing a buddy than punching him.

"Come on." Zeb clearly wasn't letting this drop. "No crushes? No secret gay porn stash?"

I very nearly choked on my pizza, making a noise not unlike this one indignant goat I'd encountered in the Azores. "Um…"

"Oh?" Zeb's eyes went wide. "Come on, spill."

"No crushes. I've worked in male-dominated fields forever. If a thought in that direction were to ever enter my brain about *any* subordinate or coworker, I'd quash it immediately. It's like I've trained my brain to never think about sex on the job or in the locker room. And honestly, that goes for women too. I don't think about specific women hardly ever, rarely ones I know, and never on the job. Stray thoughts get people killed."

"Wow." Zeb blinked. "I can't imagine not daydreaming. Especially about sex. And what about porn? Surely, when you're alone…"

"Oh God. Are we really having this conversation?" Groaning, I shook my head. I took a bite of the spicy pizza. Swallowed. Zeb was still looking at me expectantly. "Fine. I don't like most porn. Too artificial. Too staged. Except…" I trailed off, but Zeb made a go-ahead gesture. "I got kind of into solo videos for a bit. Trying to time myself to come at the same time as the other person, like a race. I started with videos of amateur women, but somehow a dude one snuck in—"

"That's been known to happen." Despite his dry tone, Zeb's eyes twinkled.

"And I did like it," I admitted. "But that's not gay. It's more competitive than anything."

"I dunno, sounds pretty gay, dude. Or bi or pan. I mean, I assume you enjoy all the chicks you get to bang that Gabe's always teasing you about."

"Gabe would be wrong. Not that much banging at all." Like under five, with a few fingers to spare, but I wasn't giving Zeb a number to tease me with more.

"Weren't you some sort of stud in high school?" Zeb demanded around a mouthful of pizza.

"Hardly. Girls like me, but I've never been someone to make the first move—"

"Evidence to the contrary."

"Point taken." A growly noise escaped my throat. Damn it. Zeb undid every measured emotion I'd worked so hard to cultivate. "But back then especially, I seemed to attract women who were waiting on sex for one reason or another. And I was fine with that. Kissing was fun, but it wasn't anything to write home about. And then, when I finally did have sex, it was…underwhelming. Figured maybe I'm just clueless at it."

"I could help you get less clueless." Zeb smirked.

I swallowed fast to avoid death by pizza crust. "You could do *what?*"

Eight

ZEB

I waited for Atlas to set aside his slice of pizza. Didn't want the guy dying on my watch. But I also wasn't about to mince words. This was my big chance.

"If you want to improve your sex skills, you should have sex with me." I looked at him, gaze not wavering, so he'd know I was serious. Showing nerves would only make it easier for him to dismiss me.

"Uh?" Atlas made a gurgling noise.

"Don't choke at the idea." Standing, I quickly fetched him a glass of water and set it in front of him. "And I'm not discounting that you could simply be not into sex at all. Maybe you're demi or ace. However, if sex with women was underwhelming…"

Atlas cut me off with a dismissive noise. "Are you suggesting I have gay sex simply because of one fantastic kiss? To rule out the possibility I've been missing out?"

"Fantastic kiss." I beamed at his compliment. Not that it was a competition, but I wanted to be the best kiss he'd ever had and more. "And yes, I know it's cliché, but if kissing women is underwhelming and kissing me was awesome, why not test my theory?"

"I don't think I could hide being bi from myself." Atlas pursed his mouth before studying his half-eaten plate of pizza like it might have the answer.

"You would hardly be the first person to manage that feat," I pointed out.

"Maybe." He flexed his jaw like he'd had to work to admit that much. "Even if I wanted to test this theory of yours, you're Gabe's little brother."

"I'm twenty-eight." I was so very tired of reminding everyone around me that I wasn't a kid anymore and hadn't been for quite some time. "And I was nineteen and legal at Gabe and Paige's wedding. I would have happily banged you then too."

"Jesus." His expression went from uncomfortable to pained. "Don't say those kinds of things, Zeb."

"Why not? It's true. And I saw you watching me dance." That, along with his perpetually single status, had given me almost a decade's worth of hope. "Maybe you're not as straight as you've always thought."

"You're fun to watch. I like your…enthusiasm. In all things." Atlas Orion, smooth military operator, blushed. Like legit pink cheeks and all. "But I can't have sex with you no matter how old you are. You're still my best friend's little brother. He'd have a fit."

"Gabe is too busy worrying about everything else to care what we get up to in private here." I gestured with my slice of pizza. "I'm not suggesting he needs to know. But we've got a month, right?" I wasn't under any illusion that I could talk Atlas into more than that. He was married to the navy, and I was tied to Kringle's Crossing, and those were the facts. But also facts? Our combustible chemistry.

"A month is more than enough time to see whether all sex is underwhelming for you, which would be fine. Maybe you're some flavor of ace, and then we shake hands and go back to being buddies. Or maybe I'm right, and you just haven't had sex with the right person yet."

"The right person being you." Tilting his head, Atlas looked down at me.

"Well, I am here." I spread my hands wide. "And a fantastic kisser."

"You're not going to let me forget that, are you?"

"Nope." I grinned at him, then turned more serious. "But I'm also not going to twist your arm. You want to have sex, test my theory? You know where I live."

I didn't want to merely wear him down and talk him into having a fling with me. That wouldn't be at all cool. I wanted him to want this too.

"Because I live here too. At least for now." He groaned, back to looking pained. His gaze darted over my shoulder toward my front door. "Jesus. I need air. I'm going for a walk."

He pushed away from the table, leaving one piece of pizza half-eaten. I could beg him to stay and eat more. And talk. But Atlas was a grown adult, and if he needed time to think, I could offer him space. He knew this town enough that I wasn't too worried about him getting lost.

"Don't forget your jacket," I called after him as he strode toward the door. "And gloves. It's cold out there."

He glanced back over his shoulder, and the strangest expression crossed his face. His eyes widened like he was surprised, but the rest of his features softened, a tenderness I hadn't seen from him before. The rare display of emotion from him made it easier to watch him walk away.

I trusted he'd be back before bed, and perhaps the

thinking time afforded by a long, cold walk would warm him up to the idea of a hot experiment with me. And if not, well, I'd tried. I wasn't going to regret making the offer, but I also wasn't going to be a jerk if he didn't want to take me up on it.

Atlas was gone longer than I'd expected. Even given his military levels of fitness, it was still a damn chilly night. Resigned, I made up the saggy air mattress with a spare pair of sheets and a comforter. As I added a pillow from my bed, Atlas finally arrived back. I hadn't bothered locking the door, and he didn't knock as he walked back in, stopping by the closet to peel off his gloves and jacket.

"How was the walk?" I yawned like I'd been the one trekking across town.

"Cold." Voice grim, he frowned down at the air bed. "You're sleeping out here?"

"Figured it was for the best. I don't want to pressure you." I kept my tone pragmatic. He didn't need a guilt trip or the weight of my disappointment. "I want to have a good time with you, not be a huge regret. You want something. All you need to do is ask."

"I can't." He said it simply, no extra emotion, but the pain in his eyes said it all for him. He'd wrestled with the decision. Face still pink from the cold, he rubbed his arms. I wanted to warm him up in the worst way, but I needed to respect his choice.

"Okay." I kept my voice low and measured. "Goodnight, Atlas. Sleep well."

"You too." He paused for what seemed like the longest second on record, gaze darting back and forth between me and the air mattress. Finally, he sighed heavily and headed to my room.

Click went the door, and with it, my hopes of getting lucky that night with Atlas. And probably ever, given how resigned he'd sounded.

Not surprisingly, I couldn't sleep. The mattress started out mushy and worsened from there. I tried adding air, which made a racket. Still mushy and, if anything, flatter than ever. Attempting to will my body to sleep, I closed my eyes only to have the bed lurch and roll like I was on a rowboat at sea.

Hiss. Too uneven to lay on, it rapidly deflated, especially after I rolled off the thing. I tried again to add air to no avail.

"What's going on?" Atlas appeared in the doorway. *Crap.* The last thing I needed was him feeling guilty or thinking I was angling for an invite to my bed.

"Nothing you need to worry about." Forcing a smile, I gestured for him to return to the bedroom. "A little problem with the mattress staying inflated, but you can go back to bed."

"No, I can't." He glared at me, frustration clear even in the dim hallway light. "Not with you thrashing around out here and turning the motor on and off."

"Sorry." I quickly grabbed my pillow and wrapped up in my comforter like an uncomfortable burrito on top of the flat air mattress. "Here. See? I can sleep like this, no problem."

"Don't be an idiot." Atlas crossed the room to come shove my shoulder. When that didn't work, he freed one of my arms and hauled me upright. I had no business getting aroused, but I couldn't deny what a turn-on his strength was. And his commanding tone. "You're not sleeping on the floor."

"I'm not sure I trust myself in a bed with you," I admitted. Atlas had been the one to sleep-cuddle last night, but I didn't trust my body not to defy my best intentions and end up on his side of the bed.

"I'll take my chances." He pulled me toward my room. "Come on, Zeb. Come to bed."

Nine

ATLAS

I couldn't sleep. I'd slept on planes, transport trucks, buses, and even my much-hated nemesis: helicopters. I'd slept in war zones, barracks, a few fields and beaches, not to mention a cave or two. But never had sleep been as elusive as lying next to Zeb. When I'd discovered him huddled on the floor in his comforter, trying to make the air mattress work, I'd been physically incapable of leaving him there. I'd foolishly figured that my long, cold walk, combined with the retail shift earlier in the day, might have worn me out enough for sleep.

Wrong.

I'd walked from Zeb's apartment, past downtown, past Seasons, past the Christmas tree lot, the teeny grocery store, the high school that looked unchanged from fifteen years ago, and I'd ended up at the park. I'd followed the entire fitness loop, hammering out pushups, pullups, running a length of tires, and more. I'd sweat enough to discard my jacket, yet I couldn't outrun that kiss.

Or Zeb's offer to be my sex experiment.

The worst part was how damn tempted I was to take

him up on it. I'd always expected more from kissing and sex. I tried not to dwell on it, but the mediocre results thus far had been frustrating and disappointing. And then I'd kissed Zeb, which had been the opposite of underwhelming.

More like overwhelming, all-consuming, and damn if I didn't want more. If a single kiss had been that good, I might not survive the sex. And I was almost willing to take the risk. Almost. If Zeb weren't Gabe's little brother. If he wasn't so nice. He deserved better than some secret holiday fling.

If only. I'd learned the hard way not to make wishes. Every time I'd wished for my parents to put down roots, they'd seemed to move on that much faster. I'd wanted us to be more like the Seasons family. I'd wished for them to be stable, *normal* parents, and well, we all knew how that had turned out. However, as I lay there in the dark next to Zeb, I couldn't help dwelling on how much I wanted things to be different. And it didn't help that Zeb was also wide awake. He wasn't even trying to disguise his breathing or rigid posture.

It was only a matter of time before one of us spoke.

"You know what I keep thinking about?" Zeb asked conversationally like it was the middle of the afternoon and we were on lunch break.

"That kiss?" Oops. I usually had more control over my mouth, but this evening had proven me wrong in multiple ways.

"No, actually." Zeb rolled toward me, going onto one elbow. I could almost *hear* him beaming. "But if that's on your brain…"

"How could it not be?" I groaned.

"It was good, wasn't it?" He sounded far too pleased

with himself, and when he flipped on the dim bedside lamp to peer down at me, I didn't protest. His smug expression was too cute to miss.

"Amazing." I couldn't lie. "But we shouldn't…"

"And we don't have to if you don't want to." Zeb was far too jolly for the hour and the subject matter. It wasn't fair, but I wanted him to beg me, cajole me, maybe even dare me into kissing him again. Anything to take the choice out of my hands. But he was far too nice for that. "There is another option, one that might help us both sleep."

"Oh?" My voice came out huskier and more seductive than I'd ever heard it. "Tell me."

"Well, there is one thing that always makes me fall asleep. And earlier, you mentioned enjoying solo porn. Something about a race? Trying to come at the same time? What if we had…a competition?"

"Yes." The word rushed past my lips and good sense both. "That. We could jerk off. Not much different from watching porn if we don't touch."

"I mean, we could touch…" Zeb trailed off with a wistful sigh. "But I can be good. I said no pressure. If you'd like to try the jerking off idea though…"

Damn it. He was going to make me say it twice.

"Yeah." I managed to make my tone almost indifferent. "Gotta sleep sometime."

"Yep." He chuckled as if he didn't buy my lack of care. "How do you want to do it?"

Every way. All the ways. Ways I don't know yet. A strangled noise escaped my throat.

"I meant, do you want to keep the light on?" Zeb's voice was unsteady. He was majorly overthinking this, which was adorable. "Whatever makes you the most comfortable."

"Lights on. I wanna see." Already, I was breathing hard, simply from picturing Zeb touching himself. Yeah, I totally wanted to see that. "And I want to hear too. Hearing is the best part, so don't be quiet."

"Oh, you are good at giving orders." Zeb lay back against his pillow, running a hand down his torso and over the front of his pajama pants, which already sported an impressive tent.

"Get it out." If he liked me in charge, then commanding I could be. This might have been Zeb's idea, but I really liked directing him. Slowly, as if trying to tease, Zeb withdrew his dick. Other than porn, I'd never seen another erect cock in person. Zeb's was ruddy, a duskier pink than I'd expected, and thick, especially at the base where a hint of hair peeked out of his fly. He wasn't as long as some porn dicks, but I found his cock way more intriguing, especially the oval head, slightly off-center slit, and thick meandering vein. "Touch it."

"Uh-huh." Zeb grunted softly as he fisted his cock. And that was unexpectedly sexy, the way his shaft seemed to perfectly fit his hand. He gave a couple of strokes. My gaze was riveted to the motion of his hand as I cataloged all the little details. His fist was tighter at the base, looser on the upstroke, thumb slightly angled. And I liked how his abs tensed and relaxed with each pass of his hand. His other hand was splayed across his belly, and his forehead was creased with concentration. Fascinating.

"This won't be much of a race if you're not competing." Zeb stopped to glare at me.

"I am. Trust me." I ran a hand down to my groin, but I didn't actually touch my dick. As turned on as Zeb was making me, I didn't trust myself not to shoot too soon. "I'll play catch-up. Just wanna watch you for a second."

And watch I did, inhaling with Zeb, our shuddery breaths syncing. I was utterly mesmerized by his every movement and soft sound, and I made a noise of protest when he stopped again.

"I want to see you too." His demand came out closer to begging, and hell, if I could deny him.

"Yeah." I pulled my aching cock out. Unlike Zeb, who had a perfectly proportioned dick, I had an awkward erection—too thick for my fingers to meet, not quite big enough to warrant a second hand, and a wide head that made my few forays into condom-wearing difficult.

"Geez, Atlas." Zeb whistled low. "Warn a guy that you're packing a missile."

"Sorry—"

"Did I sound like that was a complaint?"

Considering Zeb's eyes were the size of coasters and locked on my dick, I supposed not, but I merely made a noncommittal grumble, unsure what to make of the praise. "You wouldn't be the first. Apparently, it can be uncomfortable…"

"And God gave us lube for a reason," Zeb said reverently, moving his hand like he might be about to pat my shoulder before abruptly dropping it. "Trust me that size is not an issue for me for any activity you might dream up."

"Don't tempt me," I growled a warning.

"I'd apologize, but I do like tempting you." Raising his gaze to meet my eyes, he grinned at me. "I'd like to tempt you and that monster more."

"Better not make me pin you down and cover your mouth."

"Mmmm." Zeb made a hungry noise straight out of porn. "That's hardly a threat, Atlas."

"Fuck. Fuck." I had to let go of my cock before something embarrassing happened.

"Sorry," Zeb chirped. "I teased too far—"

"Not. Too. Far." I squished my eyes shut, but that hardly helped because all I could see was that image of me pinning Zeb to the bed.

"*Oh.*" Zeb's mouth made a perfect circle. "You were close?"

"Get back to stroking, Zeb. Enough questions."

"Fine, fine, make me pleasure myself." He gave an indulgent stretch, a full body roll complete with a groan. He stroked himself slowly, clearly showing off, unconstrained by time, nosy neighbors, or thin walls, the sort of luxury I'd seldom known. Watching him enjoy himself made my pulse hum and my dick throb.

As long as I didn't touch myself, I could probably last—

"*Ahhh.*" And then Zeb went and made a noise so primal and blatantly sexual that precome beaded up at my tip and coming untouched became a distinct possibility.

"Fuck. More noises like that." I gave the order, knowing full well I was signing my doom.

"You like it loud?" Zeb smiled over at me, playing his reactions up, squeezing and teasing, varying his strokes and finding ample cause to moan. I wanted to be the one coaxing those sounds loose so much that my hands shook. Only inexperience and some last illusions of nobility kept me from reaching for him, especially when Zeb shuddered. "I'm close."

Body tensing like he was preparing to come, he rucked up his T-shirt with his free hand, revealing a fuzzy stomach with reddish hair. Fuck. Even his belly was sexy. Made me want to rest my head there and...

Nope. I couldn't let my brain follow that thought unless I wanted to detonate like a stack of C-4.

"So close," he moaned, repeating the warning.

"Not yet. Wait." I had no business giving that command, seeing as how I was clinging to the edge by a fingernail myself. "It'll be better if you wait."

"It'd be better if you'd give me more of a show," he countered.

"Fine. Watch me." Barely hovering my hand over my shaft, I traced the length with a single finger, up and back.

"No fair teasing." Zeb leaned closer, and his hair smelled like autumn: cinnamon and apples and good memories. Lord, the scent alone would get me there, not to mention Zeb's voice, eager and intent. "Show me how you usually do it."

"I'm incredibly efficient. Not sexy." I gave a self-conscious laugh as I shrugged out of my T-shirt and wrapped it around my right hand.

"I'll be the judge of that." Zeb's chuckle was far kinder. "Of course, all you have to do is breathe, and you're sexy as fuck."

"Not exactly helping me not come." My voice was all strained. The familiar combo of loose grip and soft cotton had my back arching.

"God. You're gonna get me there." Zeb sounded nothing short of awestruck. His tongue darted out to lick his lip, and my last thread of control snapped.

"Come here." I motioned him closer with my left hand, but to my surprise, Zeb didn't budge.

"I thought you said no touching."

"Come here." I made my voice sterner, and that did

the trick, bringing Zeb right up next to me where I wanted him, at the perfect distance for yanking into a near-brutal kiss. My cock pulsed, and that I didn't come was a fucking miracle because he tasted even better than I remembered. Zeb's little whimper of surrender was the sweetest sound I'd ever heard. "Fuck. Fuck."

I held Zeb so tightly against my side that I could feel the subtle motions of his arm as he resumed stroking. I tried to do the same, and the barest brush of my hand had my dick leaking more.

"I need to come," he panted against my lips before kissing me again. His urgency was so sexy, the way he seemed to crave this. I'd never had anyone so damn *hungry* for me before, and I was rapidly becoming a convert for Zeb's haven't-had-the-right-partner theory. Because *damn*, all sex should be this good. And we weren't touching, not really. Just kissing and stroking ourselves, and God, I was right there as well.

"Me too, baby. Me too." My eyes threatened to close, but I forced them to stay open because I didn't want to miss a second of Zeb coming. "Tell me when."

"There. Oh. Fuck. It's right there." Zeb's motions and moans both intensified. I stilled my hand long enough for a rosy flush to spread up his neck, across his cheeks, and for his eyes to flutter shut. He stroked himself far faster and tighter than I would have dared. I held my breath, tensing right alongside him.

"That's it," I urged, and the second he grunted, white creamy fluid erupting over his fist, I was coming as well from the barest movement of my hand. I came into my shirt, hard, almost painful waves that made my body bow and everything from my teeth to my toes ache.

"Damn. Damn. Damn." Never, ever had I come so

hard, so quickly, or from doing so little. If my few prior attempts at sex had been a disappointing appetizer, this was a goddamned Vegas buffet with a five-star chef at the helm, and I wanted to gorge on the sheer pleasure for hours. Rather than stifle my breathing as I ordinarily would, I let myself moan and shudder and float slowly, gently back down.

"Oh wow." Zeb peered down at me, gaze amused and amazed both. "Did I win or did I lose?"

"Everyone won." I groaned and tugged him back down. He rolled away to remove his shirt, cleaning up the mess on his belly before flipping off the light. I made a sound of protest, and he returned to my side, head on my shoulder, little sleepy breaths huffing against my neck.

"Congrats to us." Zeb gave a short, tired laugh.

Long after he drifted off, I lay there. I'd lied. We hadn't won a damn thing. In fact, I'd lost because I wanted to do that again and again and again until spring emerged, and then I wanted to do it in the sunshine. Every damn *season*. I wanted it all, but I couldn't let myself have any of it.

Ten

ZEB

28 SHOPPING DAYS UNTIL CHRISTMAS

The knitters were at it again. All weekend, Gabe's bright idea to place all the yarn-based crafters in a row for the handmade gift bazaar had been tempting fate. Someone was going to get stabbed with a giant pointed needle before this Sunday night was over. Quite possibly by me. I glanced over at the bar area where Atlas was serving up drinks for the crafters' dinner.

He'd been avoiding me for almost forty-eight hours. Forty-eight long hours. All Saturday, he'd kept busy wrapping purchases and running errands for Gabe. I'd had a prescheduled livestream gaming event in the evening. Atlas had gone to Gabe's for dinner and stayed over on the pretext of letting me work, but I knew the truth. He'd liked the kissing and the jerking off far too much to let himself have a repeat and didn't want to risk a real conversation with me.

Eventually, we'd have to talk, but I'd been run ragged by work at Seasons and trying to keep my gaming channel active and relevant. I'd spent most of Saturday and Sunday trying to untangle the verbal gnarls and knots the fiber artists kept hurling at each other.

And now it was Sunday evening, and tensions had reached a fraying point.

"Muriel Akin, you're a lying thief of a knitter." Three crafters stood near the line for drinks, and the one speaking had a pinched expression, short burgundy hair, sharply angled glasses, and a sharper tongue. "You stole that mini-sweater ornament idea from me."

"Mopsy Tucker, I should have known you'd act like you were first to put a sweater on an ornament hanger." Muriel had a riot of silver curls, matching silver glasses, and an ample chest festooned with a half-dozen bead necklaces in holiday colors. "You're a self-righteous—"

"Ladies!" The third crafter held up a hand. Connie was a retired elementary school teacher with super short salt-and-pepper hair who'd done a brisk trade all weekend in crocheted potholders.

"Connie, you stay out of this." Mopsy made a *tsking* noise. Her real name was Margaret, and she worked in the Kringle's Crossing post office when she wasn't busy running the local knitting guild. I'd had enough dealings with her over the years to know she was pickier than Gabe and never missed a chance to press a point. "You crocheters all share patterns loosey-goosey anyway. In addition to being first in the area to offer the sweater ornaments, I'm selling my pattern online."

"Good for you, Mopsy." Muriel gave an epic eye roll. "Some of us don't need patterns."

"I agree. I came up with my Disney tea cozies on my own," Connie added brightly.

"You're courting a cease-and-desist letter from an angry movie studio." Mopsy clucked. "And as for—"

"Who needs a drink?" I pitched my voice to be as cheerful as possible, angling myself out of knitting needle range while steering the trio closer to the bar.

"Me!" Connie stepped up to the bar. "I'll take that peppermint cocktail everyone is raving about."

Mopsy snorted. "I don't hold with hard liquor."

"We *know.*" Muriel, who was also part of the knitting guild, had the tone of someone who'd put up with a frenemy for decades.

"We have tea and soda." Luckily, I'd grown up in customer service and could keep my tone bland and soothing even with the rudest patrons.

"I make a mean mocktail." Having finished with the earlier drink rush, Atlas turned his attention to the feuding crafters. He pointed at the hand-lettered drinks sign Paige had made. "Pick your nonalcoholic poison."

"Well, I suppose I could try the cranberry spritzer." Mopsy patted her hair, expression far less homicidal.

"It's delicious." A new crafter to this year's lineup, a blond silversmith, leaned against the bar, his gaze blatantly undressing Atlas as he handed over a few bills. "I'll have another. Keep the change."

"Sure thing, Jon."

That Atlas already knew the blond's name made heat gather at the back of my neck and the collar of my white waiter's shirt itch. I was neither blond nor hot, and suddenly, my offer to teach Atlas about sex seemed more than a little foolish. What did he need my help for?

"Tell me more about what you do in the navy," Jon demanded as Atlas passed over the drink.

"Can't tell much." Atlas gave a humble shrug. "Mainly, I get folks home. Extraction."

"Oooh, top secret and noble." Jon's unnaturally blue eyes sparkled as he dared to touch the anchor tattoo on Atlas's forearm. And I'd had enough.

I coughed. Loudly. "Atlas? Can you help me bring out the desserts?"

"Sure thing." Affable as ever, Atlas followed me to the kitchen, where two carts with neatly stacked plates of pie were waiting.

Unfortunately, three seconds after we entered the kitchen, Gabe came sprinting after us.

"Why is no one working the bar?" He glared right at me, guessing correctly that I was the culprit. "And why are you making Atlas do the desserts? I asked you to handle bringing the pies out."

"I…uh…"

"We need Atlas behind the bar." Gabe pointed at the kitchen door as he scolded. "Not only is he popular with the ladies, we're offering a cash bar tonight. We could use the extra income."

"I'm on it." Sparing a second to give me one hell of a searching look, Atlas darted back out to the dining room.

Gah. Of course Gabe had picked up on Atlas's *popularity*. He didn't miss much, which was another reason I had no business dreaming of a secret fling with Atlas. Gabe might have the gender wrong, but he'd likely cheer any experiments on. It would be my sort of luck to plant the seed of bisexuality or whatever, only for Atlas to test the theory with someone else.

Studying the cart of pie to avoid looking at Gabe, I blew out a long breath, ruffling my badly-in-need-of-a-trim hair.

"You okay?" To my surprise, Gabe put a hand on my shoulder. "You've seemed off all day. Am I working you too hard?"

"Nah." I waved his concern off. "And I could say the same thing about you. Wasn't this supposed to be one of our best weekends for sales?"

"Yeah. But we're down from last year. That new shopping complex down the interstate with all the big box stores keeps luring customers away." Gabe twisted his hands helplessly before shaking them out and turning to straighten the pie plates. "Just can't seem to get ahead."

"We'll get there." I slung an arm around his too-thin shoulders. "You need to stop stressing out so much."

"I can't help it. I'm about to be a dad. It's what dads do."

"I know. I remember." My voice went soft and faraway. "We were lucky to learn from one of the best. I know you'll be a good dad, Gabe."

"Sorry." Gabe's expression echoed my own blend of nostalgia and grief. "I'll try to stop nagging as much. I just want everything—"

"To be Seasons Special." I did a pitch-perfect imitation of our grandfather, smiling when I got a chuckle out of Gabe. "I get it, bro. Just maybe lay off a little? Yourself included."

"I'll try." Gabe moved so I could wheel the cart to the door. "Thanks, Zeb."

That rare apology and agreement from Gabe was why I'd kept working here long past needing the money. This was *family*, which was why Gabe's critique sliced deeper, and why his welfare, as well as that of the business itself, mattered. He might be a neurotic boss, but he was also my big brother.

Brain swirling with worries about Gabe's stress level, I set up the dessert buffet and almost forgot about my cheap ploy to get Atlas away from the flirty silversmith. Almost. I had to haul a tray of glassware to the bar, and one pointed look from Atlas was enough to remind me what an idiot I'd been.

To his credit, Atlas waited until there was no line at the bar to turn every ounce of his naval chief persona on me. "What was that all about?"

"All what? I wanted some help. That's all." I was a terrible liar, but I had to at least try playing stupid.

"Come on, Zeb. You wanted to get me away from the fighting knitters? Why?"

I groaned. Unlike me and my fake ignorance, Atlas was painfully clueless. "No, dude, I was saving you from the uncomfortable flirting."

"Flirting?" Atlas scrunched up his face. "All I was doing was mixing drinks."

"Seriously?" I kept my voice low but let my skepticism show. "That silversmith was all over you."

Stepping closer, Atlas tilted his head, studying me far too intently. "Were you jealous?"

"Jealous? Me? Nah." Even my scoff sounded fake, and I wasn't surprised when Atlas frowned.

"I think you were. I'm not sure I get why though. Am I supposed to not talk to the customers?"

"Yes. No. I don't know." I threw up my hands. "And you might not have been flirting back, but the customers definitely were. Hell, if you wanted it, I'm sure Jon the Silversmith would be game for a parking lot meetup after your shift."

"A...*oh.*" Atlas's eyes widened. "You thought I'd be down for that?"

"Wouldn't you?" I hissed, a hurt, angry whisper.

"Because I kissed you?" Atlas had also whispered, but his tone had been far more befuddled. The man was going to make me go gray before thirty.

I made a frustrated noise. "Because you haven't kissed me since!"

"Because I'm trying to do the right thing." Atlas stepped closer, eyes trained on my mouth. This was dangerous territory. A dining room full of crafters, none of whom were paying us any attention, but we'd get noticed in a hurry if I planted one on Atlas like I wanted.

"Says you." I fisted my hands to keep from reaching for him. "How about doing the wrong thing and seeing how that feels instead?"

Atlas inhaled sharply. And crowded room or not, I braced for an angry kiss.

"Zeb!" Still in kitchen whites, Nix sauntered up to the bar. "Quit bugging Atlas. The dinner food on the buffet needs clearing now that everyone's moved on to dessert."

"I wasn't—" I sputtered, unsure exactly what Nix thought they'd seen.

"Eagles lost today. That's all." Atlas shrugged, a far better liar than I could ever hope to be. "I owe Zeb. Later."

"Football? You guys were betting on football?" Nix blinked. "Does Zeb know the kicker from the quarterback?"

"Yep." I nodded a bit too enthusiastically. "The kicker does the kicking."

"Uh-huh." Nix looked doubtful but wandered off in the direction of the buffet table.

Atlas put a hand on my arm when I turned to follow them. "Zeb—"

"*Later*. We'll settle up." Echoing his lie about owing me some sort of payback I had no intention of holding him to, I tried to brush by him.

"Wait." His eyes widened as if he couldn't believe I was putting him off.

"Seriously, dude." I shook my head. Lord, spare me self-righteous naval chiefs who were a little too used to having their orders followed. "Later."

"No. Something's wrong at the knitters' table." He pointed across the room before taking off at a sprint, leaving me no choice but to follow.

Eleven

ATLAS

"What's wrong?" Zeb charged after me, and we reached the knitters' table at approximately the same time.

"Mopsy choked." I'd seen her coughing from across the room.

"I'm...okay." Clutching her napkin, she was no longer choking, but I studied her closely. Something was off.

"Oh, Mopsy's just being dramatic." Muriel waved a hand, silver curls bouncing.

"Are you sure, Muriel?" Connie, the crocheter and apparent peacemaker of the group, leaned closer to Mopsy.

"Choked. On pie crust." Mopsy's speech was slurred, and I knew for a fact she hadn't had a drop of alcohol.

"Has that happened before?" I asked.

"Choking?" Muriel answered before Mopsy could. "Everyone does it when they eat too fast."

I barely heard Muriel because my gaze was trained on Mopsy. Was one pupil bigger than the other? I couldn't tell, but the way she opened and closed her mouth like she was struggling to speak worried me further.

"That wasn't an ordinary choking." I crouched to better look at Mopsy's face. "Put your hands out."

She did so, and the left had a very noticeable tremor.

"Got your phone?" I asked Zeb in a low voice before returning my attention to Mopsy. "What's today's date?"

"Date?" Mopsy frowned.

"Mopsy." Muriel sounded way more concerned now. "How many stitches to the inch for a pair of house socks?"

"Stitches…itch. Itch." Mopsy sounded close to tears, voice wavering, and I didn't like the way her face sagged at all.

"It's okay," I soothed, taking one of her slim wrists to check her pulse. "Breathe for me. Nice and steady."

"I've got my phone." Zeb bent close to my ear, and for once, I wasn't hyperaware of his nearness. "Want me to make the call?"

Whatever our argument earlier, Zeb had clearly set it aside and was following my train of thought. Good. I liked a sharp-minded person.

"Yep." Straightening, I stepped to the side, motioning him to follow. "Call 9-1-1. Tell them we've got a suspected stroke. Facial weakness. Difficulty swallowing. Hand tremors. Trouble thinking. High pulse. Pale, clammy skin."

While Zeb made the call, I searched the room for Gabe but didn't see him. At least the knitters' table was in the rear of the room, and others lingering over dessert didn't appear to have noticed what was going on. I returned to Mopsy's side, dread gathering in my stomach at how her eyes kept fluttering shut.

"Muriel, you and Connie help me get Mopsy to that sofa." Luckily, a narrow sofa had been moved to the back wall to make room for the dining tables. As soon as we got

Mopsy situated, she slumped, exactly as I'd feared, alertness decreasing markedly.

Phone in hand, Zeb rushed back over. "The Kringle's Crossing clinic is closed for the weekend. The nearest hospital is going to be West Chester, and that's at least forty-five minutes away. And 9-1-1 says the EMT crew from our fire station is working a car accident. They've got another crew on the way from Woodville though."

"Not fast enough." Like Zeb, I kept my voice low. "She's losing consciousness."

Zeb relayed that information into his phone. "The dispatcher is checking on availability for a life flight helicopter. Problem is these downtown streets are so narrow and hilly."

"Let me talk to them." I held out a hand for the phone. If there was one thing I knew how to do, it was getting a chopper inbound into a tight spot. And sure enough, after a brief conversation with the dispatcher that included my qualifications, we had a plan.

"Okay, Zeb, I need you to keep Mopsy calm. Keep talking to her, nice and soft, even if she's not speaking back." I waited for Zeb to nod before moving to the center of the room. By this point, some people had started to notice the happenings in the back of the room. "Everyone, listen up. I need you to stay calm, but there's a medical emergency, and we're going to need everyone's help. We've got a chopper on the way. ETA: ten minutes. The flattest, widest spot is this parking lot. If you have a car in the lot, we need you to move it now. We need this lot empty."

"In ten minutes?" Gabe emerged from the kitchen, quickly followed by Nix and the kitchen crew.

"And we're gonna do it with time to spare," I said after filling him in. "Gabe, you make sure no one comes into the lot other than the EMT crew if they beat the chopper. Waitstaff, I need you available to move cars for people who are unable to drive and to direct folks out of the lot, keeping everything orderly. No fender benders, but also no dilly-dallying."

I didn't *want* a medical emergency, but I couldn't deny I was in my element and had missed the adrenaline rush of bringing an operation together in record time. I walked back over to the couch where Mopsy was reclining, flanked by the other two women. I did a quick check of her vitals to relay to the ER dispatcher.

"Now, who here knows Mopsy's next of kin?" I asked the women. "Have they been called?"

"She lives alone. Never married. There's a sister, though, somewhere over by Villanova."

"Good info." I kept my voice neutral even though my mind flashed to the last time I had to fill out paperwork for the navy. As always, I'd struggled with the *in case of emergency* sections. Who to call? Who would want to know? Would I want Aunt Lucy to have the burden of settling my affairs? Morbid thoughts like those had played chase in my brain until I'd finally filled in Gabe's name and number, hating adding that to his responsibilities. But like Mopsy, I ticked those *lives alone* and *never married* boxes. My chest pinched, but I forced myself to ignore it. "Connie, you search her phone. See if you can locate the sister."

"What can I do?" Muriel asked as she fiddled with her necklaces. "This is my fault. I made her so angry."

"You didn't cause a potential stroke." I took a moment to pat her shoulder. She needed something to do. "Can you make a list of what Mopsy's going to need at the hospital in Chester or Philly if they send her there?"

"I can do that." Muriel nodded as sharply as any new recruit. "And I'll call her supervisor at the post office."

I headed back to check the parking lot. A few minutes later, the Woodville Fire Department crew and a police cruiser pulled in to prepare for the life flight helicopter. The EMTs quickly took over assessing Mopsy's condition, and the lead EMT took a moment to check in with me.

"ETA on the chopper is two minutes," she reported as she unzipped her thick winter parka. She had pale blonde hair and sharp eyes. "How on earth did you clear that lot so quickly?"

"He's a freaking superhero." Zeb, who had been standing nearby, answered for me. The amazement in his eyes was good for my ego, but I knew better.

"Nah. Just good at organizing."

"I'll say." The EMT gave a short laugh before her radio crackled. She returned her attention to her crew. "Okay, chopper is incoming. Let's get her loaded up."

"What?" Mopsy roused briefly as the EMTs transferred her to a stretcher, wrapping her in blankets for the cold night outside.

"You're going for a ride." I stepped closer to the stretcher, surprised at how scratchy my throat had turned. "Helicopter. They're going to take good care of you."

"You're going to be okay, Mopsy," Zeb added.

We both followed the stretcher and crew to the parking lot, hanging back while the EMTs transferred Mopsy to the helicopter crew. I couldn't help my shudder as the chopper prepared to liftoff.

"What's wrong?" Zeb asked, touching my arm after the helicopter departed and we could hear each other again. "Bad sense about Mopsy?"

"Not that. If they can get her into surgery, her prognosis is decent." I tried to pitch my voice to be reassuring, but my apprehension came out anyway. "I just don't like choppers."

"Says the guy who got one here pronto." Zeb rubbed my biceps. "And you ride in them all the time, right?"

"Yeah. Don't have to like them though." I jammed my hands in my pockets. "All it takes is a few rough landings for the novelty to wear off."

Zeb studied me closely. "You ever think about getting out of the navy? Then you wouldn't have to ride in helicopters."

His cautious tone said this was more than a casual question, but I couldn't let myself think of the deeper implications right then. A different place, a different time, and yeah, we might have…

Nope. Not letting my brain go there.

"Nah." I met Zeb's caution with faked indifference. "I've got my sights on making senior chief before I do my twenty. I want that retirement. Security my folks never had with a steady paycheck. But also, I've got a team counting on me." My voice turned more serious. Zeb needed to understand this part too. "My team…it's the closest I've got to family."

Zeb frowned. "You've got friends. Like Gabe."

"Gabe's got his own family now."

"True." Zeb measured out the word. He and Gabe might be biological brothers, but he understood what I was saying. Depressing but true. He glanced back at the building. "Speaking of my brother, I better get to cleaning up. Sooner I get that done, sooner I can get home. You staying with me tonight?"

"Yeah." Probably wasn't smart with all this adrenaline. I needed to do something smart before I followed Zeb's earlier advice and did the wrong thing. Too bad the wrong thing was so damn tempting.

Twelve

ZEB

"You're really good at that." Atlas's voice startled me into swiveling away from my monitor. I'd missed the sound of the shower shutting off while recording a quick video for my channel. He'd waited till I flipped the mic off, but the compliment made my skin buzz like static from a wonky audio. I wasn't used to in-person critique or praise.

"You were watching me record?"

"Just the last few minutes. I like listening to you talk." Atlas sounded slightly puzzled as if he were reasoning something important out. He'd seemed off ever since the emergency at Seasons. He'd been amazing with spotting the crisis, getting the helicopter in, and getting Mopsy the help she needed with a good chance to save her life. While we were cleaning up, we'd heard that she was already in surgery, thanks in large part to Atlas's quick thinking.

But instead of acting triumphant, Atlas had been quietly reflective. Reminded me of a friend I'd had during one of my attempts at college who'd been the type to get calmer with a buzz on rather than loopy and extroverted. Atlas had headed for the shower as soon as we'd returned to my apartment, giving me little chance to ask if he was all right.

"Well, I like talking." Exiting out of my recording program, I turned more toward Atlas as he crossed the room. He had a towel around his neck, but he was otherwise dressed in sweats and a NAVY T-shirt. "People say I'm entertaining. I hope so."

"I think you are." Atlas stood right next to me. Close. Really close. Definitely not a friends-only distance, but hell, if I could read his mood. "I don't even play that new *Odyssey Online* game, and I thought it was fascinating."

"Do you play any video games?" I had to work to keep my voice steady as he touched the back of my chair.

"Sometimes the guys on base talk me into it. The first-person shooter game from *Space Villager* is always popular, but I'm not very good."

"I could teach you." I smiled up at him, trying to cover how shallow and shaky my breath had become. "Show you some tricks."

"I bet you could." Was Atlas flirting? Did he do that? And then, before I could think of an appropriate retort, he touched my hair, letting the strands fall softly through his fingertips.

"What are you doing?" I asked, knowing full well that he'd stop as soon as I pointed it out.

But he didn't.

"Your hair was in your eyes again." He kept right on petting my hair like I was some new breed of Irish Setter. He continued to sound dazed, as if his actions and words were surprising him too. "And maybe I like touching you."

"I like it too." I dropped my voice to a whisper lest I break whatever spell he was under. "You can keep going."

He didn't say anything, but his touches became more

deliberate head caresses, fingers trailing down to my neck and back up.

"Just don't turn weird after and ignore me for two days." Me and my big mouth.

Atlas dropped his hand. "Sorry."

"Don't be sorry." I grabbed his hand, returned it to my neck. "You're clearly working some things out." I took a breath, needing another hit of courage. "But…you could work them out with me."

"Like the other night?" Atlas sounded way more intrigued than horrified.

Excellent. I couldn't sound too excited, so I waited a moment before replying. "Is that what you'd like? A repeat?"

"No." He didn't stop touching my hair, but I deflated anyway. So much for going out on a limb.

"Oh."

"No, I mean yes. Not the jerking though." He quirked his mouth. "I want…more. Like that. But more touching? Is that a thing?"

"It is definitely a thing." My pulse sped up at the idea of showing Atlas all the joys of frot. I glanced over at the limp air mattress on the side of the room. "Please tell me you won't kick me to the air bed after."

"Never. You're staying with me."

I wish. Not very likely long-term, but a guy could dream. "Good."

Before I even finished the word, Atlas pulled me out of my chair and hauled me toward my room so forcefully that my feet scarcely touched the ground. But hell if I would tell him to slow down.

Especially since as soon as we were in my room, Atlas peeled off his T-shirt.

"You don't have to get—" Whatever chivalrous impulse I'd had died as Atlas pushed off his sweatpants. I'd seen him in only a towel the other day, but I'd been actively trying not to gawk. And I'd seen his cock in the dim light of the bedside lamp on Friday, but now I could see the whole package, and what a package it was indeed. Tall. Jacked. Tats, including that phoenix over his pec. It was an impressive piece of body art, but the tat had new meaning since he'd revealed more about his family situation. And the tats were simply the beginning of his hotness. Dark, dusky wide nipples and the cock every aspiring porn star dreams of having. "Oh, hell yes. *Damn.* Do you get your mail at the gym? Sleep there too?"

"I'm not all that." Atlas frowned, looking down at his chest and, apparently, seeing something far different from what I saw.

"Trust me, you very much are, and I might never remove my clothes again." Compared to Atlas, I was a movie extra. No one was mistaking me for a porn star or action hero, and even fluffers were undoubtedly hotter than short, nerdy, and bearded gamers.

"You better." Atlas practically growled the words. "Maybe I should remove them for you."

"Please." I didn't even try to play reluctant, eagerly helping him pull my shirt off. I wasn't ripped, but hopefully, enthusiasm counted for something. And then Atlas stunned the hell out of me by dropping a kiss right in the center of my belly as he bent to push my jeans down. I inhaled sharply. "*Oh.*"

"I like your body." The smile he offered me was downright dopey. "I can't explain it, but you're…warm. Homey? Comfortable? I'm not making sense—"

"I'll take the compliment," I said quickly before he

could compare me to a teddy bear or something cuddly. After sending my jeans to the floor, Atlas straightened and moved to sit on the edge of the bed, tugging me onto his lap. Being naked and on Atlas Orion's lap was more awkward than I would have guessed, and my skin heated. Trying to regain some sense of inner control, I shifted until I was straddling him. "That's better."

Continuing to seize the initiative, I brushed my mouth across his. But Atlas immediately took the control right back, claiming me in a kiss almost bruising in its intensity. For someone without a ton of experience, Atlas sure knew how to kiss. And kiss. He sipped at my lips, nudged my tongue, and held me close as his hands roved over my back. Each pass of his broad palm and wicked tongue made me shudder until I was unashamedly grinding against him, and we were both breathing hard.

My cock rubbed against his rock-hard abs, and given enough time, I could undoubtedly come from the one-two punch of kissing and friction. However, Atlas kept making sexy-as-fuck impatient noises while kissing me with a fervor I hadn't known before.

"What do we do now?" he asked against my lips, voice low and urgent.

"This." Reaching between us, I aligned our cocks and started a slow stroke.

"Oh." Atlas groaned, eyes closing and head tipping back. He let me play for a few more strokes. Trying to get my hand around both of us was a challenge I was happy to accept. I leaned back to allow more room so I could add my other hand, but the resulting motion was as awkward as it was erotic. Eyes opening, Atlas stared down at our cocks. "Can I try?"

"Please." I happily readjusted my position so Atlas

could use his bigger, broader hand. His grip was perfect, the way he used pressure from his thumb to keep us aligned. "Oh my fucking God."

"Nah." He gave a strained laugh. "You're the spectacular one."

"Spectacularly homey?" I had to tease. Laughing was good because it meant I wasn't coming in record time quite yet.

"Just spectacular." His gaze was locked on his fist and the slide of our cocks. "I love how your cock fits against mine."

I frowned. I agreed that we looked sexy, but the position also emphasized our size difference. "Mine isn't as long—"

"Hush. It's perfect." He stroked and teased the back of my shaft with featherlight fingertips before resuming jacking us together.

"So is your hand."

"Kiss me." Even before he finished the demand, he sought my lips with a ravenous mouth. He kissed like someone had started a countdown timer to the end of the world, desperate and needy, as if he needed to inhale every possible moment of pleasure.

"I can't decide what I like better," I gasped. "The kissing or the touching."

"Both." He jacked us more purposefully as his tongue delved deep. I loved how his grip tightened at the top of his stroke, pushing my cockhead against his shaft, allowing me to feel every ridge and vein. My cock leaked more precome than ever, and my balls kept lifting and tightening right along with my thighs and ass.

"Atlas. I'm gonna come."

"Not yet." He gritted out the words. "I don't want this to end."

"We can do it again later. Promise." I gave a breathless laugh.

"Oh, there's an idea." He mouthed all along my neck. "Seconds."

"And thirds."

That got a chuckle out of him. "You're highly optimistic for a guy pushing thirty."

"Hey, I dream big." Really, I dreamed of Atlas, had for years, but he didn't need to know that. And every kiss and touch made me dream that much grander. I wanted more. Wanted everything.

"I know." Atlas kissed me hard before I could ask what he meant. He stroked us faster, breath coming in harsh pants against my mouth. "Fuck. Now I'm there. Get there with me, baby."

"I am. God. Tell me." I didn't truly need his permission to come, and it wasn't a game I'd ever played before. Somehow, though, I wanted it. Wanted him to order me so I could comply and bask in pleasing him.

"Come. Come now." A low rumble escaped his chest as the pressure of his hand increased. He swept his thumb back and forth, and that was it. Moaning, I erupted all over his fist.

"Good. So good. Zeb." Atlas's praise was the sexiest thing ever, and I managed another spurt as he also came. "Goddamn."

"I'll say." I laughed giddily before stretching in his embrace, delighting in the way he held me that much tighter. "And tell me you're serious about seconds."

"And thirds, apparently."

"I'm serious." I tried to glare at him, but I was

undoubtedly too come-drunk to pull it off. "No freaking out?"

"No freaking out." He sighed, resigned but not miserable. As long as he wasn't drowning in regret, I could work with that. "I mean, I'm not really looking for a lecture from your brother—"

"We can keep it on the down-low," I said quickly. "But no reason not to keep it going."

"While I'm here." Atlas apparently needed to clarify, and I frowned. I could do without the reminder that any time together was short and finite. Yawning, he nuzzled my neck. "Damn. The adrenaline is finally wearing off. Seconds later. Promise."

"Good." I didn't particularly want to believe he'd only come to me because of adrenaline from the emergency, but if it had propelled us to this wonderful place where he'd agreed to keep things going, I'd take it. "Sleep now."

Long after we'd haphazardly cleaned up and snuggled under my covers, I watched him sleep, a protectiveness I'd never felt before blanketing me. Rather than being upset about him using sex to deal with adrenaline, I reframed it as something special I could offer him. It might be temporary, but I would happily be his recharging port.

Thirteen

ATLAS

18 SHOPPING DAYS UNTIL CHRISTMAS

"Easy. Easy. Slow," Zeb coached in patient tones. How he managed to make rearranging the window display at Seasons sexy, I had no clue. But I'd been half hard the whole time we'd been working. The frequent changing of the items in the large picture window in the Seasons store was a holiday tradition. Zeb's grandmother had started it, then his mom and Paige had kept the practice going. Gabe was busy working on the accounts, so Zeb had volunteered us to rotate the display.

"There." I stepped back from the window area. Zeb's plan had been to bring in an assortment of the ceramic holiday village pieces the store offered, and I'd had the idea of arranging the buildings to look like the historic downtown of Kringle's Crossing, complete with hardware store, florist, and construction paper roads and miniature trees and holiday lights. I'd fussed far longer than necessary with the details, but the end result was worth the time. "That may do."

"May do?" Zeb laughed fondly and bumped my shoulder. We were the only two in the store at the moment, so we could get away with a few of the touches I was fast getting addicted too. Long glances. Sneaky touches. Late-night kisses. I loved it all so much more than I'd ever thought possible. And the warmth in Zeb's voice touched long-neglected places in my heart. "It's perfect. You did amazing, and it looks so good that I'm going to put a picture up on the store's social media sites."

My skin heated. I swore I'd blushed more in the past few weeks than over the previous ten years. "You think everything I do is great."

"Because it is." Zeb gave me a toothy grin before sobering. "No, seriously. I see you trying. You're not simply killing time here. You seem invested in Seasons. That matters a lot. And you're a quick learner."

"Yeah." I had to glance away, studying the far wall of ornaments. Zeb saw so damn much, more than anyone else, possibly ever. And his praise came so easily, whether I was wrapping gifts or playing one of his games with him at night. While it seemed I could do wrong, there was also nothing fake about Zeb's enthusiasm. He truly did value the effort more than the results. "Thank you."

"You're not used to compliments, are you?" He touched my shoulder, getting me to return my gaze to his face. His eyes were kind and soft. With him, I could reach a level of honesty I simply couldn't with others.

"Not really, no." I shrugged. "Not like I've gotten a ton. In the navy, competence is assumed. Demanded really. Tough love, so to speak. And growing up…"

"Your folks weren't the cheerleading type?" Zeb finished my thought for me.

"God, no. Nothing like your parents." A wave of

sadness washed over me. Zeb and Gabe's parents had been the gold standard. Zeb's drawings on the fridge, Gabe's test scores proudly displayed, both boys bragged about, and frequent hugs handed out. Watching them had made my chest hurt, and now that they were gone, I didn't know what to do with the grief. I missed them, but I also missed what I'd never had myself. "I... A lot of times, it felt like my parents didn't see me. They were wrapped up in their own lives, partying, travel, friends." I released a weighty sigh. In so many ways, my current situation with limited contact was better than the years I'd spent hungry for their attention. I'd always felt like if I did better, was that much closer to perfect, they might finally value me. "Getting them to notice I was there was hard enough."

"I'm so sorry." Zeb rubbed my shoulder. With him, I didn't have to be perfect. I only had to try, and that was such a blessing that I gave him a quick, tight hug before he continued, "All kids deserve cheering on, and you, in particular, deserve all the praise. And noticing. You're awesome and pretty hard to miss."

"Thanks." My voice came out all gruff, but I might have said more had the front door not chimed right then.

A bundled-up kid strode in. Somewhere between eight and ten, she wasn't our first pint-sized patron. Several Kringle's Crossing families had the tradition of letting kids come in and pick a gift for someone special. This girl had warm-toned skin a few shades darker than my olive complexion, a purple wool coat with big flower-shaped buttons, a patent leather purse, and a riot of curly hair someone had attempted to smooth into submission with a ponytail.

"Hey there." Zeb strode over to greet her with a wide smile. I hung back because I'd noticed over the last few weeks that I tended to intimidate the younger customers while Zeb was an absolute natural at helping them. And a pleasure to watch. "How can I help you, madam?"

"I'm not a madam." She let out a charming giggle as she fished a crumpled bill out of her little purse. Her smile was missing several teeth, and her smattering of dark freckles became more vivid with every excited bounce. "But I have twenty dollars. Paper money, not a card. See?"

"I see." Zeb craned his neck to see beyond the girl. In the parking lot, a newer sedan with an older female driver had parked right by the door.

"Grandma is waiting in the car." The girl gave a wave before returning her attention to Zeb. "Grandma says I can get a present for Mama and Daddy. And I get to pay all by myself. And remember to get it wrapped and get the change."

"We can do that." Zeb matched her serious tone as he steered her to a nearby display of hobby ornaments popular with younger shoppers. Toolboxes, sewing machines, video game controllers, and more jockeyed for space. "What sort of things do your mom and dad like?"

"Like? Hmm." The girl wrinkled up her face, clearly thinking hard. "Daddy likes football. But Mama says it's bar-bare-ical." Her toothless grin more than made up for her butchered pronunciation. Zeb showed her several football-themed ornaments, but she shook her head at each one.

"How about Mama?" Zeb stayed patient through all the rejections.

"She makes mac-n-cheese so good." The girl rubbed her tummy. "And she sews bee-uuu-tiful blankets. We made one together for Grandma's present."

"That's great. Now, let's look over here." He held up a

miniature sewing machine followed by a few potholder ornaments. "See any you like?"

"Not yet." She scrunched up her face, and I braced for a whine. "It has to be perfect."

"I get you," Zeb soothed. "Now, how about—"

"That one." The girl went from pouty to enthralled, walking over to a display of locally made hand-carved ornaments representing different families. They were gorgeous but on the pricier end of what Seasons offered. Picking up an ornament featuring a white father, a Black mother, and a child arranged on a sofa, the girl made a happy noise. "We all watch TV together. Every night. And it looks like us. See?"

"Absolutely." Zeb plucked the ornament from the display and deftly removed the price sticker before handing it to the girl. "Is this your pick?"

"Yep." She beamed as she turned it around in her hand. "Wait. How much is it?"

"You're in luck. It's on sale." Zeb was such a good liar that I almost believed him myself. He turned the girl toward the display of holiday candy near the register. "Fifteen dollars, which means you have enough money to add a piece of candy if you'd like while Atlas wraps it for you. What color paper do you want?"

"Ooh." She carefully peered over the counter at the rolls of paper before pointing. "Dancing Santas!"

"Excellent choice." I got to work carefully packaging the ornament and doing one of my best wrapping jobs with a big, gaudy bow that made the girl squeal with delight before she hurried back out to her waiting grandmother.

"You're so good at this job," I said to Zeb as the door shut behind the girl.

"Yeah?" Zeb gave a small smile and a big blush. Apparently, I wasn't the only one who had trouble with compliments. "I guess it's in my blood. My mom was the best at picking ornaments."

"I remember her personal collection." I closed my eyes, visualizing the Seasons' annual tree at their old farmhouse. Senior year, I'd helped Gabe haul the tree in and set it up. "Each ornament was unique and had its own story."

"Gabe and Paige still have the collection." Zeb's voice had a wistful note. He shook his shoulders like attempting to shrug off sadness. "Anyway, helping kids is fun."

"It's no wonder kids love you." I let him change the subject as the wheels in my brain turned. I couldn't bring back his parents, but perhaps there was something I could do to help him carry on traditions. "You're so patient."

"I try."

"I see you." I held his gaze, and the moment stretched between us, potent with unsaid words. Damn. I liked him so much it was scary. Being around Zeb simply felt *good*, better than anything I could remember.

"I see you too," he whispered. That was it. We *saw* each other, a rare and perfect gift. I saw the ways in which he'd grown and reformed, the effort he put into his gamer channel and here at Seasons. And he saw me without requiring anything more than my presence.

It was heady stuff, and I might have gone for a sneaky kiss, but Nix chose right then to bustle in with two small plates.

"Dessert tasting!" they announced as they handed each of us a plate with a brownie drizzled with white and pink icing. "I'm getting ready for that college party tomorrow. These brownies are my ode to peppermint bark."

"Wow," I said after a big bite at the same time that Zeb added, "Amazing."

"Thank you." Nix beamed even wider than the kid had. "Also amazing? That window display." They gestured over at the front window area. "Paige will be proud of you."

"Atlas did most of it." Zeb's loyalty and humbleness were among his more attractive qualities, and I had to school my expression against showing too much pride or affection. The last thing we needed was someone guessing what we were getting up to in private.

"Good work." If Nix suspected anything, they did a great job of seeming indifferent as they turned toward me. "Big plans tonight?"

"Uh…" Crap. I had no idea what I was doing tonight other than Zeb, which would totally be the wrong answer.

"Takeout and gaming." Zeb rolled his eyes at me. "It's kind of our thing. A friendly thing."

Fuck. Between the two of us, we sounded rather guilty, but Nix merely smiled.

"You have a thing. Cute." They chuckled. "A+ roommates. I take back my bet on you two killing each other two weeks in."

"No one's getting killed." Zeb smiled broadly, but I was none too sure either of us would survive the month with our hearts intact.

Fourteen

ZEB

"Damn. I won!" Atlas celebrated his victory by bouncing on the bed before giving me a high five. We were playing the first-person shooter *Space Villager* console game, and not surprisingly, Atlas had proven to be a natural at using his lightning-fast reflexes. He didn't truly need all my tips, but pretending to coach him the last few weeks had been too much fun to pass up.

"You did." I laughed and captured his hand, swinging it in the air before releasing him. God, I loved nights like this, sitting in my bed, side-by-side, able to touch whenever we wanted. The remnants of our latest takeout feast were on the nightstand. One of these nights, we were going to need to actually cook. But like I'd told Nix earlier, gaming and takeout were kind of our thing. "You did awesome."

"Did you let me win again?" Atlas's tone was teasing, but his eyes narrowed.

"What do you mean, again?" I played ignorant. "I don't let people win. Especially not you."

That wasn't entirely truthful. I *would* let Atlas win if I thought he needed the victory, and I'd been known to let other friends or gaming collaborators win occasionally, when it served the greater purpose of fun for everyone. But Atlas was legit good at this particular game, and tonight's victory had been a fair one.

"The hell you don't." Atlas saw through me as usual. "But thank you. You're a good teacher."

"It's what I love." I grinned widely. He always seemed to react positively to compliments, and I loved how the longer he was here, the better he was at handing them out as well. We fit together well that way—both of us needing praise, but neither of us being the best at taking it. "I love finding ways to make the game more fun for people."

"You're excellent at it." Atlas ducked his head, capturing my mouth for a kiss before I realized what he was after. Swallowing back my surprised gasp, I kissed him back. If he wanted to move from gaming to our other favorite pastime, I was all for it. But before I could press my case with some quality groping, he released me.

"What was that for?" I sounded all breathless, and Atlas chuckled, eyes sparkling with pride. He enjoyed being able to rattle me a little too much.

"Maybe I like you." His tone was flippant, but my breath caught nevertheless. We were both so careful to not mention the future, not give a name to emotions, or define what was happening between us. *Like* was a vast understatement as to how I felt about him, but something in the simplicity of his answer struck me square in the chest. Atlas liked me. Really *liked* me. It was everything I'd ever wanted from him, but now that I had it, a million new wishes rose to the surface.

Before I could reply, my phone buzzed with an incoming message. Paige wanted to know what I thought of prime rib versus ham for Christmas dinner.

"Gah. Paige is in full-on nesting mode, I swear." I shook my head because she was also adorable and one of my favorite people. I typed a fast reply that we should have whatever was easy and whatever the pregnant person wanted most. "She's already planning Christmas dinner at the house."

"You don't want to go?" Atlas tilted his head as I returned my phone to the nightstand. We'd both lost the elf shirts as soon as we'd come in from Seasons, and our pants had hit the floor in a round of speedy pre-dinner rubbing off. Near-naked gaming was fast becoming one of my favorite activities with Atlas, and I groaned because I didn't want to think about the fast approach of Christmas. Christmas meant that much closer to Atlas leaving. "What's wrong?"

"Nothing's wrong," I lied. "And, of course, I want to go to Christmas dinner."

"Zeb…" Atlas studied me more closely, peering deep into my eyes before huffing out a breath. "It's not my place to dig, but you tense up whenever your old house is mentioned."

"It's Paige and Gabe's place now," I said flatly.

"Yeah, but that doesn't erase the years you spent there." Atlas put an arm around me, tucking me against his side and making it harder to be sullen.

"No, I guess not." I dropped my voice to a whisper like that might make the truth easier. "It's difficult. Paige and Gabe there, Mom and Dad not. I should be happy for them…"

"But you miss your folks." Atlas rubbed my shoulder. "And, of course, it's hard. You have all the memories of those great holidays you had at the house while growing up."

"Exactly." I managed a small smile because Atlas always did seem to get me on a level few others did. So many people went out of their way to never mention our parents out of worry they might upset us. But Atlas seemed to sense when I needed to talk. "The house is so different now. Not bad, not worse. Just…different. Some of the same traditions, like Mom's ornaments on the tree, but new ones too, like Paige's solstice candles. And they've remodeled some, but…"

"The memories linger. I get it." Atlas paused to bite his lip, expression going uncharacteristically uncertain. "I… God, I can't believe I'm going to confess this. But one of the reasons I think I stayed away so long, other than ill-timed deployments, was I miss them too."

"My parents?" It was my turn to study him. I hadn't ever considered that before. But given Atlas's unsatisfactory relationship with his own parents, it made sense that he would have looked up to mine. And he, like so many others, had lost something important when they passed. My back tensed. I should have guessed, and I sure could have been more understanding.

"Yeah." Atlas's voice was soft and distant. "You guys were like the definition of a happy family. And then they were gone, and it felt so weird, being in Kringle's Crossing without them."

I wrapped my arm around him, rubbing his side. He deserved comfort too. And he deserved to find comfort here in town too. It sucked that what was a place of solace for me had hurt him. I wished I could give him a *home*, that sense of belonging that reassured me even as it sometimes frustrated me. Atlas deserved a place to come back to.

"Join the club." I let my head drop onto his shoulder. "And my parents were relationship goals. Totally. It took me a long time to cope with their absence as well. That's part of why I knocked around from college to college, couch to couch, eating too much bad food, and escaping into my games." I could admit that to him, could share things I'd never said aloud to another soul. "It hurts not having them. But the last few years, I've come to…not really peace, but acceptance."

Atlas nodded solemnly. "They'd be proud."

"Yeah, Gabe's done a great job."

"No, they'd be proud of you, Zeb." Atlas used the tip of his finger to dig into my upper arm. "You."

"Oh." I wasn't sure I agreed with him.

"You pulled your life together." He squeezed me close. He sure sounded like he believed his words. "That's pretty impressive. And they loved you so much. Naturally, they'd be proud of you, bragging to the whole town about your gaming channel."

"Wow." My eyes burned. He wasn't wrong. My parents had been world-class braggers, but I hadn't allowed myself to feel their pride in years. "They'd be proud of you as well." I gave him a pointed look because maybe he also needed to hear it. "And happy you made it back here. Happy we're all together."

"Yeah." He gave an unsteady exhale, gaze darting everywhere but at my face. "Hey, is missing them why you don't decorate your place?"

"Huh. Good question." My mouth twisted as I thought. "Not like I'm gonna stash a tree here in the bedroom. I've always just left decorating to Gabe and Paige. They kept all the ornaments and stuff."

"Maybe you need your own traditions." Atlas's expression took on a thoughtful cast. "Your own collection like your mom's."

"Maybe." I liked the idea, but the weight of the conversation made me weary. I could indeed start my own holiday traditions, but that might mean another layer of acceptance, another degree of moving on. I could do it, but I didn't really want to dwell on it then, not with a warm and wonderful Atlas at my side. "Another round?"

Atlas gave a knowing chuckle, but he let me change the subject the way he always did. "Gaming or sex?"

"Either. Both." I shrugged before giving him a goofy look. "Maybe not at the same time though."

"Oh, we could try." Atlas offered me a wolfish grin in return. Heat gathered low in my belly, my cock already anticipating how damn good we could make each other feel. My heart, too, if I were honest. All my parts enjoyed him so damn much.

"Let's." I made the conscious decision to not think about anything heavy. Not my parents. Not Atlas leaving. Not how close Christmas was. None of it. All I wanted was to live here in this moment forever.

Fifteen

ATLAS

17 SHOPPING DAYS UNTIL CHRISTMAS

"All set on glassware?" Zeb bustled up behind me at the bar area, a common occurrence over the last week, but I was still startled, neck prickling, senses dancing with fresh awareness.

"Yep." Having a secret fling was the best worst idea I'd ever had. Best as in the time kept flying by in a haze of late nights and stolen kisses.

"So…about those Eagles?" Zeb's gaze darted around the room. Gabe was across the dining area, talking to the organizer folks from the college IT department hosting this night's party. And that would be the flip side of the best time of my life: an onslaught of corporate Christmas parties and anxious best friends. I hated knowing that Gabe, my oldest and best friend, would be upset if he knew I was messing around with Zeb on the sly. Bi-surprise aside, he'd have the biggest issues with the lying and sneaking and risking Zeb's big heart on what could only be a short-term fling.

"Believe there's a game tonight," I said all casually, like I had any idea of the playoff football schedule. And even with Gabe right there, knowing he'd hate what we were doing, I wasn't about to end things with Zeb. The best worst thing, indeed.

"Excellent. Later then?" Zeb grinned slyly at me. I was such a goner. I loved how genuine his smiles were, with no pretense or calculated motives. He smiled for the simple reason that I made him happy, and that was a power I was trying hard not to take for granted.

"Definitely later." I smiled back. Not too wide because that would be obvious, but enough that Zeb knew I had zero intention of finding a game to watch and every intention of having him for a late-night snack.

"Did the beer delivery finally show up?" Gabe strode over, dabbing at his forehead with a handkerchief.

"Yep." I pointed at the fully stocked bar area, ready for more partygoers to arrive. "You look even more anxious than usual. You okay?"

"Yeah." Gabe moved his jaw from side to side, clearly trying to seem more relaxed and failing miserably. "This is our first party for Stanton Anthony College. I'd like more of their business."

"Understandable."

"How is Paige?" Zeb asked, doffing Gabe lightly on the shoulder. From our late-night talks, I knew that he was also worried about Gabe's anxiety level. "Doctor appointment today?"

"Paige is great." Gabe beamed with pride. "And yes, we had an appointment. That's why I left earlier. We had to go into West Chester for another scan. The babies look great, but the doctor says they could come any time between now and New Year's. It's getting real."

"Get my Uncle of the Year award ready." Zeb grinned before turning his bright smile on me, a challenge flashing in his eyes.

"Hey!" I protested, taking the bait. "How do you know I won't win?"

Zeb shrugged. "I'll win by virtue of proximity."

He was right, of course, but the reminder of the distance between us still stung. He'd see the babies grow up day by day while I'd be lucky to swoop in on sporadic visits.

"Absence makes the heart grow fonder," I said lightly.

"True." Zeb gave me a tender, meaningful look that hurt more than the tease. He'd miss me when I was gone, and I hated that almost as much as I hated how much I would miss him. Turning back toward Gabe, Zeb went from thoughtful to impish. "And speaking of proximity, if the date is getting close, you and Paige need a babymoon."

"Ha." Gabe snorted. "With what time or money?"

"I'm serious," Zeb persisted, and I nodded in support. "You don't have to take a whole week away or something, but take a night off, bro."

"He's right." I would have agreed even if I wasn't sleeping with Zeb, but the way he lit up at my praise made my chest warm. "Take an evening and take your lovely wife downtown, see the city lights and Christmas Village. Eat some good food."

"Whose side are you on?" Gabe wrinkled his nose before giving a strained laugh.

"Yours. You need a break." I rarely used my chief voice on civilian friends, but I trotted out the sternness for Gabe. "Take a date night to recharge. Let Zeb and I handle one of the upcoming events."

"The Zimmerman wedding," Zeb said decisively. I

liked him in bed, warm and compliant, but I also greatly enjoyed when he showed his determination and ability to stand up to Gabe or others. "It's just a rehearsal dinner this Friday, not a whole wedding. Atlas and I can handle it, no problem."

"Absolutely." Trying to seal the deal before the party here got more underway and Gabe wriggled out of our great idea, I pulled out my phone, clicking over to a dining app I mainly used for takeout delivery back in Virginia. But it was also handy for recs and reservations. "Done. Reservations for two at this little Italian place downtown with four-point-eight stars and lots of people calling it the most romantic place in Philly."

"What do you know about romance?" Gabe gave a good-natured scoff before shaking his head. "Fine. You guys win."

"Yay, more work for us." Zeb gave a fake cheer.

"How about you worry about getting through tonight's work? Here come the party guests." Gabe pointed as the wide double doors that led to the entry foyer opened to admit a cluster of people. A chill wind followed them. The weather kept predicting we might get the first real snow of the season this week. Since snow was such a novelty in Virginia, I was looking forward to it, especially if it meant being snowed in with Zeb.

The three of us settled into our established party roles —Gabe greeting, Zeb working the buffet, and me mixing the seasonal cocktails the organizers had selected along with an assortment of nonalcoholic options.

"Two of the Kringle Jingle cocktails." A shorter man wearing glasses and a jaunty holiday bow tie stepped up to the bar.

"Coming right up." Out of habit, I looked around to see who he might be getting the second drink for.

"The other is for my husband." Bow-tie guy pointed at an uncomfortable-looking late-forties guy in a black shirt in the far corner of the room. "He's propping up the wall over there."

"A time-honored tradition of introverts everywhere," I joked as I assembled the cocktails.

"Paul's a good guy." The fellow nodded so earnestly I feared his bow tie might pop off. "He's the best really."

"I'm sure." I'd done the bartender gig enough to know to always agree with the patron's assessment of their spouse. "How long have you been together?"

"Three years this holiday season." Bow-tie guy looked adoringly over at his stern silver-haired husband. *Love.* I'd never been in it, never close, but one couldn't miss the love arcing between the two of them, even across the room.

"Holiday fling you just couldn't quit?" I mused. How did one go from just-for-December to forever-and-ever? Was there any chance…?

Nah. I couldn't allow my brain to register that thought. What Zeb and I had was different. Not epic like the bow tie and Mr. Stern. We didn't glow for each other, didn't watch each other across a crowded room.

"Whoops. Careful with the cookie tray." My head instantly swiveled to find Zeb helping one of the young servers avoid catastrophe. And okay, maybe I *did* know where he was most of the time. But it was a working necessity. Not…

"When you meet the one, the time of year doesn't much matter." The bow-tie guy spared me from finishing my earlier thought even as he supplied an even worse one.

What if Zeb was my "one," but the timing doomed us anyway? Five years down the road, I'd be near retirement from the navy. Ready for what? I still wasn't sure. Five years previous, and maybe I wouldn't have decided to go for the full twenty. Heck, zoom forward or backward any number of years, and Zeb and I would have likely never happened. What made this year so special? And what did it matter how rare and special Zeb was if there was no path forward? Jealousy for this other couple I barely knew bubbled up in my chest, making my throat bitter and scratchy.

"Here you go." I passed over both drinks and earned another smile in the process.

"Thanks. And good luck."

"With bartending?" I frowned. Tonight's crowd was particularly easy, mainly light-drinking geeky types and their assorted spouses.

"With whatever has that faraway look in your eyes."

"Huh." I hadn't realized I was that damn obvious. I'd have to work harder to keep my emotions under wrap, something I'd never struggled with before. "Sorry. Guess I've got a few questions rattling around my brain."

"Bet you already know the answer." And with that bow-tie guy was off, returning to his adoring spouse and leaving me with even more questions.

I wouldn't take the bet on me having the answers. When it came to Zeb, all I had was the increasing certainty that everything I'd thought I'd known was wrong.

Sixteen

ZEB

12 SHOPPING DAYS UNTIL CHRISTMAS

"Everything must be perfect." Betsy Zimmerman's mother, Bonnie, had been in epic mother-of-the-bride mode from the moment the family had walked through the doors of Seasons. They had come in advance of the Friday night dinner for their out-of-town guests, which was also doubling as a rehearsal dinner. The wedding was taking place at a Christmas tree farm with a reception at a large hotel afterward, but they'd chosen Seasons for the rehearsal dinner. I didn't need Gabe to tell me that the wealthy family's business and potential word of mouth were crucial. But Mrs. Zimmerman was going to require every last drop of my patience and tact.

"Absolutely." I mimicked the affable, customer-first tone Gabe always adopted. "Now, to review, you requested seating for forty-eight."

"I said fifty-seven in the last update email I sent your brother." Mrs. Zimmerman did ruffled hen better than anyone I'd met. Even the embroidered bride and groom on her Christmas sweater puffed up at the implication that we'd dropped the ball somewhere. "Where is he anyway?"

"A well-deserved babymoon." I waved a hand to ward off more questions. After much urging from Atlas and me, Gabe had reluctantly agreed to take the whole day off. I also didn't like Mrs. Zimmerman's attitude that Gabe would be better suited to handle her lengthy list of demands. Not that she was wrong, but I was tired of always being the younger sibling and not being taken seriously. I'd grown up here at Seasons as well and knew all the event tricks. "We can roll out another two tables. No problem." I smiled far broader than I felt. "And we've used the red and green table linens."

"I suppose that will do." She sniffed loudly. "I'd hate to make you redo." Liar. She'd love nothing more than to make us strip the tables and redo to her lofty expectations. "But I was hoping for more gold accents."

"I'll see what we have in the decor closet as far as centerpieces and accents like some beads or tinsel." Tinsel was a pain to clean up, but it would undoubtedly add the over-the-top feel Mrs. Zimmerman wanted. I steered her away from inspecting the linens to three draped rectangle tables set up along the far wall. "And as you can see, the decorate your own cookie station is ready to go."

Nix had provided trays of sugar cookies in assorted shapes along with bowls of various toppings, decorative elements like sprinkles, and icing bags.

"This is going to be so messy." Mrs. Zimmerman made a clucking noise.

"Mom. I saw the idea online. Everyone will love it." Blessedly, Betsy Zimmerman chose that moment to emerge from the restroom. Like her mother, she wore a red Christmas sweater, but hers spelled out B-R-I-D-E in glittery embroidery across her chest. "Thank you, Zeb. Everything looks great. However, Anderson has been trying to bring up both our playlist and the slideshow, and we can't seem to connect to your A/V system."

She gestured over at the plump fellow in the green G-R-O-O-M sweater. I'd directed him earlier to the shallow closet where we housed the system for the large screen display we positioned for events that needed the video option. Anderson worked in IT and had seemed confident enough in his skillset that I hadn't worried.

I should have worried.

The screen itself was fine, but the hub that controlled the various adapters and inputs/outputs had chosen today of all days to give up the valiant fight after a solid five years or more of loyal service. I had a solution, but time was of the essence. I tracked Atlas to the bar area, where he was arranging items for the signature cocktails the happy couple had selected.

"We've got a problem."

"Oh?" Atlas raised a single bushy eyebrow, eyes flashing with alarm as his gaze dropped ever so slightly to my waist.

"Nothing to do with…football." I grimaced because his reaction was a good indicator that he was no closer to being okay with Gabe or anyone else finding out what we were up to. The time since Thanksgiving had been like a cozy cocoon, and while I'd loved showing Atlas endless variations of frot and making out, I couldn't help but yearn for something I couldn't quite name. Not dating precisely, but something more than the sex lessons I'd promised. Time was running out to figure out what precisely I wanted from Atlas, but right then, other things had to take priority. "We have an issue with the A/V System. I can fix it, but I need to run back to my place for some of my gear."

"Need me to hold down the fort here?" Atlas asked. "I'd offer to go, but you know your equipment better than me."

"Please." I offered him a grateful smile. His recognition of my competence felt like a warm caress, the antidote to my earlier feeling of being underappreciated. "The bride's mother is kind of—"

"Zeb." Mrs. Zimmerman rushed in our direction, the glitter and ornaments on her sweater bouncing in time with her frantic movements. "What's this I hear about the vegan entrée not also being gluten-free?"

"Go." Atlas waved me toward the door. "I'll handle this."

As I grabbed my coat, Atlas spoke to Mrs. Zimmerman in far more patient tones than I had managed. "Let me take you to meet our chef, and we can discuss your concerns."

I hurried back to my apartment and collected the items I needed. The air was crisp and dry with rapidly falling temperatures. After a cold but dry November, it finally felt like winter was well and truly on the way, with snow expected any time. Returning to Seasons, I quickly used my spare laptop and cables to get a temporary solution up and running.

"It's working!" Anderson cheered. His future in-laws had already left for the rehearsal part of the evening, and he skedaddled after them, leaving us with a lull before the dinner guests started arriving.

"Hey, Zeb." Atlas tapped me on the shoulder as I was checking the A/V setup one last time. "Do you know anything about the champagne delivery? The father of the bride was worried about us running low on the bottles they custom requested."

I straightened and turned to face him. "Let's go check the storeroom."

Dutifully leading the way to the storeroom where we housed extra liquor, wine, and beer for catered events, I flipped on the light right as Atlas closed the door.

"I think the champagne is right over—" I pointed to a stack of wine crates only to be cut off by Atlas pinning me against the wall. "What the—"

"Hi." He grinned at me, as mischievous as I had ever seen him. Tracing my lower lip with the broad pad of his thumb, he hissed out a breath when I lightly nipped his finger. And then he replaced his thumb with his warm and willing mouth, a kiss so hot it was a wonder the beer kegs didn't blow. Me too. Coming in my work pants from nothing more than an unexpected kiss would be all kinds of embarrassing, so I reluctantly pulled away.

"What was that?" My voice came out slightly winded and dazed.

"Something to hold you for later." He grinned at me again, the sort of smile that made ill-timed orgasms seem like a worthy risk. Lord, I would follow this man anywhere, anytime. I simply wanted him. I smiled back as he continued, "Sorry. You looked so cute when you got the A/V equipment working, I had to kiss you."

"I like that you did." Living dangerously, I kissed him back. Being Atlas, he wasn't content to let me give him a relatively chaste peck. No, he had to go and claim my mouth for a deeper, more intense, more intimate exploration. Each time our tongues met, sparks zoomed down my spine, rendering me hard and needy and panting his name. "So, no champagne emergency?"

"Nah." Atlas shrugged, pushing his body closer against mine. "I located the missing bottles on my own."

"I think I prefer kissing emergencies anyway." I gave him another fast kiss that again turned into a meandering journey back to hard-and-ready town. "Really better stop. We need to get back out there."

"Yeah." He gave me one last kiss, this one softer and sweeter than the royal icing Nix had prepared for the cookie buffet. Ironically, the fleeting goodbye kiss proved way more devastating than the intense-but-brief make-out session. It lingered in my brain as I went about the rest of the prep and started greeting early guests.

Surely Atlas felt something more than curiosity or friendship, right? There was no way he could kiss with that much emotion otherwise. Or so I hoped, and round and round my brain whirred until Betsy Zimmerman found me arranging dinner items for the buffet.

"We've got a cookie disaster," she announced with all the gravity of an incoming asteroid.

"Run out of icing?" I hoped it was that simple even as my stomach clenched. The plan had been to have the decorating station out as an icebreaker before the dinner and then serve the cookies as dessert.

"Nope. Some of the bridesmaids turned the shapes into inappropriate displays, and Mom is pissed."

"Huh." I followed her over to the table. "That's definitely not a Santa anymore. And I never thought of using a reindeer head shape for…*that*."

"How are we supposed to get pictures of these?" Mrs. Zimmerman wailed as she joined us. "Some are downright *lewd*."

"How about I see if there is a fresh tray we can use for more family-friendly cookies?" I crossed my fingers.

Nix was usually pretty good about preparing extras for emergencies, and this definitely qualified. "The bridesmaid ones can be jokes saved for the bachelorette party?"

"I love it," Betsy said quickly before her mother could start in with a fresh wail.

As I brought out the new tray, Atlas approached us with a drink for Mrs. Zimmerman.

"Thought you might need another White Russian." He gave her a patient smile as he handed over the drink.

"Thank you," Betsy said quietly to Atlas and me as her mother returned to hostess duties, drink in hand. "You guys make a great team."

"We do." I glanced over at Atlas, who nodded. As amazing as everything happening in my bed was, the ease with which we worked together was equally rewarding. Whether it was navigating party disasters here, the whole air mattress fiasco, or the gaming tips I'd been giving him after work and before bed, we got along great. I genuinely enjoyed his company, and miraculously, he didn't seem sick of me yet either.

Later, as the party wound down, Mr. Zimmerman cornered me near the buffet dishes I'd been clearing.

"This was a heck of a party. Exactly what my little girl deserved."

"Thank you, sir. We appreciate your business." Despite all the near-mishaps of the evening, I meant it. I was glad the party had been a success, glad to be a part of Betsy and Anderson's happiness, and glad to have been part of a team.

"You did good standing in for Gabe, Zeb," Mr. Zimmerman continued, ruddy expression far more earnest and kinder than his wife's demeanor. His resemblance to a certain jolly elf sure was uncanny. "Your father and grandfather would be proud."

Unable to speak, I nodded. *Pride*. I seldom felt the emotion, but that was exactly how I felt about pulling off the rehearsal dinner. I was proud. And it meant something that Mr. Zimmerman thought the two men I'd admired most would agree. Most of their paternal pride had been directed toward Gabe, who'd taken to the business far more naturally. But it was my legacy, too, and why I'd stayed connected to Seasons even when it might've been easier to break away.

"Do you drink?" Mr. Zimmerman asked abruptly, cocking his head.

"Sometimes." Not sure where he was heading with this, I hedged. "Never on the job."

"Oh, of course not." He waved a meaty hand before holding up a champagne bottle with the other one. "We ended up with doubles of the special bottles we ordered to toast the happy couple with. It's a good year. Enjoy as a token of our appreciation."

"Thank you." I took a steadying breath. Ordinarily, I might demur, say no tip or gift was needed, but the desire to taste champagne on Atlas's lips won out. Yeah, it was a very good year, and we would make excellent use of the bubbly. Outside, snow had started to softly fall, and I couldn't wait to warm Atlas up.

Seventeen

ATLAS

"This is already our best idea ever," Zeb enthused as we locked the back door at Seasons and headed into the cold December night. He tightly clutched the bottle of champagne the Zimmermans had gifted us, and I held a bag of leftover appetizers and cookies we'd raided from the catering kitchen fridge. Fat white flakes rained down on us as we stepped away from the building. Zeb tilted his head skyward, utter awe crossing his expression. "Oh look, it's snowing. Like really snowing."

"Good thing we're walking." Throwing caution to the wind, I draped an arm around his shoulders. The Kringle's Crossing downtown would ordinarily be deserted anyway this late on a Friday night, and the snowstorm added to the feeling we were the only two souls awake and outdoors. Tomorrow morning, kids would be out in force, attacking the sledding hills as they woke to the first real snow of the season. Grumpy parents would shovel sidewalks and hand out reminders to be careful while weary shopkeepers moaned about a down day for Christmas shoppers. But right then, the world was simply Zeb and me and his perfect reaction to the same weather he'd seen for twenty-eight years.

"I love how magical everything looks all white. No tire tracks or footprints yet. And the holiday lights reflecting off the snow make it seem like the world is glowing. It looks like some sort of iconic American small-town painting."

"Are you sure you haven't started in on that champagne?" My teasing came out light and affectionate, exactly like my mood. Zeb happy was the true magic, and his was the glow I wished I could capture, especially when he started kicking at the snow. I chuckled at his antics. "If it's a painting, you're the star."

"Me?" Mouth pursed and tone skeptical, Zeb turned back toward me. "I'm not all that."

"Yes, you are." I pulled him to me for a fast, frosty kiss. Brushing the snow off his forehead and the curl of hair escaping his knit cap, I pulled back enough to stare deeply into his eyes. "You're beautiful."

"Beautiful." He snorted. "You're the one who's already drunk."

"Maybe." If I was drunk, it was on him, intoxicated by his charm and inner goodness. His fast thinking had saved the Zimmerman dinner more than once, and watching him take charge had only sweetened how good it felt when he let me lead. But I didn't want to wallow too much in emotions that couldn't change the cold, hard facts. Luckily, I still remembered one thing about Pennsylvania winters. Acting quickly, I broke away to pack a snowball with my borrowed gloves. "Wanna play?"

"Oh, hell yes." He set the bottle of champagne next to the bag of food and waggled his eyebrows in my direction. "I'll have you know, I'm the Kringle's Crossing Snow Wars champ five years running."

"Ha." My cackle came from some seldom-used place deep in my belly. "And I've had Arctic warfare training."

"It's on." He launched his missile, snow hitting me square in the chest, exactly like those pesky feelings Zeb kept inspiring in me.

And since I couldn't think about that, I threw my snowball next, over-judging how far my loosely packed ball could go. It landed with a sad little plop at Zeb's feet.

"Is that all you got?" He danced around like a boxer preparing for a title bout.

"Now you're asking for it." I packed my next snowball much firmer and put more oomph into my toss, only to be hit in the face by Zeb's throw. We played like that, right in the middle of Main Street, ducking behind concrete planters and candy cane-wrapped light poles, scampering over benches and under awnings, and laughing harder than I had in thirty years. We undoubtedly looked ridiculous. Grown men playing like little kids at an hour most people were fast asleep.

And maybe that was part of the appeal, the feeling of the universe being reduced to only the two of us. Breathing hard, I ambushed him when he bent to collect more snow, flattening him into the snow-covered grass near the hardware store. Of course, it wasn't much of an ambush when he went happily and pulled me down for a kiss hot enough to melt an iceberg.

"I win," Zeb exclaimed right before he swept his tongue into my mouth and stole the last of my common sense.

"You did." Holding his face in my hands, I returned the kiss with one of my own, hotter and deeper until he shuddered under me.

"Brrr."

Oh wait. That was a shiver.

"Sorry." I rolled off him and gave him a hand up. "Now we're all cold."

"And wet." He grinned broadly at me, with no trace of regret. "Only one thing left to do."

After collecting our loot, we raced the remaining blocks to his apartment, pounding up the stairs, not slowing until we were crammed together in his tiny shower, hot water blasting our chilled skin.

The shower was a practical necessity to warm up, nothing sexual or even particularly sensual. And yet, we shared a closeness that went far beyond the close quarters of Zeb's bathroom. Even if I wanted to get sexy, there simply wasn't room, but there was unexpected joy in holding Zeb close, lathering up his mop of hair, kissing his neck.

"Better than the barracks?" He smiled like he already knew the answer.

"Light years." I groaned as he managed to soap up my chest, paying particular attention to my tats. "Trying to scrub my ink off?"

"Nah." His smile turned wistful. "Trying to memorize their colors and designs."

"Zeb—"

He cut off my protest with a blistering kiss, one that made me forget whatever I'd been about to say.

"Eeeee!" He made a high-pitched squeal as the hot water ran out.

"Bed." I'd never delivered an order while laughing so hard, but like everything else with Zeb, it felt new and wonderful. As did being snuggled under his stack of covers, naked and surrounded by plates of snacks while drinking champagne from mismatched cups.

"This is the life." Zeb stretched against me, rubbing up on my shoulder.

"It really is." I bumped back against him, an easy familiarity between us. Had it really been only a few short weeks that we'd been doing this? My leave was speeding away from me at a breakneck pace that left me wishing for the power to freeze time. Funny how I'd worried about being antsy to get back, and now part of me didn't want to leave. "I could get used to this."

"You ever think about putting down roots?" Zeb asked cautiously. "Finding a place like Kringle's Crossing, making a home? Maybe after the navy?"

"Sure, I've thought about it." I'd meant I could get used to laughing and champagne picnics and Zeb in my bed, but I also couldn't deny the appeal of more midnight snowball fights. "But I'm not sure I'm built for the settling down thing. Wouldn't know where to start with the whole home and family thing. Not like I had stellar role models in that department."

"I don't think that's a requirement." Zeb pursed his lips before snagging another spinach artichoke bite from a plastic Captain Marvel plate.

"Says the guy with the idyllic childhood."

"Yeah, and I still had to figure out adulting the hard way." Zeb's chin took on a stubborn tilt. And he didn't say it, but the pain in his eyes said he was thinking about losing his parents early. "I never really fit in at school. And after my folks died, I floundered from college to college and thing to thing. And here I am, almost thirty, living in my brother's old apartment, with an obscene investment in computer equipment and almost nothing else."

"Hey now. You've pulled it together pretty darn

admirably. You've got your gamer career. Tons of kids want to be you when they grow up."

"You think?"

"I know so. I've watched a few of your videos on breaks at Seasons." I hadn't intended to reveal my reconnaissance on his gaming stream, but Zeb's uncertainty made me want to reassure him. "The comments are always filled with tweens who idolize you. That's pretty cool."

"Thank you." Zeb leaned in for a fast kiss. "Both for watching and for saying that. It's my dream career. And it's not only the playing-games-all-day thing. I like interacting with people of all ages. Games bring people together and give them an outlet they might not otherwise have for connection."

"See? That's awesome." I kissed him right back. "And your pricey computer equipment saved tonight for the Zimmermans."

"True." He offered me a small, proud smile that touched a place deep in my chest.

"Also, sure, you're living here now, but you know what you want for the future."

"Do I?" Zeb flopped his damp head onto my shoulder. "Still feels like I'm figuring that out. I guess I'd like a house of some sort. Backyard with a grill. A mutt or two. I've always wanted one of those big dogs where no one can guess all the breeds."

The laugh that escaped my chest hurt because I could so easily picture that. Zeb with a little house with a room full of electronics for his gamer command central. Two big floppy, furry beasts at his feet. Meat marinating in the fridge for the grill. And someone—someone not me— entering through the side door. Zeb deserved all of that, even if it fucking *hurt* to think of that someone who might get to share those dreams.

"See, you do know. With me, it's different." Sighing, I leaned more against him. I wished I had a vision like his for myself. "It's wanting something I've never had."

"When has that ever stopped you?" Zeb turned slightly so he could peer deep into my eyes. "You didn't have security, structure, or long-term friends growing up, and you went out and built a life that has all three."

"Huh. I guess I did." When I'd first joined up, I'd been an angry, hurt kid, but sometime over the last fifteen years, I'd built a life I was proud of, a life that looked nothing like my nomadic childhood.

"So do that for a life after the navy." Zeb's eyes widened and color rose up his cheeks. "Identify what you'd like and then set about filling those desires. Who cares if you don't know how to do whatever? Not you. You'd figure it out."

"Your faith in me is admirable." My throat went tight, making my voice drop to a near whisper. "Possibly misplaced, but admirable."

"It's not misplaced," Zeb said firmly. "I'm not hero-worshipping you. I look at you and see someone fighting to overcome his past." He placed a hand on my chest, right below my phoenix tattoo. "I know it's not all roses and heroic deeds, and it hasn't been easy, but that's why I'm proud of you."

"Wow…" I had to stop and swallow hard. I'd had friends for years, including Gabe, who'd never seemed to see me as well as Zeb did. "I'm proud of you as well."

"Thank you. And we're both trying. That's what matters." Zeb pressed a fast kiss to my mouth. However, it was the sadness in his eyes that gave me pause. *What matters.*

What mattered to me was Zeb being happy and fulfilled. And if I thought for a second that I could do the job, I'd sign up that moment.

"Zeb, I wish—" Like earlier, he cut me off with a deep kiss.

"Shush." He placed a finger on my lips. "You know better than to say a wish out loud."

"What about a wish for another kiss?" I asked lightly. That wasn't what I'd been about to wish for at all, but we didn't need to go there right now, not when everything felt so right. Being here in Zeb's bed was all that mattered.

"That I can grant." Deftly, Zeb set the plates of food next to our cups of champagne on the nightstand.

"Figured you could." My smirk turned to a gasp as Zeb slithered down my front.

"I can kiss more than your mouth."

Eighteen

ZEB

"Can you?" Atlas sounded lazy but interested, which was a good sign. I licked a line down his sternum before grinning up at him.

"I can." I was deliciously buzzed on expensive champagne and Atlas. He turned me on simply by being in the same room, but with added snowball fights, picnics in bed, and bubbly drinks, I'd reached new heights of horniness. I peppered his well-defined pecs and the colorful tattoos with kisses, gradually working my way down his body, taking the covers with me until all his gorgeous, tanned flesh was mine.

"This okay?" I glanced up so I could study his reaction. We'd made an exhaustive inventory of every possible variation on making out, rubbing off, and using our hands. I'd loved all of it more than I could ever adequately express, but I was also dying to taste him. However, since he was essentially a virgin to dude-on-dude action, I hadn't wanted to rush him.

"Oh yeah." Atlas's deep voice made his stomach

rumble under me as he stretched. "Kiss me anywhere you'd like."

"Anywhere?" I raised my eyebrows before deliberately licking each of his hipbones, painting a path around his hard-and-ready cock without actually touching it.

"There. Definitely there." He groaned, impressive cock straining toward me.

Teasing, I kissed closer and closer before blowing a hot breath across his shaft. Only when he let out a needy moan did I press a soft kiss right below his plump cockhead. I flicked my tongue against the same spot, loving how he arched toward me, ready for more.

"Fuck. That's already almost too good." He stroked my head, touch uncertain, like he couldn't decide between pulling me closer and pushing me away. "Feels a little unfair though. What if I want to kiss you too?"

I glanced up at his face. Surprisingly, his eyes were hot and his skin flushed. *Damn.* He was into the idea of blowing me back, and my cock pulsed against the sheets.

"You can. After."

He made a thoughtful noise. "What about at the same time?"

"Ha." I gave a strangled laugh because the idea of attempting a sixty-nine with Atlas had me near detonation. I'd only tried it a couple of times and hadn't much liked the split attention, but Atlas's mouth anywhere near my cock was likely to be epic. "You're greatly overestimating my ability to multitask."

"They make it look easy in porn." His tone was adorably earnest.

"Been expanding your viewing habits beyond solo videos?" I teased.

"Well, yeah. What else am I supposed to do during the

evenings when you're recording gamer content?" He laughed, but his cheeks flushed a dark, dusky pink. "I want to be good for you, Zeb."

"You are." Hell, Atlas doing research for me was so damn hot. And sweet. Perfect, really. I wasn't lying—all I'd ever wanted was right in front of me. "Honestly, I've been loving our steady diet of frot. I don't *need* more than that."

"But you want?" He gestured down at the position of my head mere centimeters from his cock.

"Well, yeah, of course I want to taste you." I gave his cockhead a fast, soft lick to emphasize my point. "And do other things, but only if you want those too. I don't want you to feel pressured."

"I want it all." His reply was fast and firm. "With you, specifically. Tell me your absolute favorite thing?"

"I'm about to blow you." I leered up at him. "Something tells me that's gonna make top three at least."

"I'm serious." He lightly doffed my shoulder.

"Since you asked, I like blowing someone way more than getting blown, but I'm happy to let you try. After." I took a shuddery breath because Atlas wanting to make all my sexy desires come true had me giddier than the champagne. "Most of my experience has been hands, mouths, and frot, but I do like getting fucked." I paused to watch his eyes flare hot and dark again. Yeah, he liked that idea. "I'm so-so on topping. The who matters though, for getting fucked. I've only bottomed a couple of times because I have to really trust someone. And in case it's not wildly obvious, I trust you."

"But I'd hurt you." He pursed his mouth, but the way his cock bobbed and strained said at least part of him loved the idea of fucking.

"You would not." I patted his thick thigh. "Prep is a

thing. And I may not have bottomed very much, but I've got an adventurous toy collection."

"Oh really?" His eyes went hilariously wide, and his voice lowered. "Gonna show me?"

"Some time." I waved a hand before he could suggest I rummage under the bed right then. "I need to taste you in the next century, though, so no show-and-tell right now."

"I could get into watching. Just saying." He glanced over at my nightstand as if considering demanding a show anyway.

"I know you could." I licked his cock again. "Now, hush."

"Aye-aye, Lieutenant." Atlas gave me a funny little mock salute right before I swallowed as much of his cock as I could easily take. "Oh fuck."

I pulled back enough to chuckle. "I've barely started."

"And I like it already."

"Just wait." I started a slow and steady rhythm of shallow sucking intermixed with licks. Growing more comfortable, I went a little deeper, and he instinctually rocked toward me. I pitched my voice as stern as his often was. "Hold still. I wanna try something."

"Anything." Atlas was already panting even before I took a deep breath and slowly, so very slowly, went almost to his base. Not quite, but close. I retreated, then tried again, my nose tickling his well-trimmed patch of hair. "God. You don't…" He trailed off to moan loudly as I did it again. "Fucking hell. That's good."

"Keep holding still," I ordered as I played with this new, deeper rhythm, swallowing hard around his shaft and working him with my tongue. He was on the larger side, no doubt, but I loved the challenge almost as much as his responses.

"Zeb. Zeb, I need to come." Groaning, he pressed his body into the bed, clearly working hard at the whole staying put thing. "Or let me touch you. Please. Something."

"You can move a little now." Retreating a bit, I jacked the base of his cock, but Atlas stubbornly stayed still even as I resumed my rhythm.

"I might die from not coming." His voice was labored. "I'd rather that than accidentally hurting you."

"I trust you." Glancing up, I met his heated gaze, and a powerful current passed between us, something more than desire or need. I did trust him, more than I'd ever trusted anyone, and I hadn't known how much I'd needed that in my life until he'd landed in my bed.

"If I move, I'll come," he warned like that would deter me.

"Then come." I grinned wickedly before going fast and hard. The movements of my head and mouth turned sloppy, rhythm giving way to something involuntary and primal. He thrust gently at first, then harder as he became more comfortable.

Trust. It went both ways, and Atlas trusting me with his pleasure was heady stuff, more potent than hundred-dollar champagne.

"Now. Zeb." He pushed at my shoulder, but I didn't budge. I took him deep again, swallowing hard as I milked him with my tongue as if this were my only chance on earth to taste him. He came in big spurts, whole body heaving, big groans escaping his mouth.

"Oh, my sweet fucking God." As soon as he stopped shuddering, he hauled me up his body. "I think you sucked my soul out."

"Good." I grinned at him, already reaching for my

own aching cock, intending to finish while cuddling against him.

"None of that." Atlas apparently had a different agenda as he stayed my hand with one of his. "Get up here now."

He patted his chest, and I frowned because I wasn't exactly light.

"I'm not sure—"

"I said now," he growled while tugging at my arm.

"Yes, Chief." Laughing self-consciously, I followed his order and straddled his chest. "Hey, if I'm the lieutenant, does that mean I outrank you?"

"Hush." One hand on my ass, Atlas scooted me forward so he could take a tentative lick at the tip of my cock. "Or rather, don't hush. Tell me how to do this."

"You're doing great." I kept my tone encouraging as I tensed my abs. It wouldn't do to come three seconds into his first try. "Little licks. Whatever feels good to you is going to feel good to me."

Taking me at my word, Atlas proceeded to experiment, licking softly at first, then with more pressure, imitating the moves I'd used on him before finding his own way. He seemed to like gently sucking on the head while jacking me with his hand the most, which was more than enough to have me moaning.

"Okay, no fair being the quickest study ever."

"I do like making rank." Atlas winked before going right back to work.

"Suck a little more." My voice turned lower and more urgent. "Not deeper, just harder." I made a keening sound as he did exactly as asked. "That. That right there. Add your tongue and—*Fuck.*"

I had to clamp down my every last muscle to avoid

coming without warning, and Atlas pulled back to chuckle warmly. "I think I like this."

"Good." I groaned. "I might tie you to my bed so I can have this whenever I want."

"All you have to do is ask." His eyes sparkled, but I knew better. There was a growing stack of things I wanted desperately but could never ask for. Needing to chase those thoughts from my head, I rocked my hips to meet Atlas's hand and mouth, getting closer with every pass.

"You gonna be okay if I come?" I panted.

"I've tasted my own spooge lots of times." Color rose up his face as he gave a nervous chuckle. "I'm good. Come when you want, baby."

That was all the permission I needed as I closed my eyes and gave myself over to the onslaught of sensations. Atlas's wet tongue, willing mouth, and giving hand drove me higher and higher. He swept the hand he'd had on my hip over the curve of my ass, fingers venturing close but not quite to my rim. Didn't matter. Merely the small hint that Atlas was thinking about fucking did it for me.

"Coming." I managed the barest of warnings. My head tipped back, body arching, hamstrings burning, abs trembling. My ass clenched reflexively with each harsh wave of pleasure. I half expected Atlas to pull back, but he moaned around my cock and swallowed me down.

"Fuck. You are so damn hot when you come." Atlas released me with one last pat on my butt. "You first next time, so I can still taste you when I come."

"You keep talking like that, and we can have round two before dawn."

"Hell, yes." Atlas sounded more than game and gave a happy sigh as I settled next to him, my head on his chest. "Any chance of it being a snow day?"

"Might take a literal act of God for Gabe to fully close." Groaning, I stretched to look out the window where the snow was still coming down. "But we can probably bank on a late start if the parking lot needs plowing."

"Come on, snow." Pulling me back down, he buried his face in my hair. "Never wanted a blizzard so much."

"Me either." And I'd never wanted a man as much as Atlas. That much was certain.

Nineteen

ATLAS

Sleeping against the wall had its perks, namely getting to spoon around a warm, naked, and cuddly Zeb while my back stayed cool. Also, I was closer to the window, so I could easily check on the snow situation. A pale, gray morning peeked through Zeb's blinds. The lack of sun was a good sign that more snow was coming, and indeed, fat flakes were continuing to lazily drift down.

However, sleeping against the wall had its downsides, namely having to scoot all the way to the bottom edge of the bed and twist up like licorice candy to slither quietly past a sleeping Zeb. After checking my phone messages along with the weather, I proceeded with my plan to make Zeb some food.

Cooking breakfast was a strange, fanciful urge. Sure, I'd dated a little here and there, but I'd never cooked for someone. The sleeping next to someone else thing was new enough, but the desire to take care of Zeb was something else entirely. And it wasn't so much that I felt obligated to do something nice after last night's midnight picnic and epic orgasm swap. I *wanted* to spoil Zeb precisely because he was perfectly capable of feeding himself and because no one else seemed to notice how hard he worked.

Zeb's fridge held the remnants of several takeout feasts of ours, but I also found a couple of potatoes and eggs. I raided the leftovers for a small container of feta, some olives, a few herbs, and lemon wedges. The finished plates weren't particularly social media-worthy, but they smelled good. I repurposed a baking sheet as a tray and added mugs of coffee and the last of Zeb's juice before carrying it into the bedroom.

The door squeaked as I pushed it open, and Zeb yawned and stretched before noticing me. He blinked and brushed his hair off his forehead.

"Breakfast in bed? What did I do to earn this?"

I replied with a pointed look and raised eyebrow.

"Other than the obvious." Rather than blushing, he let the covers fall away from his torso, revealing morning wood.

"The obvious was pretty damn amazing." I chuckled as he covered back up and scooted over so I could arrange myself and the tray next to him. "And I figured you might have a champagne hangover."

"A little one." He groaned and then helped himself to a mug of coffee. "What time is it anyway?"

"Nine, but it's still snowing. Gabe texted. Tonight's party for that accounting firm is canceled and the snowplow folks are running behind. He said to take our time, and he'll text when he gets a better idea of when or if Seasons can open."

"A possible snow day?" Zeb grinned broadly. "Sounds like you got your December wish."

"Yeah." If only my greatest wish were as simple as a snow day. True, I'd wished aloud for more snow, but

CATERED ALL THE WAY

privately, I'd wished for a year of December. Three hundred and sixty-five days of Zeb, picnics, late-night sex, and lazy mornings. If wishes were snowflakes, the whole Eastern Seaboard would be buried, but instead, my wishes were more like flurries, evaporating as soon as they hit reality. *Damn it.* I snagged a piece of the toast I'd put with the eggs and potatoes.

"This is amazing," Zeb said around a mouthful of potatoes. "What is it?"

"Lemon potatoes with oregano and feta, topped with fried eggs. Hangover cure popular at this tiny Greek diner in Nafplion. You had the right ingredients, so I looked up how to do the potatoes on my phone."

"Were you on deployment or traveling with your folks when you discovered the diner?"

"Travel." I chewed a bite of eggs extra well. "I was sixteen, and I undoubtedly had no business drinking, but I was also rather stupid."

"Did your family spend a lot of time in Greece?" Zeb asked, making the same assumption as most people I encountered. "With a name like Atlas, I bet you're at least part Greek."

"You'd lose that bet." My laugh was rather dry. "We spent time all over the Mediterranean, but my whole name, including the last name, is entirely the product of having two flighty parents with wanderlust."

My name was one more reason why I'd never quite fit in anywhere I went. I wasn't an Aguirre-Bronson like my parents, wasn't a trust-fund baby or an ex-pat, loved Kringle's Crossing but never belonged here like Gabe, Paige, and Zeb, and had found my purpose in the navy, but I still had a name that stood out.

"I like it. Atlas Orion suits you." Zeb offered me a kind,

almost sentimental smile. "And it's kind of cool how much of the world you've seen."

"I guess so." I shrugged, taking a moment to eat more potatoes before continuing. "I mean, yes, I know it's a privilege, but it's also weird not having a hometown or a good answer to the 'where are you from' question."

"Like I said last night, it's not too late to acquire a home base of sorts."

"And not too late for you to travel," I countered. There were any number of places I'd like to show Zeb. Sunsets in Morocco, the stunning colors of Portugal, three-hour feasts in rural Italy, and the distinctive flavors of South Korea and Indonesia. Yeah, it would be fun to travel with Zeb.

Maybe…

"I have. Finally left the Northeast for a conference in Atlanta this year. Next year, I might make it to Seattle."

"I guess that counts." I tried to keep my voice light, not reveal any sadness. No way was a guy who saw Atlanta as far away going to enjoy gallivanting around the world with me, snatching weeks of leave here and there.

"Hey, maybe someday I'll get a passport." Zeb continued his jokey tone. "Toronto and Vancouver have major gaming conventions."

"That would be fun for you." I smiled, hoping I came off as encouraging. "The China town district in Vancouver has some of the best food I've ever eaten. And Toronto has this amazing little bakery I love."

"Too bad I can't take you along as my guide." Zeb bumped my shoulder, expression soft and open. "I do like to eat."

"I know." I sighed. The urge to think beyond December was rapidly winning out over my legendary common sense. "Me too. Maybe if I had leave—"

Zeb cut me off with a finger on my lips. "No promises, okay? We both know what this is."

Do we? But I didn't ask. That way only led to heartbreak. But the gulf continued to widen between what this was supposed to be—a fun holiday fling complete with sex lessons—and what it was—a deeply emotional friendship that kept stealing my breath and logic both. And right that moment, I *needed* to kiss Zeb.

No hesitation, no second guessing. I simply moved the breakfast tray to the floor and rolled him underneath me in one smooth move. Zeb chuckled, but I silenced him with a toe-curling kiss, delving deep into his mouth, claiming his lips and tongue and very soul as mine. I kissed him and kissed him until a vague worry about his oxygen levels made me take a reluctant breather.

"What was that about?" Eyes glassy and lips damp and swollen, Zeb gave me a dazed grin.

"Taking advantage of living in the now." I kissed him again as he hummed his agreement. Kept kissing him until he shifted, letting the sheet fall away, revealing the return of his morning erection. "God bless snow days."

Zeb went all pink and buried his face in my neck, licking and sucking while his hands swept over my back. However, when he tried to wiggle a hand between us to reach for my cock, I pinned both of his hands to the mattress.

"Nuh-uh." Voice stern, I peered down at him. "I said you first next time, a fact you conveniently forgot when we went for round two last night."

He made a frustrated noise. "But I like touching you. And kissing."

"I like it too, and right now, I like your hands right where I put them."

Zeb wrinkled his nose. "You're lucky I lo—*like* you in chief mode."

I winked at him, careful to act like I wasn't well-aware of what he'd been about to say. "I do like giving orders."

"Aye, aye." Zeb made a show of relaxing into the mattress, tension leaving his arms, hands splaying wide against the sheet. Straddling him, I took a moment to study him, not only to decide where to kiss first but also to memorize my favorite parts. I started by kissing his forehead, brushing his floppy, reddish curls aside. Then I used my tongue to outline the perfect shell of his ear and the freckled line of his neck muscles. His scruffy jaw was fuzzy against my lips, while the delicate skin below his Adam's apple and collarbones was impossibly soft.

"You don't let me do this nearly enough." I scooted lower so I could examine his rosy nipples. I pressed a kiss in the center of his chest, right over his heart.

"I'm not nearly as worthy of admiration as your muscles." Zeb squirmed under me.

"Better not let me hear you talk like that again." I scoffed at his ridiculous argument before lightly raking my teeth over his right nipple. "You're perfect, Zeb. Seriously."

Zeb's skin was warm from sleep, warmer still from my kisses and touches. He tasted faintly of soap, the result of a hasty second shower after the round two he'd promised. But he also tasted like sunshine on fresh snow, more potent than the champagne the night before, the sort of indescribable flavor I couldn't get enough of.

Accordingly, I wanted to kiss him everywhere. I crept lower still, letting my chin brush his cock, loving his intake of breath. Last night had been more of an exploration of unfamiliar territory, a chance to tease and taste, but now, with a snowy morning stretching ahead of us, I could seize more control and devour. Raising up on my elbows, I licked long stripes up his shaft.

"Atlas." His voice shook as well as his soft stomach. Taking my name as a plea, I swallowed him down, cautiously as he'd done with my cock, then more enthusiastically as I discovered how far I could go without tripping my gag reflex. I hadn't passed every swimming test the navy had handed me for nothing. In fact, it was damn fun to see how long I could hold my breath and make Zeb tremble and curse.

"Fuck. How are you this good?"

"Maybe I had a good teacher?" I winked before getting back to the job at hand. The weight of his shaft on my tongue, the slightly salty taste, and Zeb's reactions combined to make me hum happily.

"You really like doing this, don't you?" Zeb's voice was so full of wonder that I had to laugh.

"Yeah, I really do." I started to return to blowing him, but Zeb shoved at my shoulder.

"Atlas. Really want to come together. Please."

"You're lucky you're cute." I'd been fully intending to make him come with my mouth and then worry about my own insistent erection afterward, but I was powerless to deny Zeb. "And you said please."

"*Please*." He trembled as I levered myself back up and over him, lining our cocks up so I could take them in my hand. Zeb exhaled like he'd been waiting decades for exactly that. "Oh, this is my favorite thing."

"Mine too." I groaned because his dick was slick from my mouth, cockhead sliding easily against mine. Zeb was a little self-conscious about our size difference, but I honestly loved it. His cock seemed to align perfectly with every sensitive spot on mine, and the way he fit my hand

and mouth made it seem like he was made especially for me.

"Fuck me." Eyes drifting closed, he bucked up into my grip. He likely meant the plea metaphorically, but the image of him under me, welcoming me inside him, sturdy legs wrapped tightly around me was almost enough to make me come on the spot.

"Soon." I chuckled, loving how his eyes popped open, gaze hot and needy. "You said there's a way to do it that won't hurt you. I trust you to tell me if it's too uncomfortable."

Trust. It was at the heart of everything between us, and considering the life-and-death nature of my work, it was sobering to realize I trusted Zeb more than almost anyone else on the planet. And while I was still worried about possibly causing him discomfort, I believed in our ability to communicate.

"Trust me that the only uncomfortable thing will be if you stop." Zeb gave a strained laugh. "Expect a supersize bottle of top-quality lube in your stocking."

"Counting on it." An unexpected tender feeling overwhelmed me, made my grip slow and loosen. Zeb made a sound of protest, reaching between us to place his hand over mine. I welcomed the warmth of his hand against mine almost as much as his kiss as he arched toward me, lips soft and ready. "Zeb…you really are perfect."

"You sure make me feel that way." Claiming his kiss, he didn't give me a chance to tell him that it went both ways.

He made me feel special in a way no one else ever had. And not simply because I was big and ripped or competent at a challenging job, but like I was worthy merely by existing. In fact, I didn't feel any pressure to be perfect with

Zeb, which made me relax and believe his praise that much more.

"Damn, baby. That's good." Our combined grip was that much better than my hand alone. The tightness and warmth alone were driving me closer to the edge, and the increased connection only heightened my pleasure. "I don't want this to end."

I meant the words on many levels, but Zeb chuckled, eyes sparkling.

"Me either." Zeb's words came in between breathy laughs. "But my cock has other ideas. Damn. I'm close."

"Good." I kissed him with a newfound urgency, pouring all those unsaid words and emotions into the sex. Gratitude for how he made me feel. Longing for what couldn't be. Desire for him, body and soul both. All of it. I kissed him and held him close and let his hand over mine set the rhythm, which shifted from fast to frantic.

"Coming." Pulling loose from the kiss, Zeb arched toward me, head tipping back as his cock spurted all over our hands. Slick. Messy. Perfect. The increased slipperiness was enough to get me there, but it was the absolute awe on his face that made my breath catch and my pulse stutter.

"God. So fucking beautiful, Zeb," I gasped as I also came. Orgasms always hit me hard and fast, a knockout punch that usually left me drained and sleepy, but today it hit on a deeper level, one where his pleasure enhanced mine and the sensations spiraled out, a long, lazy ride back down to earth. And instead of sleepy, I felt triumphant and content, like I'd reached a summit I never wanted to leave.

"How many more times do you think we can come before the snow stops?" Zeb laughed as he lightly nipped my shoulder.

"I'm game to find out." I nuzzled the top of his head. "After another shower."

"What if it snows till Christmas?" The hope in Zeb's voice was almost too much. He was thinking exactly what I was—Christmas was too close now, the countdown truly on, and we needed to hoard every spare second.

"I hope it does," I said gruffly. I'd take all the snow the universe wanted to dish out if it meant that much more time with Zeb.

Twenty

ZEB

CHRISTMAS EVE: ONE SHOPPING DAY UNTIL CHRISTMAS

"There are certain advantages that come with age." Christine Maurice, the ninety-year-old matriarch of one of Kringle's Crossing's oldest families, was full of sage wisdom and merry humor. Her short, curly, snow-white hair was adorned with a tiara for the occasion.

"A Christmas Eve birthday party being one?" I teased as I cleared the luncheon plates from the table at the front of the event space where Miss Christine had the place of honor. I had no idea what sorcery was up with the calendar. How was it Christmas Eve already?

"After ninety Christmas birthdays, I'm entitled." At least Miss Christine was delighted at the date on the calendar, and hers was officially our last event before Seasons closed at four p.m. for the holiday. We'd reopen on the twenty-sixth with our famous Boxing Day sale, but our month-long rush was nearly over.

I hated it.

For the first time ever, I wanted December to go on and on. I wanted all the parties, all the chaos, all the disasters, and all the near-misses. I wanted whatever it took to keep Atlas here in Kringle's Crossing, working alongside me at Seasons. Screw my urge to get back to making regular content for my channel. Atlas felt way more important.

"I hope this is your best birthday yet." I managed to keep my own wistfulness out of my tone. Miss Christine had earned her large family and friend celebration, and she didn't need a mopey server. "Can I get you more punch?"

As this was a nonalcoholic event, Atlas had come up with a creative fruity and spicy punch for the signature drink, along with several other spritzers and mocktails.

"No, dear." Miss Christine patted my arm with her papery hand. Barely five feet, she had an air of fragility, but she was also sprier than many folks forty years younger. "There's a chill in the air. More snow is on the way. I wonder who bribed the weather people for the coldest December in decades?"

"Ha." *Atlas and I.* I couldn't admit to that, of course, but our wish for more snow days had come true over the past few weeks in a big way as the Northeast had been pummeled by back-to-back storms. "I'll write to the news station and demand a better forecast for you, Miss Christine."

"You're a sweet boy. We need to find you a nice girl to settle down with." Miss Christine touched her pearl necklace as I glanced over at Atlas, who was working the bar with his usual good humor, smiling as he handed out more cups of punch.

"Or a nice boy," I said it lightly with a laugh, but I also wasn't going to lie. Miss Christine and the Maurice family brought us a lot of business, but none of it was worth sacrificing myself.

"Ah. Yes. That works too." Miss Christine did an admirable job covering any shock with a wide, impish grin. She had a little spot of mauve lipstick on her teeth, which somehow made me like her that much more. "I knew your grandfather back in the day. Quite the charmer. Just like you. He'd be proud."

Charmer? Successful? Miss Christine undoubtedly had the wrong Seasons brother in mind. "It's really Gabe who has made Seasons a success."

"I didn't mean the business." She waved a hand, gold bracelet jangling. "I meant your video game channel thing. Streaming, they call it?" Her eyebrows knit together. "All the great-grandkids have been raving all afternoon about meeting you in person. Don't think I didn't notice how generous you were with the autograph requests. You're doing something right. A good example and a self-made man."

She was right that an eagle-eyed young guest had recognized me as Zipster from my channel. I didn't show my face in every video, but I was getting recognized more and more, especially after my con appearance in Atlanta. Getting asked to sign a few game cartridges and manuals earlier in the day had been a kick.

"Thank you." My chest went warm and tight like my white dress shirt had shrunk in the wash. *A self-made man.* I supposed it was accurate. My tax return identified me as self-employed, but I didn't often frame my success as one of determination and grit. Perhaps I needed to start.

"Ready to go, Aunt Christine?" Miss Christine's sixty-something niece strode over. Like her aunt, the niece had white hair and a diminutive stature.

"Me? Leave my party early?" Miss Christine's voice was strong and stubborn, belying her advanced age. "Never."

"It's starting to snow pretty heavily." The niece gestured at the windows as well as the thinning crowd. "Everyone else is about to head out too."

Miss Christine gave a regal sniff. "Well, I suppose you can fetch my coat and gloves. But I'll take one more turn around the room, say my goodbyes."

With the niece's assistance, I helped Miss Christine to her feet, which were clad in elf slippers complete with curly tips, and I fetched her candy cane-striped walker. The two ladies made their way from group to group as people readied to brave the increasingly ominous weather.

As I cleared more plates, one of the older kids came up to me. A girl in that indeterminate zone between eleven and fourteen or so, she had long, fine dark hair and purple glasses.

"Hey, Zipster—I mean, Zeb." She gave a shy smile, revealing a neat row of colorful braces. "Brian said you told him how to level up on the new *Space Villager* expansion."

"Yep. You want the same intel?" I looked around for a pad of paper to write the secret codes on, but the girl shook her head.

"Nah. I'd rather watch my brothers play while my sister and I write fan fiction about our favorite game characters. I wanted to say thanks because your channel is the only thing the four of us can agree on, and you always make us laugh."

"Thanks." I could talk for hours and hours to no one while streaming, yet suddenly, I found myself at a total loss for words. "That means a lot to me."

"Will you sign this?" She held a notebook with a hand-drawn cover featuring a grisly scene and a big, bold title of *The Villagers Fight Back*. "It's the first draft of my latest fic."

"I'd be honored." It took a few deep breaths, but I managed to sign without turning into a blubbering mess. I did, however, need a moment to collect myself after the girl walked away.

"Seems like you were pretty popular this afternoon." Last of the guests gone, Atlas wandered over to where I was stripping table linens.

"I suppose." My face heated, but I shrugged because I didn't want to put too much stock in a few autograph requests.

"Don't be so humble." Atlas gave my shoulder a friendly shove. "You were the highlight of the afternoon for those kids. I spoke with the mom of that group of four with all the B-names that kept following you around. Her husband is deployed right now. Said your content is the perfect distraction."

"Oh wow." I'd finally managed to calm myself earlier, but now I was emotional all over again. It might not be much, but I was doing something of value with my content. "I wish I could do something for them."

"A little Christmas magic?" Nix came striding over. "Did I hear you talking about Brent Maurice's family? He and Belinda graduated the same year as my older sister. What if we used some of the leftovers here and packed up a Christmas breakfast for them for tomorrow? I can deliver it on my way home. I need to leave soon to beat this weather."

With the three of us working together, we quickly packaged a festive box full of goodies for the family. Atlas undoubtedly thought he was being sneaky, but I caught him sneaking a wad of cash into a card. I added some game download codes and printed off a gift card for the most popular game-purchasing site as well.

As Nix departed, the skies darkened further, the storm worsening, and I said a quick prayer that they could complete their mission and arrive home safely.

"Well, that's a wrap." Gabe emerged from the shop area, keys dangling from one finger. "All locked up. We're almost done with the holiday rush. Just the Boxing Day sale to go."

"And Atlas and I have that handled," I reminded him. Paige had had a few false alarms, but all signs pointed to next week being a full-term arrival for the twins. "Tomorrow too. You and Paige need to let everyone else do the meal and cleanup. You've got enough on your minds."

Buzz. Buzz. "Speaking of my lovely wife…" Gabe fished out his phone and stepped away to take the call, returning pale and more than a little gray. "Babies are coming. Paige didn't want to worry me, but she and Lucy headed into Chester earlier for a fast check that turned into go-time in a hurry. I've got to get there."

"Man, it's really coming down now." I looked out the windows, willing the skies to clear.

"I have to get to West Chester." Gabe looked ready to join me in battle against the weather gods.

"We'll get you there." Atlas spoke in soothing tones, far more confident than I could be, as he rubbed Gabe's shoulder. "Promise."

Twenty-One

ATLAS

Out of all the missions I'd undertaken over the years, the mission to get Gabe to the hospital before Paige went in for a c-section to deliver the twins was one of the most critical. And perilous, given the increasingly thick snow. All trembling hands and nervous energy, Gabe was in no shape to drive, and he'd handed the keys to his four-wheel-drive SUV to me, not Zeb. I'd driven any manner of large vehicles, tanks and transport trucks included, under some harrowing conditions, but Zeb likely had more hours of snow driving than me. I hadn't missed his heavy sigh when I'd ended up with the keys.

However, I was determined not to fail at any part of the mission, winter driving included. I kept a steady grip on the wheel as we crept down the highway to West Chester.

"This has to be the worst Christmas Eve blizzard in decades." Positioned in the center of the backseat, Zeb leaned forward to peer out the windshield.

"Not helping." Gabe's eyes were tightly closed, likely praying for an alternative route to his wife.

"We'll get you there." Zeb rubbed Gabe's shoulder. "If anyone can get you there, it's Atlas."

"Thanks," I gritted out. The vote of confidence felt particularly warm, given Zeb's reaction to not driving. "And I'm going as fast as I dare. We'll make it."

We had the radio on for weather updates, and a cheery Christmas carol gave way to a crackling announcement from the DJ.

"*The governor has issued a state of emergency in the face of the latest blizzard. She is mobilizing national guard units to deal with power outages across the state, road closures, and other ongoing needs. We expect to see more highway closures in the next hour.*"

"Fuck this storm." Gabe sounded closer to tears than rage. Right as I was about to reassure him, police lights appeared in the rearview mirror, and I carefully pulled to the shoulder.

A tall officer in a heavy parka rapped at my window. ""You boys have reason to be out in this weather? Governor ordered this highway closed."

The officer had the posture, military short haircut, and commanding voice of someone who'd served, so as I produced my license, I added my military ID and made sure to let my coat sleeve slip to reveal part of my anchor tattoo.

"Yes, sir, officer." I addressed him with all the respect I'd give a captain. "I hear you on the closure, but my buddy here is about to be a first-time dad at the hospital in West Chester. Twins."

"Huh. Twins, you say?" The officer twisted his mouth as he glanced over his shoulder. "Harry, get over here. We got a situation." A younger officer made his way over to our car, and the first officer pointed at me. "Harry, this is…"

"Chief Atlas Orion out of Little Creek, Virginia." I almost never used my rank or duty station in the civilian world, but I wasn't above pulling out all the stops for Gabe. I gestured at him next. "This is my friend, Gabe, and his brother, Zeb."

My back muscles tensed. I felt more than a little disloyal to Zeb, reducing him to nothing more than Gabe's brother. In a few short weeks, he'd become so much more to me. Sure, Gabe was my best friend, but Zeb was the center of my world, an uncomfortable secret that grew harder to keep by the minute.

"Got a good buddy at Little Creek. Spec Ops." The first officer nodded as I'd hoped he might. "Did my time on the USS Enterprise. Let's see what we can do."

He stepped away to confer with Harry and was back in short order.

"You're in luck. We've got a plow coming through and a plan to get you to the hospital for your babies." Harry's chipper tone contrasted with the seriousness of the storm, but his cheer was oddly reassuring. And thus, we ended up under police escort, following a plow, making painstaking progress.

Finally, we arrived at the hospital, said our thanks to the officers, and made a mad dash up to the birth center. Gabe had a room number for Paige, but the room was empty, with the door wide open.

"Are we too late? Are the babies already here?" Gabe demanded of the empty room, but before Zeb or I could calm him, a passing nurse snagged Gabe.

"Mr. Seasons? Right this way. We're already getting Paige prepped. We need to get you gowned up, Dad."

"Dad," Gabe whispered to himself, expression wide-eyed and pale.

"Go meet those babies." I slapped him on the back, and Zeb gave him a fast, hard hug. The two of us then made our way to a waiting area where my Aunt Lucy was already sitting, knitting in hand, house-flipping TV show on, and multiple phones lined up to distribute baby news updates.

"The nurse said it would likely be an hour and a half or two until we can see Paige and the babies. But hopefully, we'll hear from Gabe sooner." Aunt Lucy knit even faster than she spoke. "Bet you two need food after your long ordeal."

"Nah—" Zeb protested, only to get a hot-pink scarf-in-progress flapped at him.

"You're not going to make the babies appear any faster pacing here." She gestured at the sign directing visitors to the hospital cafeteria. "Go. Take Atlas. Get some food and bring me back a coffee and one of those blueberry pie bars."

"Yes, ma'am." We dutifully fetched food I was sure none of us would taste before hurrying back. Zeb carried the tray of coffee while I toted a white bag full of pie and snacks, an unspoken division of labor that spoke to how well we worked together.

"Any news?" Zeb asked Aunt Lucy as she furiously ripped back several rows of stitches.

Mouth tight, she shook her head. "We should have heard something by now."

I glanced at the nearby nursing station, where personnel in various colored scrubs bustled around. "Should I go ask—"

"No." Aunt Lucy waved a knitting needle. "Gabe would text if there was news. No need to bug the staff."

After all the adrenaline of our crazy drive to the hospital, sitting there silently waiting was the worst. I wanted to be able to do something. My gaze caught Zeb's, all my emotions reflected in his eyes: exhaustion, exhilaration, anticipation, and a healthy dose of fear. I wished like hell I could take his hand, offer some strength and connection, but that, too, I couldn't do.

The hospital speakers blared with various codes being called, each one making the three of us jump. Any emergency could be Paige and the babies. Not knowing made my hands clench, feet bounce, and every brain cell jangle. Zeb wasn't the only one who needed reassurance.

Buzz. Buzz.

Aunt Lucy, Zeb, and I all lunged for the phone she'd set in front of her. Gabe's name lit up right as she grabbed the phone.

"They're here." She held up the message so we could see. "They had a last-minute wait for the OR and then a bit of a scare with some blood loss for Paige. But they're here and healthy. We should be able to see all of them in about two hours. Paige is in recovery now with Gabe and both babies."

"That's wonderful." Like Aunt Lucy, Zeb looked on the verge of tears.

"Two hours is enough time for us to worry about where to spend the night." I was still desperate for something, anything to do. "No way are any of us making it back to Kringle's Crossing in this weather."

"I'll likely end up here most of the night, helping Paige and Gabe." Aunt Lucy kept staring down at her phone as if willing more updates to arrive. "But I suppose we should snag nearby rooms if any are available."

"I'll find something." I was so damn relieved to have something productive to do that I failed to consider the implications of sorting out room arrangements. *Crap.* The last thing I wanted was to be separated from Zeb for the night, but the alternative was equally unappealing. "So one for you and—"

"One for you and Zeb." Aunt Lucy gave both of us a look more pointed than her knitting needles. "Gabe may be oblivious, but I've known you both too long not to notice what's been happening the past few weeks."

I was half-tempted to ask her to enlighten me because I was living this thing with Zeb, and I had no clue how to label what we had together. Perhaps it wasn't the worst thing that someone knew. Any sort of future was a total long shot, but a more open present might be nice. Might mean that Zeb stopped putting a finger over my lips when I tried to talk about pesky feelings and things like visits.

"Are you going to tell Gabe?" Voice dropping to a horrified whisper, Zeb went pastier than Gabe had earlier, complete with sweaty temples. And there went my thinking that being honest about our fling could be a good thing. If the thought of being found out made Zeb physically ill, well, that was answer enough for me. "If Gabe finds out…"

"Are you fourteen, Zebediah Seasons?" Aunt Lucy rolled her eyes at Zeb, tone sharpening. "No, I'm not going to tell Gabe. You're both grown adults. You can do that yourselves."

"We can't." I didn't wait for Zeb to reply this time. I wasn't going to risk Zeb's discomfort just for the chance to not hide.

"You don't think he'll be happy for you?" Aunt Lucy glanced back and forth between us.

"It's not like that," Zeb said flatly as he stood. "I'm going to walk down to the gift shop."

I shot to my feet as well. "I can come—"

Zeb held up his hand. "I need a minute. Please."

And with that, he was gone, leaving me little choice but to sink back down next to Aunt Lucy.

"Oh dear." Dismayed expression making her look older than usual, Aunt Lucy set aside her knitting. "I've put my foot right in your muck, haven't I?"

I didn't want to lie and say no, so I settled for saying nothing, simply studying my hands instead.

"Are you really going to tell me this is some no-strings hookup?" Aunt Lucy laughed lightly when I made a strangled sound. "Yes, dear. I know that word. I'm sixty-something, but I get around. Might even start dating in the new year. Hot grandma and all that."

"You should." I nodded, not even trying to hide how eager I was for a conversation topic change. "Uncle Joe would want you to be happy."

"And he'd want you and Zeb happy as well," Aunt Lucy shot right back. "Is it that you don't want to come out?"

"It's not that." I made a vague gesture with my hand. Sure, coming out would inevitably lead to some awkward questions from a few folks, but it was nothing I couldn't handle. "If I thought it would make a difference, I would. Happily. But there's no future for us."

Aunt Lucy made a clucking noise. "How sad that you live in a world without email, text, airplanes, and frequent flier miles."

"I can't do the long-distance thing to Zeb." I kept my gaze locked on the cracked leather of the chair opposite me. Aunt Lucy already saw far too much. "He deserves better. I'm a bad bet."

"And Zeb's not exactly the gambling type." Her heavy

sigh matched my own, and we sat in silence as I arranged for rooms at a nearby hotel within walking distance. Aunt Lucy continued knitting at a steady pace until her phone buzzed.

"Gabe says they're set up in the post-partum room. I can go back, then you and Zeb can follow in a few minutes."

"Guess I better go find him."

"Guess you better." Aunt Lucy gave me another pointed look, this one harder to read. I hated feeling like I was disappointing her somehow. Leaving her to head toward the room number Gabe had sent, I strode toward the gift shop only to discover Zeb emerging from an elevator holding two small stuffed reindeer toys.

"Got there right before it closed." He held up the toys but didn't smile.

"Hey," I said softly. "We can see the babies and Paige in a few."

"I know." His voice was just as flat as when he'd walked away. "Gabe texted me."

"Good. I got rooms for tonight." I took a deep breath before venturing into the murky waters churning between us. "Are you going to be okay sharing?"

"Why wouldn't I be? It isn't like we haven't been sharing a bed for weeks now." He addressed the wall map behind me rather than meet my gaze.

"True, but you seemed upset earlier." Gah. Talking about emotions was the worst, and I had no idea how to do this better.

"Of course, I'm upset." Zeb frowned like I was missing something obvious. "Aunt Lucy might be able to keep a secret, but if she knows, others have likely guessed too.

And that means Gabe could find out, and I hate that for you."

"You're worried about me?"

"Well, yeah." Zeb pursed his beautiful full lips, beard bristling as he spoke. "You're the one with more to lose here."

"Zeb." I reached for him, almost weeping with relief when he didn't dodge my touch on his shoulder. "That's not true, and we both know it."

Buzz. Both our phones went off at the same moment, but Zeb raised a hand when I went to fish mine out.

"Can we just pretend a little longer?" He finally met my gaze, and his eyes were so pained that I would have promised him the sun itself. "It's Christmas Eve, and I want to spend it with you, not fighting and not thinking about the future."

"I want to spend it with you too," I said reverently, tightening my grip on his shoulder. If nothing else, I was going to give Zeb the best Christmas Eve I could and make the most of every moment we had left. "And that part isn't pretend."

"I know." His voice was heartbreakingly certain. "Let's go meet the babies."

Twenty-Two

ZEB

As we walked through the maternity ward toward Paige's room, I tried to close all my mental tabs, shut down my internal computer for the night. I didn't want to think. Somehow, Aunt Lucy knowing about us made the end much more real. Because it wasn't truly about the secrecy or protecting Atlas. My reaction had had more to do with the fact that Atlas was leaving soon and couldn't make a single promise about when he'd be back. Which was understandable and reasonable and all those adult things, but reality still sucked. Dressing up the truth in navy blue didn't make it hurt less.

I wasn't about to let him risk his friendship with Gabe when we likely were down to days left. I couldn't protect him out there in the real world, where he confronted danger on a daily basis, but perhaps I could protect him from unnecessary best-friend awkwardness.

"Come in!" Paige called softly from her hospital bed when we appeared at the door. She was propped up by pillows with the head of the bed raised and held a small, tightly wrapped bundle in each arm. One bundle had a teeny blue cap while the other sported pink. "Meet Plum and Pine."

"You went with holiday-themed names after all?" I smiled because the great twin name debate had spanned most of the fall. "I love them."

"Can you believe I had almost twelve pounds of babies in me?" Paige grinned back. "The nursing staff is amazed at how strong the babies are. Getting twins almost to term is the real holiday miracle."

"You're the miracle, Paige," Gabe said reverently from the chair beside the bed. He kept patting the closest baby as if reassuring himself she was still there. Aunt Lucy sat knitting in the window seat, which doubled as a visitor bed.

"Who wants to hold a baby?" Paige asked. "Mom is chomping at the bit to get pictures of you guys with them."

"Him first." Atlas wasted no time pointing at me.

"Well, come over here, Uncle Zeb." Paige's eyes twinkled. Stepping forward, I peered down at the little pink bundle. Scrunched up face. The barest hint of reddish hair escaping the cap. A little fist holding the edge of the blanket. "Plum, meet Uncle Zeb."

"Sit here." Standing, Gabe steered me into the big chair and placed Plum in my arms as if conducting a ceremonial exchange of priceless royal artifacts.

"Now that's a perfect picture." Aunt Lucy's voice was tender, but I didn't bother glancing up, totally mesmerized by the baby in my arms.

"Hi, Plum," I whispered to the sleeping baby. "You, I, and Pine are gonna have some amazing adventures. Can't wait till you're old enough for board games."

That got a chuckle from Atlas, who had moved to stand next to the chair. "At least wait until they're a few days old. Maybe they make a Candyland for newborns?"

"Ha." I met his gaze, which reflected back my own wonder at the moment and also my wistfulness. Of all the things I wanted and couldn't have, being uncles together was at the top of the list. I wanted him along for all those adventures and game nights and sleepovers. I hated the idea of seeing him across the room at some future birthday party, memories of what had been hanging between us, all awkward pauses and long looks. I'd told him I wanted to pretend, and right then, I wanted to pretend all the way until spring. Hell, make that spring fifty years in the future.

"And one for you." Plucking Pine from his spot next to Paige, Aunt Lucy arranged the baby in Atlas's arms. She moved away to take photos of the two of us, but I didn't smile or pose for the camera. Instead, my gaze flitted between the two babies and Atlas's stunned face. His big hands made Pine look impossibly tiny, yet the gentleness in his posture gave an air of security. Atlas might be strong, but he, too, was undone by these two tiny humans and overwhelmed by protective urges.

"Trade me places," I said to him. "We need a picture of you with both babies."

Or rather, I needed the picture, one to pull out and reflect on. After some careful maneuvering, Atlas sat in the chair, a baby in each arm and a look of pure amazement in his dark eyes. Like Aunt Lucy and Gabe, I snapped a few pictures, but I also tried to memorize the little details my camera phone couldn't capture—the scent of baby powder in the air, the small movements of little hands wiggling free from their swaddling, the faint flush on Atlas's neck, the twitch along his jawline, the way he gradually relaxed, rocking slightly in the chair, whispering something to the babies none of us could hear.

The moment lingered like a perfect bite of peppermint

bark—layers of sweetness, one on top of the other. Long after we'd said goodnight to Paige and Gabe to let them rest, I kept seeing Atlas's awestruck expression in my mind. I wanted to be the one to put that expression on his face again and again, stealing his breath and earning his adoration. Not that I was jealous of the babies, but their presence only made me yearn for that much more.

As Atlas and I trudged through the snow to the hotel two blocks south, where he'd lucked into rooms, all I could focus on was getting him alone, warming him up, and forgetting every damn thing other than how good we were together. I waited through the check-in process, but the second the elevator door closed on us, I was on him, snowy mittens, heavy coat, and all. I kissed the snowflakes dotting his eyebrows and nose along with each pink cheek before claiming his chilly lips in a white-hot kiss.

"Wow." He pulled back, a bemused expression on his face. "What was that? I thought you might still be mad about Aunt Lucy knowing."

"Not mad. Just a realist. One who doesn't want to think about a damn thing other than getting naked with you and making this a Christmas Eve to remember."

"It's already pretty memorable." He chuckled, then ran a gloved fingertip down my bearded jaw. "But here's to making a few more memories."

The elevator doors opened on our floor, and Atlas grabbed my hand in a gesture even sweeter than my lusty panic-filled kiss. I let him lead me to our hotel room, a generic space done in shades of beige and white, notable for the huge king bed in the center of the room.

"Now that's an upgrade from my full." I laughed as I pushed his coat off his shoulders.

"Still gonna hold you all night long." Atlas tugged me close for a soft kiss.

"Counting on it." I kissed him back, continuing my efforts to undress us both.

"Your nose is cold." He kissed the tip of it, then nuzzled the snowflakes captured by my beard. "You should take a hot shower."

"We should," I corrected.

"The front desk had a small display of toiletry and pharmacy items for sale. I was thinking…"

"I love your thought." We'd talked a bunch over the last week or so about penetrative sex. Atlas had confessed to issues with finding condoms to fit comfortably, which had led me to pull up my most recent test results and Atlas had done the same. However, even after deciding condoms were optional, exploring oral and our favorite frot variations, along with the busyness at Seasons, had taken priority. However, at that moment, the only Christmas Eve present I wanted was him inside me. "I want that tonight. Merry Christmas to us. If they don't have lube, we can make do with lotion or something."

"No making do." Atlas's stern finger wag made me chuckle warmly. "Back in a second."

"I'll save you some hot water."

Twenty-Three

ZEB

I finished stripping my clothes off in record time, spurred by the thought of finally having Atlas inside me. I started with the most necessary washing before luxuriating in the hot water. I was rinsing the hotel shampoo from my hair when Atlas slid in behind me.

"That was fast," I gasped as he pulled me snugly against him.

"Mission accomplished." Dipping his head, he lightly nipped at my neck. "Name brand lube and everything."

"Excellent." I shivered from his nearness and teeth.

"Also grabbed us some cookies and chips since you didn't eat much at the hospital. Figured you might be hungry later."

"After." I sighed happily at his thoughtfulness. "A late-night Christmas Eve junk-food feast sounds perfect."

"Almost as perfect as you all warm and slippery." Lathering his hands, he soaped my already clean chest. "You're going to tell me how to do this, right?"

"I'll share what I know, and we'll figure it out together," I said lightly. I wasn't going to lie and claim tons of experience with bottoming or topping, but I also didn't want Atlas overthinking things. "I'm not worried. I trust you."

"Don't want to hurt you." He frowned as I spun in his damp embrace. "And I don't just mean the sex."

"I know. But we're not thinking about that, remember?" I made my voice a stern imitation of his. "No thinking about anything other than this moment right here."

"Sounds like a plan." He agreed readily, but his dark eyes were soft and sad. Stretching, I kissed him until the sadness was replaced by heated desire. Gasping, he flipped off the water. "Bed now."

"Abso-fucking-lutely." I hopped out of the shower to grab a towel on the rack opposite the tub. Before drying myself, I handed Atlas a towel. But apparently, Atlas had other things on his mind besides dry skin because he scooped me up, towels and all, fireman-carry style.

"Hey, I'm not light!"

"Says you." He tossed me in the center of the bed, right next to a small white paper bag.

"Oooh, God bless the lube fairy." I plucked the bottle from the bag and put it on the nightstand as Atlas stretched out next to me, damp and magnificent.

"Is that the right kind?"

"We'll make it work. Promise." I kissed his frown away, kissed him until he rolled me under him. His cock was heavy and hard against me, and I almost forgot our plans in the rush of how good his cock felt next to mine, how much I loved this, holding each other, moving together in familiar ways.

But then he hitched my leg over his hip, fingers coasting over my stomach and thigh, and I soon remembered everything I wanted. Helping him, I shifted my weight more to one side and pulled my upper leg farther back. Atlas took the hint and stroked lower, over my straining cock and heavy balls, to gently circle my rim.

"This?" he asked, biting his lip. The desire was clear in his dark eyes, but his nervousness was equally evident, especially in his unusually tentative touch.

"Yes. Feels good." Snagging the small bottle of lube, I passed it over to him. "For your fingers. And it's okay to play around, explore, have fun. Prep doesn't have to be serious business."

"Okay." Atlas continued to look like he was trying to ace a test he hadn't studied for. But slowly, he slid slick fingers over my sensitive flesh, more circles, then slightly bolder pressure. I rocked to meet his questing fingers, subtly inviting penetration, and I made sure to reward the increased exploration with lots of nonverbal feedback.

"Love that." I moaned as he went deeper. "Go deeper and curve your fingers a little. See if you can hit my prostate."

"Oh yeah. I read about that being good." Atlas nodded overly emphatically before carefully following my instructions. I arched my back and groaned as he grazed the spot.

"More," I demanded.

"More?" He glanced down at the bottle of lube like it might have extra instructions.

"More lube. More fingers. More stretching. More *you*."

"That I can do." Finally, Atlas seemed to relax, tension leaving his shoulders as he leaned over to kiss me, even as his fingers kept teasing. I used every bit of knowledge I'd gleaned the last few weeks about what he liked, nipping at his lower lip, sucking hard on his tongue, and reaping the rewards as his touches became as sure as his kisses. Gradually, he seized control there as well, finger-fucking me in earnest and drinking down my moans with more kisses.

"Now." I moaned the order, and he chuckled darkly.

"All right, Lieutenant." Fresh uncertainty crossed his expression as he withdrew his fingers and dried them on one of the towels before reaching for the lube again. "Give me a sec—"

"Let me." Sitting up in a hurry, I took the bottle from him. Nope, no way was I letting him get nervous again. And I might not be an expert, but I could at least make it sexy with lots of touching and kissing as I stroked his generous shaft with extra lube.

"In a hurry?" he teased, groaning softly as I kept jacking him with my hand. I pushed on his shoulder, and he went easily to his back, as I'd hoped.

"For you? Only for the last decade." I laughed but held his heated gaze so he'd see the truth there too. I couldn't get enough of him, wouldn't ever have enough time or chances. Hoping to take away the last of his nerves, I straddled his waist. "We can start this way, but feel free to flip me with those muscles of yours when you want to be on top."

Winking, I tried to project way more easy confidence than I felt. Atlas wasn't tiny, I wasn't particularly experienced, and the last thing I wanted was to disappoint either of us. The best I could do was go slow and hope my extreme desire made up for any miscues. Holding his cock steady with my right hand, I cautiously lowered.

"Oh." I breathed out in shallow gasps. His cockhead felt way, way bigger from this angle, and my abs and thighs trembled.

"Easy, baby." Concern creasing his forehead, he

stroked my thighs gently. "Remember, it's okay to play around, explore, have fun."

"Goof." I laughed hard at him quoting my own words. And amazingly, joking around worked. He relaxed. I relaxed. I slid a little lower, rocked, let my body adjust, slid more, then back, then tilted my hips a tiny and—

"Holy wow." I groaned low and lusty as his cockhead met my prostate for the first time, and all those worries about size and experience became irrelevant, lost in a wave of pleasure. "Feels like you were made just for me."

"Hey, I was going to say that." He gave a strained laugh that turned into another moan as I rocked faster, moving way more fluidly now. His eyes drifted shut. "Can't believe how good no condom feels. Fuck, Zeb."

"It's good. So good." I pitched my voice to reassure us both. This was working, and not only in terms of fit, but also in how damn good and joyous every little movement and breath felt.

"It is. It really is." Atlas sounded as stunned as I felt. He slowly opened his eyes, meeting my gaze. Wonder. Amazement. Joy. All those things I'd seen when he'd held the twins were there in his gaze, this time for me. "You're the hottest thing I've ever seen."

His words consumed me, making me feel so seen and cherished that I could only nod. My sinuses burned, and I grabbed for a joke rather than risk tears by thanking him. "I'd say we need to expand your horizons, but—"

Atlas cut me off with a growl and an impressive display of strength and control as he gathered me close to his chest and flipped our positions.

"No talking yourself down, remember?" He glared at me, but I merely grinned back.

"Hey, if that's what I get for some mildly low self-esteem, I've got a pile of insecurities—"

"I'm serious." Atlas put on his firmest voice as he pinned me to the bed, arms above my head, lower legs trapped by his. And damn did I love stern Atlas and the return of his usual cockiness because he started fucking me in earnest, punctuating each word with another thrust. "Only. Nice. Things."

"Okay, okay, I rock." I moaned, totally willing to sing my own praises if it meant more bone-rattling fucking. "Just keep doing that."

"Trying." Atlas gritted out the word, eyes and mouth narrow like he was concentrating hard not to climax. He wasn't the only one. I'd never gone hands-free, but I was all for trying until Atlas groaned again. "Tell me how to make you come."

"Keep looking at me like that." I chuckled at his heated glare before arching my back to drag my cock across his hard abs. "And give me your hand."

He started jacking me in time with his thrusts, picking up speed. I was close, but I kept getting distracted by the absolute wonder of watching him lose all control and composure.

"Zeb. Fuck. Please." Atlas Orion begging me to come was the hottest thing ever. The big man was totally reduced to primal need by me and this thing we shared.

"Yeah. Almost." I closed my eyes, letting his sure grip pull me that much closer to the edge. He added his thumb, a perfect amount of pressure, exactly how I loved it. "Jesus, you know me so well."

"I do." His voice was tender, and the intense look we shared as I opened my eyes was enough to push me right over the edge. Because that wasn't passion or desire in

Atlas's eyes. It wasn't lust or raw fucking. It was affection, the reflection of our shared connection, and the emotions of the last few weeks.

"Atlas." I gasped as I came hard, come jetting out of my cock to land on my stomach and chest. A few drops even made it as far as my beard. The release was blissful yet tinged with the same emotions as that look we'd shared. And I wanted to share even more. "You too. Come on. Go hard."

Thank God, Atlas took me at my word and thrust faster and harder, the last of his control shredding as he, too, came. Watching his face, knowing he was feeling it too, brought a fresh wave of pleasure. I'd wanted his orgasm as much as my own, and I felt every grunt and shudder and moan all the way to my soul.

"Oh, holy fuck." Atlas carefully pulled out before collapsing down next to me.

"More like, oh, holy night." Chortling with the sort of goofiness only climax could induce, I bumped his shoulder. "It is Christmas Eve, after all."

"So it is." He yawned big.

"Should we sleep or have our junk-food feast and watch one of the Christmas Eve services on TV?"

"Sleep is for the weak." He groaned and gathered me close.

"True." I willed my own sleepiness away. I didn't want to miss a single moment of Christmas magic with Atlas.

Twenty-Four

ATLAS

CHRISTMAS DAY

"Merry Christmas," I whispered softly to Zeb's sleeping body, which was pressed tightly alongside mine despite the hotel room's king-size bed. I wouldn't have it any other way. Early morning light filtered into the room, the grays of Christmas Eve replaced by sunshine and a world lit up by icicles and mounds of white snow.

"Merry Christmas." Zeb yawned and stretched. Last night had been all kinds of magical, from the babies' arrival to the sex to watching a regal Christmas Eve service on the local PBS station while outside, falling snow and twinkling Christmas lights mingled to create an otherworldly atmosphere. However, when Zeb groaned, certain real-world concerns took over my brain.

"How do you feel?" Rising onto my elbow, I peered down at him, but he only grinned.

"Excellent." Zeb stretched to press a kiss to my mouth. "Don't worry. I loved the sex. Every second."

"Good." I kissed him back, then chuckled when both of our stomachs rumbled.

Zeb reached between us to give my abs a quick pat, grazing my increasingly awake cock as he did so. "In fact, if I were less hungry, I'd show you again how much I love you fucking me."

"Food first." I hefted myself out of bed before Zeb's touch could distract me from what my guy really needed. *My guy.* Last night, Zeb had truly felt like mine, a piece of myself I hadn't known was missing, and something that belonged to me and me alone. *Mine.* Breakfast was the least of what I owed him. "Then you can show me whatever you want."

"Have you heard from Gabe or Paige this morning?" Zeb followed me out of bed.

"Yep. Sleepless night, so they're going to try to doze the best they can this morning without visitors." The early morning text from Gabe was what had awakened me, but I was glad I'd had the chance to watch Zeb sleep a few extra minutes. "Gabe sent a list of things they need from their house, so that's our Christmas mission if the roads cooperate. We can see them later in the afternoon or so."

"We'll make the drive." Radiating good humor and confidence, Zeb strode naked to look out the window. Luckily, we were up high enough he was unlikely to be seen. "The snow has stopped. Think we should hunt down some food and rescue Gabe's car from the parking garage?"

"Sounds like a plan." I grinned at him because I was usually the one with the plan. In my military life, entire operations and dozens of souls counted on my ability to strategize quickly yet thoroughly. My crew and I were their ticket home, and I couldn't afford to wing it. But with Zeb,

I didn't have to be in control of every last thing. Yes, he happily let me lead in the bedroom, but with other things, I could simply sit back and let events unfold in a way I couldn't with anyone else. Being around Zeb continued to be both thrilling and relaxing.

To that end, I tossed Zeb the SUV keys as we approached Gabe's vehicle in the hospital parking garage.

"What's this?" Zeb's nose wrinkled.

"The roads are better, but still not great. You've got more snow-driving experience than me, and you're more likely to have an idea of where we might be able to find food on Christmas morning."

"Oh, I've got ideas." Zeb's eyes twinkled, and the soft blush above his beard said he was pleased about being asked to drive. Which he did admirably well, navigating minimally plowed side streets, icy patches, and slushy highway to lead us to a truck stop diner partway between West Chester and Kringle's Crossing.

Rudy's 24-Hour Diner was barely bigger than a railroad car with a similar, low rectangular shape and looked to be easily seventy years old with a weathered roof that matched its faded menus. The server who seated us had long gray hair twisted into a topknot with a pen stuck in it and a crooked nametag that read: Martina. She seemed to be of a similar age to the diner. Along with the menus, she handed us a thin sheet of holiday specials, which Zeb eagerly studied.

"Oh my God, they have gingerbread pancakes." He made a near-orgasmic noise that had me regretting not going for morning sex.

"Get them," I ordered gruffly.

"Only if you do the cinnamon roll French toast."

"Deal." I chuckled because Zeb hardly had to twist my

arm to make me try something decadent on one of the few days of the year custom-made for indulgence. And cinnamon-anything was already going to remind me of him for the rest of my life.

"Coffee?" Martina, the same server who'd seated us, appeared with a steaming pot of what smelled like an excellent dark roast.

"Please." I moved so she could reach our cups. I'd worked enough holiday duty shifts myself to know what a thankless day it could be, so I added, "Merry Christmas."

"Happy Holidays to you boys too." Martina gave us a wide smile that reminded me of Aunt Lucy. "And it's a good Christmas. Steady stream of highway patrol, truckers, and stranded drivers all night. Can't beat those holiday tips."

"Glad you don't mind working the holiday." Zeb smiled back. "Feels like all Atlas and I did this month was work, so you've got my sympathy."

I frowned because I personally felt like we'd done so much more than work. The month had flown by, and the hours we'd put in at Seasons were the least of the reasons time was at such a premium. But before I could shoot Zeb a pointed look, Martina chuckled.

"Oh, honey, I volunteered. Every year since my Nadine passed, I try to take all the holiday shifts so my regular servers can enjoy the day." She offered up another winsome smile. "Owner perks, Nadine would say. I work when I want."

"That's...great." Zeb swirled his tongue over his lips like he wasn't sure of the proper response. "And I'm sorry about Nadine."

"Eh. We had a good long run." Martina shrugged. *Long run.* I tried to picture what sort of partnership could give rise to such a fond tone. *My Nadine.* And what I wouldn't give to be able to say *my Zeb.* Earlier, when he'd felt so much like *mine,* my heart had barely been able to hold it. What would a long run for us look like? Who might we become in twenty or thirty years or more? If circumstances were different, I liked to think we would have made it work, the same as Martina and her Nadine. "Two old broads running this place. We even made an episode of a show about truck stops once. Said we had the best biscuits north of Virginia."

"Don't tempt me away from the cinnamon roll French toast," I mock-scolded, which earned a girlish giggle from Martina.

"You look hungry. How about adding a half order of biscuits-and-gravy to that cinnamon roll French toast?"

"Sold." Martina and Zeb might have to roll me out of the diner, but I was determined to wring every bit of joy I could out of this weirdly wonderful Christmas.

When Martina returned with our food, she asked the inevitable. "You boys from around here?"

Like always, I had no clue how to answer, but for the first time in many years, I had a specific yearning. Or rather, the ghost of a childhood memory, begging my folks to put down roots in Kringle's Crossing, give us a real home and real friends like Gabe and his family.

And an answer as easy as Zeb's. "Kringle's Crossing. My family runs Seasons."

"That's a nice joint." Martina nodded, then cackled as she topped up our cups. "Our coffee is better."

"I'll never tell." Zeb put a finger on his lips. He waited until Martina had moved on to speak again. "This might be the best Christmas breakfast ever."

"Agreed. Pretty damn perfect. And the food's not bad

either." I winked at him, and his answering blush made my chest all warm. But I wasn't lying—the company mattered far more than where or what we were eating. "What should we do after this? It's not going to take us that long to gather Gabe and Paige's stuff for later."

"I think we need to do something easy and lazy after this carb coma, and I've got the perfect idea."

And thus, after loading the SUV with the things Gabe and Paige needed, we ended up in Zeb's bed yet again, sprawled in front of his bedroom TV, watching an animated Christmas movie neither of us had seen. The piece was surprisingly engaging for a kid's movie, and I laughed more than I had during any other holiday in memory.

"See? I was right." Zeb leaned over and kissed my cheek. "Best Christmas ever. Full from breakfast. Movies. Bed. You. I can't ask for more."

We actually *could* ask for more, way more, but perhaps Zeb was right, and we needed to be grateful for what we had, the perfection of this holiday season, and not waste time worrying about might-have-beens.

Twenty-Five

ZEB

"Congratulations must be in order." A nurse in holiday scrubs gave me a cheery smile as I hauled the last load of things Gabe and Paige had requested. The red-haired nurse looked to be heading home after a long shift, and I grinned back. Making my way through the parking garage, I carried two empty infant car seats with a bag of food stashed in each seat.

"Merry Christmas, but these aren't for my babies." *I wish.* There was a world where I might adopt a pack of little gamer cousins for Plum and Pine, but that world seemed hazy and rather lonely at present. "My brother and his wife had twins last night."

"Oh! The Christmas Eve blizzard twins! They're going to be famous. Congrats, uncle!" The nurse gave a last wave before continuing on to a small compact, leaving me to trudge up to the maternity ward on my own. Atlas and I had already made one trip, and since the car seats and food didn't require both of us, I'd left him to visit with Gabe and Paige.

I'd also deliberately volunteered for the trek because I was scared Gabe, Paige, or both would guess about Atlas and me like Aunt Lucy had. As much as I would love to publicly claim Atlas, the last month had also made me rather protective of him. Sure, he had his parents and his lengthy list of military contacts, but Gabe was family to him, and I refused to be the thing that strained that friendship. Bad enough that awkwardness would likely persist for years for Atlas and me. If I couldn't have him for myself, I at least wanted him happy, best friendship intact.

I didn't trust Gabe not to go into big-brother mode if he learned about our fling. Never mind that I was twenty-eight or that it had been my idea. Gabe, the world-class worrier, would likely have thoughts with a capital T, and dread over those opinions slowed my steps further and further as I approached Paige's hospital room.

Outside the door, I paused to peek in. Atlas sat in the rocker, the double twin pillow Paige had requested from the twins' nursery on his lap, and a twin wearing a jaunty Christmas sleeper nestled near each elbow. I wasn't sure what it was about big men and tiny babies, but a piercing want struck me square in the chest.

"Atlas has the magic touch," Gabe whispered from the daybed in front of the window. Aunt Lucy sat in a plastic chair near Gabe, and the hot-pink scarf she was working on was far longer than yesterday. Paige still occupied the hospital bed, but she was sitting up with far more color to her tired complexion than the day before.

"They're both asleep?" I crept into the room.

"Appears that way." Gabe didn't move from his sprawl as I set the car seats and food down. Luckily, I had nestled a surprise that might help revive him in between the food.

"Here." Keeping my voice low, I kneeled next to Gabe.

"Since the hospital coffee shop is closed for the holiday, I grabbed you a coffee at a gas station on the way in. Not the best brand, but at least it's your favorite hazelnut."

"You're my favorite brother." He offered me a tired smile.

"And I have cookies." Staying quiet, I unpacked the food bags for the Christmas dinner hospital picnic plan Atlas and I had dreamed up. We all had agreed to wait on any present exchanges until the twins were home, but we didn't need presents to celebrate.

"I should be the favorite something," Atlas softly teased from his spot, rocking the twins. "Not only did I convince your kids to sleep, but I also had the idea to raid the leftovers fridge at Seasons."

"Okay, you're both the best." Gabe took a long swallow of coffee.

"You're a championship team," Paige added. Aunt Lucy shot me a knowing look, but I kept my expression neutral, careful to not seem too pleased at being a team with Atlas. We did work well together, whether at Seasons, solving disasters, gaming at my place, or in bed. I simply liked being around him far, far too much.

We'd grabbed paper plates and plastic silverware, so I quickly assembled plates with assorted appetizers, ham, cheese, and plenty of cookies. While I worked, Aunt Lucy carefully transferred the twins to their bassinet so Atlas could eat. As I handed out plates, Gabe swallowed hard.

"What?" I took a seat next to him on the daybed. "Are you okay?"

"I'm fine." His quivering lower lip said otherwise. "This isn't the Christmas dinner any of us expected at all. But you and Atlas made sure it was Seasons Special."

"We tried." I set a hand on his shoulder. "And it might

be unexpected, but I can't wait to tell the twins the story of our Christmas Eve adventure, complete with police escort."

"A new family legend." Gabe's voice brightened. "The next generation of Seasons."

"Next generation?" Paige laughed lightly before turning toward me. "That's a lot of responsibility for two teeny babies. Someone better produce some cousins."

"I'll get right on that." I laughed even as my longing intensified. And what would I do if, a few years from now, Atlas showed up with someone else? Had a family? Could I imagine having one without him? Impossible though it was, every future wish I had seemed to center around Atlas.

My plate full of Nix's delicious offerings might as well have been pebbles for all the appetite I had. After we cleaned up the plates and delivered some cookies to the nurses' station, Aunt Lucy headed back to the hotel for a few hours of rest while Paige dozed in the bed. Gabe also looked well on his way to sleep. Exchanging a quick glance, Atlas and I bundled up for another chilly night.

"We'll let you nap while the babies are sleeping," Atlas whispered on our way out the door.

Once we were in the car and headed out of the parking garage, I looked at Atlas in the passenger seat. "What do you want to do now? Another movie at my place?"

"The side streets have to be better after today's sun, right?" Atlas pointed at the neighborhood opposite the hospital, where every house seemed lit up in holiday colors. "Look at all those lights. Tomorrow, most decorations will start coming down, but tonight it's Christmas. Let's drive around and look at the lights."

"I love that idea."

We started near the hospital with the cheery, middle-class neighborhood, with me driving while Atlas looked up the best areas in Philly to see holiday lights.

"Hey, you remember that college party from a few weeks back? The IT department? Apparently, one of the best neighborhoods for lights is near there. Evergreen. People come from all over to see the displays."

"Well then, let's do it." I gestured for him to type the address into Gabe's SUV's GPS. We turned on the same station we'd listened to the night before, which was playing lots of old Christmas hits. We kept cracking each other up by singing along badly and making up joke lyrics.

"Oh wow, this was worth the drive." I legit gasped as we entered the Evergreen neighborhood. The group of older brick homes was spectacularly lit up, each house lavishly decorated, one after another. The largest house on the corner had row after row of bright lights, along with reindeer on the roof and an illuminated Pride flag in the window. Multiple windows revealed various trees, and to my delight, two male figures were slow dancing by the largest tree in the front room.

I want. The feelings I'd been battling all day returned in full force. Why couldn't that be us? Was the universe truly so unfair as to give us this one perfect holiday season and nothing else?

"Pick a house," Atlas ordered softly as we drove through the neighborhood as if he, too, was under the spell of all these lights and holiday magic. "Come on. Pretend with me. Pick a house."

"Hmm." I pondered which I might choose if I were in the market. "We're a bit far from Kringle's Crossing."

"Ah." Atlas made a sad, knowing noise.

"Sorry." I hated feeling like I was letting him down, and I exhaled hard. Apparently, even in my daydreams, I had a hard time leaving Kringle's Crossing. "Wait. I like that one." I pointed to a small two-story home on one side of a shared driveway. I pulled closer to it, idling near the curb so other traffic could get around us if needed. The holiday light display was all at precise angles with a celestial theme. "That's clearly well-wired. It would be fun to program a light display like that."

"I could see you having fun with that for sure." Atlas smiled over at me, expression tender yet distant. "Looks like there's a little fenced backyard for your future mutts."

"Garage big enough for a spare fridge for all our leftovers." I played along, not even tripping over the *our*. In this little fantasy existence, there was most certainly an *us*, a future, and a home somewhere, whether in this neighborhood or another. "Bet I could make a soundproof recording studio in the basement for my game streaming."

"I'd be up for learning more renovation tricks." Atlas placed a hand over mine near the gear shift. "Seems like the sort of neighborhood with an overly active local association. There's not a single house without lights. Might be fun to be part of a community like that."

You could. My heart hammered, and my tongue was suddenly too thick to speak. Yearning clogged my chest. I didn't just *want* this future. I *needed* it. I wanted it for me, yes, but for Atlas most of all. He'd never really had community, a place to put down roots and call home, and I could be the person for him.

There was no traffic behind us, no reason to move on, and I turned toward him precisely as he shifted my direction as well. Our mouths met, saying things our voices simply couldn't, giving me the courage to—

Brrrrriiiiiiinnnnnng. A ringtone I'd never heard shrieked out of Atlas's phone, making us jump apart, and my heart sank. Somehow, I knew even before he answered that I was about to hate whatever came next.

Twenty-Six

ATLAS

"I have to leave." As I ended the call, I set my phone on my lap, knowing full well it was likely to ring again. Zeb had remained silent and parked by the celestial lights house while I'd been on the phone with my commanding officer.

"I know," Zeb said flatly. Even hearing only one side of the conversation, he'd likely deduced the seriousness of the call. "When? Guess we should head back to my place and get you packed."

"Tonight." I couldn't keep the pain out of my voice. "No time to go back to Kringle's Crossing."

"Christmas night?" Zeb echoed my tone. The stunning light display reflected off the windshield, but after my news, the sparkling lights felt eerie rather than festive.

"There's a crisis in…" I trailed off because this particular shit show hadn't reached the news yet, and while I trusted Zeb, I also knew security protocol.

"You can't say where. I get it." Zeb sounded more resigned than hurt now. He put the car in gear, heading out of the neighborhood and toward the interstate. He flipped to the GPS screen on the SUV's dashboard. "New Hanover?"

"Yup. I've got to get to McGuire ASAP." I took over, entering the base's destination into the GPS as Zeb continued to drive out of the picturesque little neighborhood and back to our real lives. "They're sending a chopper to take me to the rest of our team before we're wheels up. They need me to start my new role a few weeks early. Nothing like hitting the ground at top speed."

"Your own chopper?" Zeb gave a tired laugh. "Too bad you dislike helicopters because that's a pretty sweet Christmas present. Must be nice to be that important. Chief Big Deal on your new team."

He chuckled again, but his white-knuckled grip on the steering wheel and tight mouth belied his joking tone.

"It's more that I have the experience they need to get some SEALs in and out of a…delicate situation." Again, I couldn't say too much, but the higher-ups wouldn't have sent for me if my experience wasn't mission-critical to this particular operation. The SEAL team involved included personnel I'd worked closely with for years. I didn't simply *need* to go because I was ordered. I *wanted* to go, but guilt over my divided loyalties made my stomach churn. "I'm not sure I trust anyone else to get this job done."

"I was kidding, Atlas." Zeb exhaled harshly before merging onto the interstate. "Of course you're important enough to warrant a helicopter. Unquestionably, the navy needs you. You're the best at what you do."

"Thank you." I swallowed hard. Other words crowded my throat, thoughts and sentiments, none of them helpful. No matter what I said, I couldn't change the reality.

"I do wish you had time to go and get your stuff, however. Don't you need a uniform, at least?" Zeb shook his head, taking the exit that led to 276, which would take us out of Philly and into New Jersey. And away from Kringle's Crossing, but that went without saying.

"No time." I glanced down at my phone, a flurry of incoming messages underscoring how serious the situation was and how rapidly the mission was coming together. "I've got my military ID to get on base, and a buddy from the barracks is handling getting my uniform and stuff like that. I'll worry about my other stuff later. Even if traffic is light, it's still going to take us around an hour to get to McGuire."

"Okay." Zeb seemed zapped, all his usual sunny energy gone, like a holiday light display with a blown circuit. And it was all my fault.

"I'm sorry."

"Why?" Zeb spared me a quick glance. "This is your job. And you love your job, and it's vital to the whole damn nation. You don't have to apologize for needing to work, especially not with so many people counting on you."

But he'd been counting on me too, and we'd both been counting on at least one more night. I rubbed my temples. I hadn't bothered shaving that morning. Even my appearance was in vacation mode, and I wasn't ready to report for duty.

"I can still be sorry I have to cut my stay short and sorry that I'm leaving you on Christmas." I wanted to touch him in the worst way, but I knew better than to distract a driver in thick Philadelphia-area highway traffic.

"It was a good Christmas." Zeb's tone was resolved like he was willing himself to stay positive and not get overly emotional. I understood, but I almost wished he'd let himself be upset. Perversely, Zeb being all matter-of-fact made it harder for me to outrun my own tsunami of mixed emotions.

"It was the best Christmas I've ever had." I tried to match his even tone, but I also wasn't lying. The last forty-eight hours had been heartbreakingly wonderful. "I didn't get to give you my present. It's hidden in the bottom of my duffel under some T-shirts. Open it when you get home."

"That's no fair." Zeb pursed his lips. "Mine for you is at my apartment too. I wanted you to have it before…" He paused to swallow hard. "It's okay. It'll keep."

"I'll get it when I come get my stuff."

"Sure." Zeb sounded the exact opposite of certain.

"What? I'm coming back, Zeb." Trying to keep my emotions in check, I made my voice firm. "I might not know when, but I'll be back for my stuff. And you."

"I'm sure Gabe and I could figure out how to ship you your clothes and whatever else if needed." Zeb stared straight ahead at the line of traffic stretching down the dark interstate. Nothing to see but taillights and billboards. "I know you have no idea how long this deployment will last."

"Is that you saying you'd rather not see me?"

"Of course not." He managed the weakest of smiles. "Any time you can make it back, you should. You'll want to see the twins as often as you can. They'll change a ton this first year especially."

"And you?" I pressed.

"I'm always going to want to see you." His smile went from barely there to bittersweet to downright sad.

"Somehow, that's not all that reassuring." A nervous chuckle escaped my throat. God, I hated this.

"I'm not sure what you want me to say."

Say you'll wait for me. Say you'll be right where I left you. Say there will always be a place for me in your bed. In your life. Say we can have next Christmas and the one after that.

But of course, I couldn't ask for any of that. It wouldn't be fair to Zeb, and I cared for him far too much to make selfish requests, but damn did I want.

In the distance, houses draped in holiday lights sped by, a blur of bright colors. Elsewhere, it was still Christmas night. Kids playing with new toys. Exhausted parents dozing. Grandparents picking up wrapping paper. Family and friends munching leftovers. Others, like the cars around us, were on their way home. *Home.* If I knew where that was, I might miss it as much as I was going to miss Zeb.

"Say you'll miss me," I said at last, tone light, just this side of flip.

"You know I will." He said it softly but surely, as if he knew all the other things I'd been tempted to say.

"But you'll be able to get back to work now that the holiday rush is done." If Zeb could put a brave face on things, so could I. "You can pull as many all-nighters gaming as you'd like. And you'll sleep better without me hogging three-quarters of the bed."

"Ha." He laughed, but the resulting smile barely made it past his full lower lip. "Yeah, back to real life. I just wish…"

"Me too." We reached for each other at the exact same moment, holding hands near the gear shift. We drove on in silence, all our unsaid wishes and hopes riding along, making each breath feel that much weightier and more significant.

As we exited the highway near the base, traffic thinned further. We stopped for a red light, and Zeb inhaled sharply before turning toward me.

"If you're serious about coming back—"

"Shush." I stole his go-to move and placed a finger on his lips. "No promises. I can't ask for that."

"But I can offer." He gave me a crooked little smile before kissing my finger.

"But you shouldn't." I made my voice chief-level stern and somehow managed not to weep as the light turned green and he drove on. As we approached the checkpoint at the base gate, time seemed to further speed up, every second another one closer to goodbye.

I readied my ID and ensured Zeb was ready for the guard's questions and possible car search. Someone had evidently briefed the gate crew on my arrival because the guard who took my ID and checked over the vehicle nodded at a young recruit standing near a government-issue Jeep. The kid was probably fresh out of basic training and clearly not accustomed to either waiting or the cold as he kept stamping his feet.

"Heard there's a bird on the way for you." The gate guard motioned the younger guy forward. "Johnson here will take you to your chopper."

"Guess this is goodbye," Zeb said softly.

"Yeah." I made no move to open the door handle.

"Don't worry. I'm not gonna do something stupid like cry or kiss you in front of your fellow naval personnel." Zeb laughed, but I didn't.

Since when did I give a flying flock of reindeer about what these guys thought? I wasn't scared of coming out or being with Zeb publicly. I should be so lucky.

"Maybe I like stupid." I leaned in for a fast, hard kiss.

"Thanks." Zeb licked his lower lip as I pulled away. "Stay safe. I know you can't promise that, but…be careful?"

"Always." I kissed him one more time before breaking away and opening the door. His eyes were wide and sad, and I couldn't look more than a second or two. "Okay. Gotta go." My voice came out all gruff. "Drive safe on your way back. Thanks for the ride."

As I walked toward the waiting Jeep, I mentally kicked myself. *Thanks for the ride.* Out of all the things I'd wanted to say, that had to be among the dumbest. Zeb was so much more than another buddy dropping me off on base.

He was my everything. I glanced back over my shoulder, intending to meet his gaze, tell him with my eyes what I'd failed to articulate, but he had already turned the SUV around and was driving away.

I watched his taillights for a long second.

"Chopper waiting," Johnson reminded me.

"I'm ready," I lied. I wasn't sure I'd ever been less ready to go wheels up. Was every future mission going to hurt this badly? God, I hoped not, but I had a sinking feeling my life had been divided irrevocably into before and after Zeb.

Twenty-Seven

ZEB

BOXING DAY: DECEMBER 26TH

I didn't open Atlas's present on Christmas night. Didn't go hunting through his duffel bag, didn't do anything other than crawl into my now too-big bed, hugging the pillow that still smelled like him, and willing sleep to claim me so I could stop worrying about him and what he might be facing in the line of duty.

And missing him.

Needing him.

I spent most of Boxing Day working the annual Seasons sale on autopilot. *Half-off. Everything must go. Year-end clearance.* Funny how it felt like my heart was the thing on the markdown table, battered and worn and unlikely to be needed again anytime soon. I didn't hold my breath on anyone swooping in to claim it either.

Not that I'd want anyone other than Atlas.

In the late afternoon, after the initial rush of bargain hunters was over, Belinda Maurice appeared with a handwritten thank-you note and a small box of homemade fudge.

"I wanted to thank you all for the food box and help for the kids."

"No problem." I smiled my first smile all day because she didn't deserve my bleak mood, and the memory of working with Nix and Atlas was still warm and wonderful. Funny the difference forty-eight hours could make. "It was fun to pull together, and you've got some great kids."

"Yeah, we're blessed." Belinda sighed, worry lines deepening around her eyes and mouth. Her dark hair had a few more gray strands than the last time I'd seen her as well. "This latest deployment has been a super hard one. I mean, they're all hard, but the older the kids get, the harder it is to pretend…sorry. You don't need to hear my complaints."

Actually, I did, more than she'd ever know. I'd vaguely understood the sacrifices home-front families made, but the reality of caring for someone in the military was so much more heart-wrenching than I ever could have anticipated.

"I'm happy to listen." I held her gaze, not wanting to make this conversation about me but wanting her to know I was sincere. The shop was largely empty, late afternoon sun rapidly fading, and the bargain bin was well picked over. Another long, lonely night stretched in front of me, making me more talkative. "And it sucks for all of you. How…how do you keep going?"

I probably shouldn't have asked, but I'd spent the last day desperate for answers. Hell, knowing which questions to ask would be a decent start.

"I don't." Belinda shrugged, the pain in her eyes echoing deep in my chest. Yeah, I shouldn't have asked. "Okay, that's not true. Obviously, I do go on. I get up, I get the kids to school, I manage to get to work, I make the dinners, and I fall asleep alone. I'm the opposite of a superhero. There are weeks like this one when going on with Brent deployed utterly sucks, and there are weeks when I remember the dream."

"The dream?" I hoped this was less of a bad question.

"We're twenty-two months away from his twenty-year retirement and our lives as full-time national park nomads. We've wanted this for years. Homeschool the kids for a year or two, see the country, get a sweet RV, and figure out the next great adventure. We've spent eighteen years dreaming together. Kids. House. Future plans. The dream gets us through because there's no one I'd rather dream with."

"Wow." Swallowing, I wished I knew her well enough to offer a hug. *No one I'd rather dream with.* I knew exactly what she meant. "That's beautiful. Truly."

"Thanks." She gave me a fast pat on the back of my hand. "Anyway, I better get back to the kids. Take care. Tell Nix and Atlas thank you too."

"I will." I didn't tell her that Atlas had been deployed. She had enough worries of her own. But long after she departed, I mulled over what she'd said—the parts where she'd admitted life as a military family was super hard and the parts where she'd revealed why it was worth it for them.

I didn't doubt that being a family with Atlas would be worth it. I wasn't sure he wanted it, wasn't sure how to get us from here to there, and wasn't sure I was anywhere near as strong as Belinda Maurice. All I knew was I missed him more and more with each passing moment.

Twenty-Eight

ZEB

DECEMBER 27TH

Not surprisingly, by the twenty-seventh, I was the mopiest of mopey uncles as I helped Gabe, Paige, and Aunt Lucy bring the twins home.

After the twins passed their car seat tests and all the various medical personnel signed off on the discharge, it was late in the day, and everyone was more than a little cranky. Gabe and I hauled multiple loads of belongings out to the SUV in the parking garage. I'd accidentally parked in the same space I had on Christmas and the memory of longing for what couldn't be kept smacking me square in the chest. I glanced across the parking garage toward the neighborhood Atlas and I had driven through. As predicted, most of the lights had been removed, packed away, another season over. I sighed hard enough that Gabe turned toward me, frowning.

"What's up with you?" He slammed the back hatch shut. "I thought you'd be happy the holidays are almost over so you can get back to your gamer life. Pizza, energy drinks, and endless raids."

"Gabe…" I shook my head. For once, I couldn't let the teasing slide. Something had changed in the last month. Atlas had seen what I was trying to accomplish with my life. Others had too. The kids wanting autographs thought I was pretty awesome. Heck, if ninety-year-old Christine Maurice could see the value in what I did, Gabe could damn well make an effort. "I earn a good living at my gamer life. I have an accountant who ensures I do all the self-employment stuff above board. I have health insurance and a savings account. I'm not some kid futzing around with a channel with three subscribers. Fans know who I am. Fellow creators respect me. Why can't you?"

"Oh." Gabe paused, turning back to the car and looking at the rear door for long moments. "That's…that's a good point." He licked his thin lips. "You're my little brother. My job is to take care of you."

"You're a great big brother, but I'm twenty-eight. The days when I needed you protecting me on the bus and after school are long over. And I miss Mom and Dad as much as you do, every damn day. But you can't save me from that grief either. At some point, you've got to let me be an adult."

"Yeah." Eyes distant and glassy, Gabe nodded. "Maybe I got so used to taking care of you, I didn't realize how much you're taking care of yourself these days. I'm sorry."

"I get it. And I am taking care of myself." I put a hand on his shoulder. "I'm happy to help out with Seasons. I am. It's our heritage, and its continuation is your dream. I support all your dreams, but the gaming channel is mine. And I'm tired of you talking it down."

"I'm sorry. You're right. I do tease—okay, maybe it's

not all teasing." Gabe's mouth twisted as he slumped against the car. "I give you too much shit. But it's because I care and because I worry." Groaning, he rubbed his temples. "God, I'm so tired of worrying about every little thing. Last night I couldn't sleep. And not because of the usual hospital noises, but all the worries in my damn brain. Were the babies warm enough? Too warm? Full? Dry? And so on."

The last month raced through my head, all the times Atlas or I had said how anxious Gabe seemed, far more than normal. Maybe there were other hard truths I needed to share with Gabe. "I say this with all the love in the world, but you need help."

"Help?" His nose wrinkled. "Like a nanny for the twins?"

"No, help like medication and therapy." I met his gaze. "I've met several people at gaming cons who live with clinical anxiety disorders. You don't have to be miserable. You deserve to be happy."

"I am happy. And blessed." Gabe scrunched his face up like one of the twins stubbornly resisting a nap. "I just wish I could shut my brain off."

"You can. Call your doctor. Today. Please." I sounded very much like the older brother, a reversal of our usual roles, but it also felt right, being the one to take care of Gabe for a change. Spending time with Atlas had shown me how good it could feel to take care of another person. "If not for me, do it for Paige and the babies."

"Okay. I'll set a reminder." Gabe pulled out his phone. "When did you get so wise?"

"Oh, I'm not wise." I gave a harsh laugh. "I'm a fucking idiot. But one who loves you and wants what is best for you."

"Ditto. I want you to be happy. Whatever that looks like for you." Gabe gestured widely. "Even if that means working less at Seasons or not at all. If you're working your dream job, you shouldn't have to prop mine up too."

"Hey. It's family. We're family. I'm happy to help. Your dreams matter." I glanced away. In the past, I would have ended my thoughts there, not given enough weight to my needs and wants. "But you're right that I need to chase my own dreams."

"You do." Gabe pulled me into a swift, tight hug before releasing me. "I don't know what I'd do without you."

"I'm not going anywhere." I wasn't. I couldn't. Could I? All the questions of the last few days came roaring back. How could I leave Gabe at such a critical moment? How could I not?

"Hey." Gabe motioned for me to look at him again. "Don't you try to give me a run for the title of family worrier. I didn't mean I needed to tether you to Seasons and Kringle's Crossing. I need you in our lives. That's all. Go where the dream takes you."

"Huh." I made a thoughtful noise, and my thinky thoughts about dreams, both shared and personal, lingered long after we'd returned to the hospital room, long after the tiny bundles were loaded in their car seats, and long after everyone was settled back at their home. The twins' nursery was my old room, and I left the new family with a sense of rightness. For years, I'd had trouble adjusting to the place where I'd grown up being Gabe and Paige's place now. Maybe I'd had a little trouble moving on myself. Like I'd said to Atlas, growing up and figuring out adulting wasn't easy.

But with the twins installed in their home, the place seemed further removed from my past and more a part of

Gabe's family's future. And what was my own future? That was indeed the question, one that distracted me as I did a livestream play-through of a new expansion pack.

Unfortunately, I kept making error after error, rookie mistakes piling up despite my larger-than-normal audience.

"Sorry, folks," I said as I restarted the level I'd been attempting. My gaze drifted yet again to Atlas's duffel bag across the room, near the hall closet. I'd moved it from my bedroom, but I hadn't found the courage to dig inside. "Guess I'm just not on my game tonight. Either that or my skills are rusty from my holiday break."

Ping. Ping. Ping. Predictably, the chat window started to blow up with fans telling me my skills were fine while others wanted to know if I was okay.

"Oh, that's sweet of you all to care," I said aloud. "It's nothing, I promise. Sometimes I wish I was an NPC, no backstory, no love life, no distractions other than the game goal."

I probably shouldn't have said love life because the chat flooded with commiserations and bad breakup stories.

"Not a breakup." I groaned. "At least, I don't think." Could there be a breakup if we had never been an official couple? And we hadn't exactly parted badly. But we *had* parted, and hell if I knew anything anymore. Keeping my headset on, I rushed to Atlas's bag, not pausing to overthink yet again, and dug out a small wrapped box. I wasn't ready to open it, but holding it while I checked out the chat window made me feel marginally closer to Atlas.

Be easier on yourself, one of the chat commenters wrote. *You're only human and you have a heart.*

Another commenter added, *Maybe your love life sucks, but, dude, you're making bank streaming.*

Another good point.

"Yeah, you're right. I am only human. And I have a great life. I do. I was saying that to my sibling earlier. I have my dream job. And that's thanks to all of you who tune in. So thank you for making that possible."

Ping. Ping. Ping. A bunch of fresh tips came in as a gratifying reminder that people cared about what I did. I had the type of job a lot of people envied—set my own hours, worked from home. Work from anywhere I had Wi-Fi and the ability to stream. But what good was all that flexibility and fun without someone to tell about my day? Someone to care about?

"Thanks for the tips," I said into the microphone as my brain whirred. *Anywhere.* I flashed back to my conversation with Gabe but also the way I'd stubbornly insisted on a Kringle's Crossing future, even when Atlas had wanted to play that silly pick-a-house game. "If only it were that easy to solve my…" I took a breath because I'd been about to reveal more about my love life than I needed to. Logically, I knew I was the only one who could escape the limbo land I occupied, but emotionally, I yearned for someone with a crystal ball to simply tell me what to do. I turned the small present over and over in my hand, the ribbon coming loose. Perfect wrapping job, exactly how I'd taught Atlas.

The chat conversation predictably picked up on my lengthy pause and everything I hadn't said.

Dude. You're crushing on someone.

Yeah, he is.

Come on, man. Just tell whoever it is how you feel so you can get your head back in the game.

"Tell them how I feel? I think they know…" I trailed off as I remembered all the times I'd stopped Atlas from talking about the future or feelings. Did he know how I felt? Or was I simply assuming he'd guessed? And if he didn't know, would it make a difference if I spoke up? "Okay, maybe I'm an idiot." I chuckled aloud. Without waiting for permission from my brain, my fingers undid the tape on the present. "And talking would be a good idea. Too bad that's not an option here."

Taking a deep breath, I opened the present the rest of the way. A small ornament fell into my hand. A small wooden picnic basket dangling from a hook cradled a champagne bottle and two slices of pizza that looked suspiciously like the Mafia Meat Trio. While the ornament was obviously handmade, it wasn't one I recognized from our stock at Seasons.

Which meant he'd tracked it down, especially for me, likely after our conversation about how much I liked helping shoppers find the exact right ornament to gift. And he'd done exactly that here. The pizza was so realistic I could almost smell the pepperoni and taste our first kiss. The champagne bottle looked freshly chilled, needing only some plastic cups to serve up a taste of that midnight picnic. A piece of paper fluttered out of the package onto the ornament.

Maybe this can be the start of your own collection.

As I looked at his familiar handwriting, my chest ached. Atlas was so much braver than me. The present was perfectly sentimental. He wasn't afraid to care. I was the one who had held back, trapped by my fears.

Ping. Ping. A few more chat messages rolled in.

Where there's a will, there's a way.

Hey, dude, back to the game? I wanna see you conquer this level before I sleep.

"Yeah, yeah, back to the game," I said to my audience as I set aside the ornament, placing it near my monitor so I could see it even as I played. Wait. *The game.* Maybe that was it. When it came to gaming, I was legendary for thinking outside the box. I was a freaking master of last-ditch efforts and high-risk plays. And yet, when it came to my own life, I'd played it far too safe for years now.

Maybe, just maybe, there was a winning strategy out there for Atlas and me if I was bold enough.

Twenty-Nine

ATLAS

"Good work." The SEAL lieutenant I'd worked closely with the past few days strode over to me as I finished my satellite phone call to mission ops. All around us, hot and dusty SEAL team members lounged on large boulders and the ground, exhaustion rolling off each of them. They'd been awake far more hours than me and without food or water for a good chunk of that. Now that they'd reached the relative safety of the extraction point, the SEALs were slugging back electrolyte drinks and polishing off MRE packets as we awaited the chopper I'd arranged for.

"Thank you, sir." Getting this team out had been a relatively short mission, but despite the brevity, it had also been one of my most challenging. Our SEAL support division had been pushed to its limit as much as the SEALs themselves. But in a major victory, everyone was present and accounted for with only a few minor injuries.

"What's the ETA on that bird?" The lieutenant scanned the sky, wind whipping through his blond hair as yet more dust and dirt swirled around our feet. The cloudless sky was gray as temperatures dropped. "Weather's kicking up."

Cooler weather was good news for the sweaty SEALs but alarming for everyone else, especially this time of year at this elevation.

"Should be any minute now." As soon as I said that, my phone beeped with an incoming message. "Make that three minutes."

"Knew we could count on you, Orion." He gave me a sharp nod before clapping his hands and raising his voice to the rest of his team. "Look alive! Bird coming in. I need everyone to listen to Orion here. We need to load up fast and smart, get the hell out of these mountains before the wind worsens."

The helicopter arrived as the sky darkened further, giving an ominous, chilly edge to the increasing wind. We loaded up quickly, but I didn't like the concerned looks from the flight crew or their murmurings as they, too, kept glancing at the sky.

On board, we were packed in tightly, and I found myself next to the team's newest member, who groaned with every lurch of the chopper. "Why is turbulence so much worse on helicopters?"

"Not sure." I grit my teeth as my own stomach rolled. It wouldn't do to puke in front of all these SEALs, but this was one of the bumpiest rides I'd had.

"We'll be all right." The SEAL on the other side of the newbie, a bomb specialist nicknamed Rooster, whom I'd worked with several times before, had a far more reassuring voice than me. After my month in Kringle's Crossing, I also really liked Rooster's Philly accent. Made me miss Gabe, Nix, and most especially, Zeb, whose accent only really showed up when he was excited or super stressed. I suppressed a sigh as Rooster dug in his pocket. "Here. Have a piece of gum."

He offered squares to the newbie as well as me, and the dry, minty flavor was a welcome distraction from the turbulence.

"This is the same type of weather that caught that other chopper a few weeks back." One of the SEALs across from us was less than helpful with his observation, and I shot him a harsh look.

"Why aren't we landing?" Predictably, the newbie continued to fret as we approached the base, flight conditions about as rough as I'd been in, and I went from trying not to hurl to quietly praying. Damn. I did hate choppers.

Chief Big Deal. Even as he'd teased, Zeb had understood the way he understood so much about me. Hadn't judged me for my dislike of helicopters or found me lacking valor. God, I missed him so much. I'd been careful not to think about him much the last few days. The heightened danger made any stray emotions or lack of focus potentially deadly. But now I was here on this bird, nothing to do but picture Zeb's face right before I'd walked away.

There were so many things I wished I'd said. *I could offer…* His voice rang in my ears, louder than the drone of the chopper. We'd both done an A-plus job of dodging hard conversations the last couple of weeks. First, Zeb had been reluctant, then me, and then we were simply out of time.

And I refused, utterly refused, to believe we wouldn't get another chance. That *I* wouldn't get a chance to make things right. I'd been afraid of committing to Zeb, to Kringle's Crossing, to my own future, but here on this lurching chopper, I knew true fear. Being afraid to get the one thing I wanted most in this world was nothing compared to the fear of never having it and losing the chance for good.

Below us, the base appeared like blocks in a kid's play set, the ground crew scurrying like ants as we readied for another approach.

"Fuck this weather." If even the stoic and ever-optimistic Rooster was cursing, we were truly in a bad place. The chopper's com speaker crackled with an announcement from the cockpit.

"Gonna need y'all to brace for a hard one. We're only gonna get one shot at this."

I held tight to a nylon strap, bending forward and bracing my feet as I tried to protect my head. But there was no protection from my rising fear or increasingly doomsday thoughts.

What if Zeb never knew how I truly felt?

As the chopper dipped with its approach, I saw Zeb's shining face the night of the snowball fight. I could hear his laughter, see the snowflakes glistening in his beard, taste his frosty lips, and smell his cinnamony goodness. What wouldn't I give to have another night exactly like that one?

I'd rushed into battle for far lesser causes, so why was I so reluctant to fight for a future with Zeb?

Bang.
Rattle.
Shake.
Boom.

We landed hard enough that my teeth rattled, my ass shook, my biceps burned, and my feet ached from the jolt. But somehow, we stayed upright and didn't tip or crash.

"We made it. Thank God. We made it." The newbie was close to tears, and I offered him a discreet, reassuring pat.

"We did."

All of us were in a hurry to get the hell off the chopper. The line for the chance to call home would be super long, and I wasn't entirely sure what I wanted to say yet. No way was my stomach interested in food either, so I headed off in search of some rack time.

"Orion!" However, before I got far from the helipad, a chief I hadn't seen before flagged me down. "Not so fast. Orders came in to get you on a transport back to the States. Some sort of strategic meeting they want your ass in-person for. Transport leaves in forty-five, so no time for anything except hauling ass across base."

"Got it." God bless the hurry-up-and-wait navy. Hours and hours of flight time for what could likely be a thirty-minute meeting. I schooled my expression even as I did internal calculus on whether I had time to grab a cup of coffee. Or breathe. Breathing would be nice.

"Hey, man, at least you get a New Year's Eve arrival back home, and hopefully, you'll be stateside before the ball drops."

"Wow." My math shifted to how in the hell mere days had passed since I'd left Kringle's Crossing. When I'd arrived at Thanksgiving, New Year's had seemed so far off, and now, here it was, the time I'd originally had to leave anyway.

"Arrival time will let you get a couple of hours at home and some good shuteye before whatever the brass has in store for you." The chatty chief gave me a last smile before adding, "Safe travels."

I was almost to the landing field the giant transport planes used when I heard my name again. "Hey! Orion!"

Expecting yet another change in plans, I stifled a groan as I turned around. My would-be groan turned to a smile, though, as I saw the bomb specialist from the SEAL team trucking toward me at top speed. The dude was fit.

"Rooster, my man, shouldn't you be passed out in your rack already or in line for a hot shower and some decent chow?"

"In a minute." He smiled back at me. "Heard the LT say you're headed stateside."

"Yep. Assuming the wind doesn't ground the transport flight as well, but sounds like the plan is to get me stateside ASAP."

"It'll likely be New Year's Eve when you get back." Rooster's smile turned wistful. "Can't believe the holiday season is almost done. I'm missing getting to spend it with my guy like crazy. I'm hoping for a phone call home soon, but I was wondering if you could deliver a personal message and a belated Christmas gift for me?"

"Absolutely. Consider it done." I didn't even have to consider the request. I'd grant it for anyone, but I'd worked several missions with Rooster, had even had a couple of meals with him and his guy, Caanan. The two were crazy in love, just like me and...

Oh. There it was. That realization I'd been circling around all day. And the words I'd been searching for were right there when I probably wouldn't get to use them any time soon.

Not wanting to burden Rooster with my relationship woes, I took a deep breath as he fished a thick envelope out of his pocket.

"Not much shopping time on this mission, so I improvised." He gave me a lopsided grin that revealed dimples. "Bunch of index cards became IOUs for dish duty, chores, and a couple of...personal favors."

"You guys are couple goals." I carefully accepted his

precious cargo, taking time to stow the envelope where it wouldn't get creased. "Now go get some rest."

"Will do." Rooster jogged away, leaving me alone again with my thoughts. I was half a planet away from Zeb and keenly felt every mile, but for the first time since departing on Christmas, I felt hope. Maybe Zeb wouldn't want to hear what I had to say, but I had hours of flight ahead of me to figure out exactly how to fight for us.

Thirty

ZEB

DECEMBER 29TH

"Sleeping babies are the best." I smiled down at Plum, swaddled in a lilac blanket and matching hat. We'd scored the rocking chair, the same one my mom had used to rock Gabe and me. Gabe and Pine reclined on the couch, Pine dozing with soft little snores on Gabe's chest in a green sleeper. Their personalities were starting to emerge—Plum loved rocking and snug swaddles while Pine preferred endless marching around on one of our shoulders and hated any blanket or wrap. "Go us. Simultaneous nap time for the win."

"Thanks for your help." Gabe offered me a sleepy smile. I'd come for the morning so Paige and Aunt Lucy could rest. "You and I make a pretty good team, bro. I don't know what we'd do without you."

"About that…" I'd come to visit to see how the babies were faring at home, but I'd also arrived with a secondary purpose. My pulse pounded. The Seasons annual after-Christmas sale was done, and the shop would be closed until after New Year's in keeping with our traditions. This was my best opportunity, both for this conversation and for what I needed to do, but that didn't mean I wasn't terrified.

"What's wrong?" Gabe barked, which made Pine give an angry huff before going back to sleep. "Sorry. That came out harsh. You were right the other day. Anxiety continues to be a big issue for me. I've got a doctor's appointment on the fifth though."

"Good for you." I offered him a reassuring smile. "And it's okay. Nothing is wrong, but I did want to talk to you."

"Shoot." His tone was far gentler now, which gave me the shot of courage I needed.

"I need to take a leave of absence of sorts."

"From Seasons?" Gabe's forehead creased as he patted Pine's little rump. "So you can focus on your gaming channel? Yeah, that makes sense."

"Kind of. That's part of it, but I'm…taking a trip." Gah. I'd expected this to be hard, but each word felt sharp and icy and dangerous.

"A trip?"

"A road trip. To Virginia." I inhaled sharply. Eventually, I'd get the whole truth out.

"Oh." Gabe nodded, then his eyes went wider. "*Oh.* Is there something else you'd like to tell me, Zebediah?"

"I'm in love with Atlas." I rocked a little faster in the chair.

"No shit. You've had a crush since…" Gabe trailed off as he peered more intently at me. "Wait. You're serious. Like *serious*."

"Yeah. I'm serious. I love him."

"Like, in theory, or like you guys have been carrying on in secret? That's it, isn't it?" Gabe kept his voice low enough to not wake the babies, but his pain came through loud and clear. "Because you thought I'd judge?"

"It didn't start out…" I quirked my mouth. This wasn't the time for excuses. "I'm sorry. The secretive thing was shitty. But I didn't want you to go all overprotective big brother and ruin your friendship with Atlas."

Gabe took a long pause, breathing in and out like he was counting. "I suppose that was a valid worry. I do have a track record. But I like to think I've also been supportive."

"You have. Always." From the moment I'd first come out, Gabe had always had my back. "Keeping on the down-low was all about your long-standing friendship rather than worry you'd be judgmental."

"Well, if you're both happy… I mean, I take it he feels the same way?" Gabe smiled nervously.

"I think. I'm not sure." I shrugged, heart starting to hammer again. "But regardless, this is a leap I have to take. I need to find out. Need to give this—him, *us*—a chance."

"Wow." Gabe took another of those measured pauses. "As someone who knows a thing or thirty about unrequited and complicated feelings, the leap can be worth it." He looked fondly down at baby Pine. "But you also have to protect your heart. And if he hurts you…"

Shifting Plum to one side, I held up a hand. "No big-brother theatrics, remember? He doesn't know I'm telling you any of this. But I couldn't leave town without an explanation. And we're brothers. Family. I owe you the truth."

"Thank you." Gabe nodded. And I did owe Gabe the truth, not some half-baked excuse for why I was traveling, but not being able to ask Atlas his opinion on telling Gabe sucked. I'd been more adamant than him about staying secretive, but he deserved a choice in who we told and when. I could only hope he'd understand.

"I'll turn that warning right back on you though." I stared Gabe down. "Don't hurt Atlas. Your friendship is everything to him. He's not out. Might not want to be out. And he might not feel the same way as I do about the future. If that's the case, it'll be awkward, but I'm not gonna let either of you trash your friendship over something silly."

"You are not something silly. You matter, Zeb," Gabe said firmly. "And he'd be an idiot not to return your feelings."

"Thanks, bro." Sighing, I gazed down at Plum snoozing away. "But if he doesn't, at least I will have tried. And either way, you don't get to give him shit about any of this."

"Look at you. All cocky. All grown up." Gabe laughed softly, then sobered. "I'm sorry I didn't see your maturity sooner."

"It's okay." I shrugged because what mattered was that Gabe was trying now, not harboring resentments over the past.

"When are you leaving?"

"After this visit." Heat rose up my cheeks. I had a plan, but that didn't mean it was sane. "Weather is finally clear. I don't know how long Atlas will be deployed, but I want to be there when he gets back, whenever that is. It's important. I worked out a deal on housing with a gamer contact. And I'm blessed that I can work from anywhere. I can afford to be patient."

"You can." Gabe opened his mouth like he had a lot of warnings to issue, but surprisingly, all he did was swallow hard before giving me a small smile. "Go get your man, Zeb."

"I'm sure going to try." I smiled back, trying not to tear up at how hard Gabe was trying. "I'll be back though. Promise." I gazed down at my precious bundle one more time, taking in Plum's little rosebud mouth and button nose. "Uncle Zeb is going to be around a ton, no matter what."

"Uncle Zeb is always going to have a place here." Gabe made his voice Atlas-level stern. "Atlas will too. Promise." He chuckled. "Still not sure how I missed you two…"

"You were a little distracted." I joined his laughter.

"Just a little." He patted Pine's little back as the baby stirred. "Be safe? Text when you get there."

"I will." I had no idea what was coming next, but I knew where I had to go. I was the master of winging it, famous for last-ditch efforts and crazy schemes. I had to at least give this a shot.

Thirty-One

ATLAS

NEW YEAR'S EVE

If I couldn't get a midnight New Year's Eve kiss of my own, at least I arrived stateside in time to complete my mission for Rooster.

"Are you sure you don't want to come in for a snack or some cocoa or something?" Canaan and his grandfather were the nicest people. They'd answered the door late on New Year's Eve. After I'd delivered Rooster's package, they'd also invited me in and tried to get me to join in the New Year's Eve appetizer party they were hosting with some neighbors without making me feel like an imposition.

"Nah. I've got a ride waiting." Not only did I not want to intrude on their plans, but I was also utterly exhausted. I'd slept like crap on the long flight back. But I'd made Rooster a promise, so I hadn't even stopped by my quarters in the barracks. I'd used my ride-share app to go directly from base to this small Virginia neighborhood full of older homes. Further, as usual, the navy didn't care tomorrow was New Year's Day, and I had an early meeting with mission ops. My thrilling New Year's Eve plans included microwaving something easy from the convenience store and collapsing in my bunk after I managed to reach Zeb. "I didn't mean to crash your party, but I wanted to get you Rooster—Renzo's message before midnight."

"Thank you." Canaan clutched the envelope to his chest. "You have no idea how much this means."

"I think I might." I managed a tired smile. Seeing Canaan and Rooster and their enviable bond gave me hope. Some military families did make it work, lengthy separations and all. And if they got happy endings, maybe I might be worthy of that too.

"What's that?" Canaan grinned back. "Did the eternal bachelor find someone on leave?"

"Think so." Felt weird but good to admit it aloud at last. "Not sure the person in question knows it yet. We need to talk, but I battled a dead phone the whole trip back to the States. Soon as I get back to base, I'm tracking down a charger for my phone."

"Let me see what type yours is." Stern expression on his usually playful face, Canaan held out a hand. He nodded as I held up my older model smartphone. "I've got you." He grabbed a charging cable from the hall table near the door. "We're drowning in chargers, and loaning you one is the least I can do. This one should work in the car too."

"Thanks." Pulling my jacket tighter around myself, I headed back into the chilly night and the waiting newer model sedan from the ride-share app.

"Back to base, boss?" the driver asked as I slid back into the car. The man wore a jaunty wool hat and had a heavy Chicago accent with an accommodating demeanor.

"Yep." I located a USB port near the backseat where I was sitting. "Is it okay if I plug my phone in here?"

"Of course, boss." He turned to nod at me before putting the car in gear. "There's water and some snacks back there too."

"Appreciate it." I wished I could order him to drive all the way to Kringle's Crossing. I wouldn't make it by midnight, but it would be worth the five-hour drive to see Zeb's smile. However, that meeting in the morning loomed large.

Zeb had been right that I loved my job. I was good at it, and I played a necessary role in national security. At that moment, though, I hated it, hated the priority it had to take, hated the time away from Zeb, and the delay in talking things out with him.

However, the job wasn't something I could walk away from either. While I was desperate for the chance to finally make things right with Zeb, I still hadn't found a magic wand that could change the realities of military service. I wanted to fight for us, but that meant asking Zeb to accept all of me, job included. After all the hours awake on the frigid transport flight, I had something of a plan there, but I wasn't sure it would be enough.

Step one, however, was getting my phone functional again, and as we sped back toward base, my phone powered up with two percent battery life. Predictably, a rush of messages came in one after the other, the product of days without service.

A bunch of baby pictures from Aunt Lucy, Paige, and Gabe all came in at once. I scrolled pictures of the twins that made my chest tight and achy, accepted New Year's wishes from friends stationed in other time zones, and deleted spam from various online merchants as other messages continued to load. When a message came in from Zeb, my pulse sped up like an inner drumroll.

I'd half expected him to not message at all, but he'd written, more than once even. A few more pics of the twins, one of him holding the ornament I'd given him as a present, and then a message from yesterday showed up as well.

> I'm not sure when you'll see this, but when you're back, something is waiting for you at 1111 North Clover Lane.

Oxygen suddenly in short supply, I read it again, trying to make sense of the words. Was this a scavenger hunt? A clue to something else or a waiting message? Or Zeb himself? I didn't want to let myself hope too hard, so I took some steadying breaths.

"Okay back there, boss?" the driver asked, glancing at me in the rearview mirror.

"I'm good. I think." If this turned out to be a joke of some kind, I was going to legitimately weep. I was hungry, exhausted, and emotionally depleted, but no way could I ignore Zeb's message. "Change of destination."

Thirty-Two

ZEB

New Year's Eve found me in a new location in a new state but with the same livestream tradition as the last several end-of-year celebrations. Even though I was alone in an unfamiliar place, it was hard to feel lonely with record numbers of watchers and an active chat scrolling by.

"And that's a wrap on our review of the new *Space Villager* drop." Leaning forward, I spoke into my microphone, hoping the tinkering I'd done with the sound settings helped to mitigate the echo some viewers had noted earlier in the evening. I'd packed my little car full of all my most essential computer equipment with just enough room for some clothes. Priorities. "Happy New Year shortly to my fellow East Coast Americans and the rest of the world's time zones as well." As I said *world*, I wondered for the millionth time which time zone Atlas was in. Was it already New Year's there? Was he missing me? But I couldn't dwell too much on the possibilities with an audience to entertain. "Thanks again for tuning in for this livestream with me and for the patience with my new setup. I'll iron out the acoustics in my new location soon."

The chat box filled with commenters trying to get their own wishes and last-minute questions in before I ended the broadcast.

> Happy New Year!
>
> Thanks for another great year of content!
>
> Best wishes!
>
> Hey, how did your love-life dilemma the other night turn out? Got a hot New Year's Eve date?

"Ha." I laughed aloud. "Your chat comments are great, as always." I liked how invested my viewers now were in my love life, but I wished I had something, anything to report. "And I've got a date with pizza any minute, along with a warm shower and a pint of ice cream. Hot times, indeed. The rest of you stay safe. Signing off."

Patience. That was the name of the game. I'd barely been in Virginia for twenty-four hours. Enough time to unpack my equipment and set up shop in the second bedroom of this small bungalow. I'd updated my address in my meal delivery app and found decently-rated local pizza. Baby steps forward.

While warmer than Kringle's Crossing, the weather was far windier, and the older bungalow was drafty. I'd been counting down to my shower the whole livestream and couldn't wait to be less chilled.

Buzz. Buzz. The friend I was renting from had talked me through setting up my phone with a doorbell app for deliveries. Since I knew the buzzing was my pizza, I didn't bother clicking the camera app and instead strode toward the door.

When the buzzing on my phone was joined by a rap at the door, I called out, "You can just leave the pizza. The tip is on the app."

"What pizza? Is that you, Zeb?" a familiar voice called back.

"Atlas?" I raced the rest of the way to the front door, scarcely daring to hope, but there he was in my entryway in dusty BDUs, looking cold and exhausted with deep lines around his eyes and mouth. But he was *here*. "Oh my God, you came."

"You asked." Shrugging like he'd grant any command I made, he gave me a small smile. His eyes narrowed, though, confusion clear. "Not sure what you're doing here, but I came."

"You did." I tugged him into the house, letting the door shut behind us. The entryway featured mocha-colored walls, optimistic art typical of vacation rentals, and warm lighting from a faux Tiffany lamp on a small table. The light cast amber shadows across Atlas's face, making him look that much more tired. But also more real. More *here*. "That was a quick deployment."

"Some missions are like that. Have another meeting in the morning." Atlas sighed as his eyes continued to search mine. "I wouldn't be surprised if they ship me out again as part of my new role, but I'm here now."

"I'm here too."

"I see." He looked beyond me into the furnished living room, expression even more befuddled when his gaze returned to mine. "Zeb, what are you doing?"

"Well, that's a pretty broad question." Hedging, I offered him a lopsided grin.

"Okay, what are you doing *here*?" He motioned at the house around us.

"I've got a gamer friend, fellow streamer, who has a side hustle of vacation rentals around Virginia Beach. Slow season for him, so I worked out a deal on an open-ended long-term rental on this place."

"Open-ended?" Tilting his head, Atlas considered me more closely.

"I wasn't sure how long your deployment would last." It was my turn to shrug, to act like this leap of faith was no big deal. "Or whether you'd want me to stick around after you were back."

"Of course, I want." Atlas made an exasperated noise. "But, Zeb, your whole life is in Kringle's Crossing."

"And my whole future is right in front of me." Moving to stand directly in front of him, I reached for his hand. "I came to show you that I believe in us. I believe we can have a future."

Atlas let me take his hand even as he vigorously shook his head. "You can't leave Seasons, your family, your community simply for *me*."

A knock at the door startled us both into jumping apart. "Pizza!"

"Thanks," I called to the delivery person before collecting the pizza. Returning to Atlas, I gestured at the living room. "Come in. Let's eat." I grabbed two soda cans from the otherwise empty fridge and handed one to Atlas. We sat side-by-side on the couch, the pizza box open on the coffee table in front of us, the sausage and cheese aroma joined by a distinct stiffness between us.

"This is…good. Thank you." Atlas was being kind because the pizza was light on the sauce, heavy on bland cheese, and missing the zing of real Italian sausage. The Mafia Meat Trio it was not.

"If not for you, maybe I can leave Kringle's Crossing

for mediocre pizza?" I laughed. Atlas didn't. "And why can't I use you as a reason?"

"Because." Atlas's tone was more stubborn than stern.

"You're more than worth it." I patted his thigh. "But I'm also doing this for myself. I owe it to myself to take this leap and to take a chance on us. I've spent my whole life in Kringle's Crossing, playing it safe. I need to prove to myself that I can be this brave. I want to have a life that's fully my own. I don't want to look back in a few years and wonder *what if*."

"I don't want that either," Atlas said softly, much of the fight gone from his voice. "But I hate the idea of prying you loose from your heritage and Seasons. Your brother is going to be mad enough at me."

"Seasons will survive. And so will Gabe." I looked away at the imitation Eames chair across the room. "I...uh... kind of had to tell him about us." That admission earned me a gasp from Atlas, but I kept going. "Sorry. But I couldn't leave town without an explanation."

"Of course you couldn't just up and leave. That's my point. And it's okay that you told him—that part was inevitable."

"Inevitable?" I wrapped the word around me like a fuzzy blanket. "Does that mean you're letting me stay?"

"I'm never going to be able to turn you down." Atlas sighed like he couldn't decide if this was a bad or good thing. "I'm surprised my phone isn't already smoking from Gabe's wrath though."

"I warned him not to go all protective big brother." I decided to cling to the "never going to be able to turn you down" part instead of Atlas's continued reluctance. "And I'm sure the distraction of the twins doesn't hurt."

"The pictures sure are cute." After pausing for another

bite of pizza, Atlas narrowed his eyes. "And what happened to being so worried about my friendship with him?"

"I decided my happiness matters too. We matter." I touched the back of his hand. "This thing between us matters. And also, Gabe and you are grown adults. It's not on me to try to save your friendship." In talking with Gabe about his anxiety, I'd realized that he was far from the only anxious, overprotective Seasons sibling. "But, for what it's worth, I trust Gabe to keep you around whatever happens."

"You're right. We do matter." Atlas surprised the hell out of me by capturing my hand with his, squeezing it tightly. "And I'll talk to him. His friendship is important to me, no doubt, but you've got my whole heart, Zeb."

"I do?" Relief coursing through me, I smiled hopefully. Atlas's resistance to my presence and plan had made me question whether he did indeed return my feelings.

"Of course you do." Atlas wrinkled his face like this had never been in question. "And I was going to come tell you exactly that as soon as I could get leave. You beat me."

"Winner, winner, chicken dinner." I waggled my eyebrows at him, needing a real Atlas laugh in the worst way. "And if you were coming for me, why take issue with me exploring a potential move? Of the two of us, I have far more flexibility in where I work."

"You do. Which I both love and hate." He swung my hand lightly. "I guess I was expecting to have to negotiate, offer you incentives to spend more time in Virginia."

"Oh, feel free to offer away." Tone all seductive, I batted my eyelashes.

Atlas groaned at my antics. "I didn't mean sex bribes."

"Darn."

"I meant more that if you can give me your present, I'll give you my future."

"Yes." That required absolutely no consideration on my part.

"You're making this too easy." Atlas finally gave me that real, deep laugh of his I'd been craving. Showed off all of his dimples too. "I thought I'd have to apologize. And not simply for how we left things, but for all the times I didn't visit. Yes, I've been deployed a lot, but I also didn't try hard enough. I can admit that now and hopefully make up for it. I don't want more regrets."

"I don't want regrets either," I said softly.

"I've got five years left in the navy before my twenty. I know that seems like a long time right now, but if you can bear with me, be patient, we can go back to Kringle's Crossing every chance we get and then move home after I take my retirement."

"Home, huh?" Hearing Atlas call Kringle's Crossing *home* felt even better than I'd hoped.

"Yeah. Turns out you were right. I do like the idea of settling down. Putting down roots. Making a family. You. Me. A couple of mutts. And maybe Kringle's Crossing has always been that home, even when it hurt to think of it that way."

I nodded so enthusiastically that my neck hurt. "And I'm right about us too. We can make this work. Like you said, we can visit a ton. And yes, I feel bad leaving Gabe and Paige and Seasons, but we deserve our dreams and happiness too."

"Yeah. Exactly. And I have a plan that may help all of us in both the short and long terms."

"You are good at plans." I leaned in to kiss his jaw because I was about to die without further contact.

"Since my parents blew a literal fortune, I've been obsessive about saving while in the navy. It's why I don't own a car, still live in the barracks, and like checking my savings account balance far more than spending money. However, I think I've finally found something worth spending on. I want to invest in Seasons."

My eyes went so wide my temples ached. "You want to buy Seasons?"

Thirty-Three

ATLAS

"Not buy. Invest." I licked my lower lip. I'd been parched even before the long plane trip back to the States, and eating pizza plus worrying over Zeb's reaction had my skin tight and dry. While Zeb stayed wide-eyed and slack-jawed, I paused to take a large swallow of the soda he'd brought me. "A partnership. Gabe needs a cash infusion, and I see Seasons as a part of all of our futures."

"Yes." Zeb nodded so hard it was a wonder he didn't strain something. "That's brilliant. I don't have a huge amount of savings, but my channel is doing well. I could invest too. All of us going all in on a future for Seasons."

"Exactly." I took his hand again, more for reassurance than to make my point. He was so warm and alive and here, *right here*, where I hadn't dared to hope to find him tonight. "Seasons will always be your family's past, but maybe it can be my future. Those roots you want me to put down."

"I love this idea so much, but you don't have to put your savings into Seasons to prove to me that Kringle's Crossing can be your home."

"*Our* home," I corrected simply to see him glow like a searchlight. "And I want to. You asked what I wanted to do after I retire, and if Gabe is up for it, I can't think of anything better than helping to run Seasons, making a life with you, and preserving your family legacy."

"*Our* family," Zeb shot back, still beaming. "You're part of Seasons now."

"I like that." I leaned in, intending a kiss, but I ended up resting my heavy head on his shoulder. Simply being close to him felt so good. He smelled familiar: cinnamon, sugar, pizza, *Zeb*. The tension that had plagued me ever since leaving Kringle's Crossing melted away. I couldn't even stifle a big yawn.

Zeb laughed tenderly. "I'd say we should call Gabe right now with your brilliant idea, but you seem exhausted. How many hours have you been awake?"

"A lot." Another huge yawn escaped before Zeb stood and hauled me to my feet.

"You need rest." He stuck the rest of the pizza in the nearly empty fridge in the cramped but homey kitchen off the living space. "Shower first, then bed."

"Not gonna make me sleep on the couch now that you have one?" I teased, only for Zeb to playfully swat me on the ass.

"Don't make me withhold that shower. You're going to like the bathroom. It's a big improvement from my apartment."

"Aye, aye lieutenant." Laughing, I followed him down a narrow hallway that led to two bedrooms with a large bathroom between them. One of the bedrooms held much of Zeb's computer equipment on two folding tables, while the other featured a big, cushy king-size I couldn't wait to face plant on. "You're in charge."

If Zeb wanted to boss me around so I didn't have to make another damned decision all night, I was all for it. I let him order me out of my clothes as he turned on the hot water in the walk-in tile shower.

Naked, I stretched and made a pleased noise. I was so damn happy. The place could have been a rusty outdoor shower for all I cared, but the surprisingly spacious room heated quickly from the steamy water. The all-white decor further added to the retreat-like feel. After my last week, I almost wanted to weep from how much I needed this taste of home comfort. And Zeb. Mainly Zeb.

"Do I want to know how you got those bruises?" He cast a critical eye over my ribs. I also had a few on my right biceps and a big one on my thigh. I was a mess, but nothing out of the ordinary for my line of work.

"Probably not." I was nothing if not honest.

"Fair enough." Zeb tugged me into the shower, arranging us so I got most of the spray and draping himself against my back. "But you know I'm here if you ever do need to talk about what happens out there."

"I know." I turned so I could kiss his forehead. "We had a hard helicopter landing."

The words popped out before I could censor myself. That was one of the things I loved so much about Zeb. He was easy to talk to. Didn't judge or dismiss. Actually listened.

"Sounds scary." He gathered me tightly against him, warm water sluicing over both of us.

"Yeah. But we made it." I returned his embrace, hugging him hard. "I'm here now. In one piece and everything. No biggie."

Zeb frowned at my attempt at a joke. "It's all right not to like every aspect of your job, Atlas."

Grabbing the soap, he started lathering my chest and arms, quick, efficient movements that served to relax me.

"Yeah, you're right." I exhaled hard. I was so used to having to pretend to love every bit of military life because outsiders didn't often grasp the complexity of choosing this way of life. "Helicopters suck, and I was so afraid I might not get the chance to be here with you or to tell you how I feel."

"And how do you feel?" Reaching down, Zeb gave my ass a meaningful squeeze. I chuckled, chest and heart both light, loving how he'd sensed I needed the humor right then.

"Good. Great. Keep going." Pulling him even closer, I gave him a thorough kissing before releasing him to peer deeply into his eyes. "Grateful. I'm grateful to have had the time we did in Kringle's Crossing, grateful for whatever I did to deserve someone like you. And I'm so damn grateful you came here."

"Well, technically, no one has come yet…" Zeb's eyes sparkled as he lightly tickled my sides before soaping up my back. "You want to rectify that here with some shower fun or in bed?"

"Bed." I both laughed and yawned at the same time. "I'm so tired I'm not sure my old knees can hold me upright if I come."

"Well, in that case…" Zeb soaped himself with the efficiency of a recruit in week four of basic training, rinsing us both before hopping out of the shower. "Race you to the bed, old man?"

"Race is gonna be more of a slow trot." I laughed more as he handed me one of the big, white, fluffy towels. Despite his challenge, he waited for me to dry off and held out a hand so we could walk together to the bedroom.

"Maybe we both won the race?" I suggested as he tossed back the covers.

"Absolutely." Giving an impish smile, he pushed me backward onto the bed. As with earlier, I was happy to let him boss me around a little. He peered down at me with stern eyes. "Since you're so exhausted and all, you should lie there and let me do all the work."

"Uh-huh." I made a happy noise as he straddled my waist. "So this is work now, is it?"

"Back-breaking hard work." He lightly smacked my abs with his cock. Loving this display of confidence, I grinned up at him.

"You look so very taxed and stressed." I groaned as he started rocking against me, dragging his cock against mine. Over the past month, I'd come to love grinding with him, but I'd spent the week since Christmas Eve dreaming of a repeat. "Please tell me you packed lube?"

Zeb had shown me that sex didn't have to be uncomfortable or awkward, and I couldn't wait to see how good seconds might be.

"Along with all my computer equipment, yes." Gleeful, he reached over to the nightstand where he'd already stowed the same lube we'd had at the hotel. He tossed it next to me on the bed before revealing a small wrapped object. "Oh, and your Christmas present." He placed the small package in the center of my bare chest, right under my tat. "I loved your present for me, by the way. Totally the start of a collection."

"Keep me around, and I'll add to it every year," I promised as I studied the perfect wrapping job.

"I'm keeping you." He gave me a swift kiss before sitting up again. "On Christmas, I had it in the pocket of a parka for you. You'll get that later."

"You got me a coat?" Even after all the events of this evening, I still marveled at Zeb's kindness and caring. He made being taken care of feel amazingly right. And safe. With him, I could let down my guard, admit mundane things like being tired or cold.

"Well, you can't spend more time in Kringle's Crossing freezing in that light jacket."

"True." I opened the box to reveal an old metal compass. "It's a compass?"

"From Grandpa Seasons. It was his, and then he gave it to me the year you and Gabe graduated. I thought he might like me passing it on so you can always find your way back to me and Kringle's Crossing. To home."

"I love it." I swallowed. I looked at the ceiling. I looked dead-on into the bedside light. I closed my eyes hard. Opened them. Nope. Nothing helped. A tear escaped my eyes. But Zeb made it safe to feel big emotions too. He gently ran a finger down my cheek.

"And I love you." He kissed right where a tear had landed. "But you probably guessed that."

"Maybe. You did up and move on a few days' notice." I stretched to kiss his mouth. "But I like hearing it. And I love you too. That's the real thing I wanted to tell you, and I was terrified I might never get the chance."

"But you did." Zeb gave me the most tender smile before adding a devilish wink. "Now, back to our regularly scheduled fucking."

"Please." I groaned as he moved against me again. The gift, the sentiment, and simply being here were almost too much. The distraction of sex was exactly what I needed to avoid drowning in a sea of emotions. "You going to ride me again?"

"That's the plan." Grabbing the lube, he preened on

top of me. "You being so weary and all…" He gave a dramatic sigh before making a show of prepping himself with the lube, hand dipping behind him while he made little breathy moans. "Guess you'll just have to watch me…"

"Come closer." Making my voice stern, I crooked my finger.

"What's that?" He feigned surprise before we both broke out into chuckles. "Finding some energy?"

Cupping his face, I looked directly into his mischievous eyes. "You're trying to goad me into fucking you through the mattress."

"Guilty." Zeb cackled right as I gathered him close and deftly reversed our positions, pinning him with my thighs. "Whoa."

"Well, your plans, all of them, are working." I shook my head, continuing to marvel that he was here, that he was staying, that he *loved* me. And the need to show him how much all that meant to me in the most primal way possible kept building until we were kissing furiously.

Unlike the first time, where I'd been tentative and so afraid of hurting Zeb, now I trusted that he was strong, far stronger than anyone else gave him credit for. And I also trusted him to speak up, to know what he wanted, and to want me, all of me, size and aggressiveness included.

I could kiss Zeb and drink down his moans and frantic little noises and grind hard against him, and it wasn't too much. It wasn't enough either. Grabbing the lube, I took over where he'd left off with prep. I hitched one of his legs over my arm to give me more access, and he met my fingers eagerly, rocking up.

"Fuck me. Please. Now," he chanted as he rode my fingers.

"You got it." None of my first-time nerves, I handled the additional lube quickly and moved between his legs.

"Go hard," he ordered. "Hard as you want. I want it too, promise."

"Yeah." I moaned because he had indeed asked for what he wanted, what I wanted too, and all that was left was for me to push into his tight, welcoming heat. "That good?"

"More." He gave needy moans with my every thrust, spurring me on faster and faster until the bed rattled and squeaked. Zeb wrapped his legs around my waist, pulling me in deep. I'd never fucked like this, raw and open, nothing held back. But then, I'd never made love either. Never felt so much with every movement, every breath, every touch.

Rather than waiting for me, Zeb worked a hand between us, jacking his cock in urgent time with our fucking. Later, we could try for an endurance record. Later, I could kiss him slowly, whisper how much he meant to me, and touch him softly and lovingly. We'd have time for all that. But what we both needed now was this frantic pace, galloping toward climax, all our longing and a week of missing each other coming out in an all-consuming race to the finish.

"I'm gonna…" he moaned, arching his back, taking my cock that much deeper.

"Do it. Please." I didn't let up or hold back, fucking him right through his orgasm, white streaks painting his soft belly and fuzzy chest. And when he grinned up at me, sleepy and satisfied, I could no more stop my orgasm than I could harness the sun. I thrust fast, loving how he moaned and urged me on until the world seemed to explode around me.

Boom. Boom. I collapsed against Zeb only to raise my head. *Boom. Bang.*

"Wait. Are those actual fireworks?"

Zeb laughed so loud the bed shook one more time. "You thought we were that good? Damn. I aspire to be so impressive, but it's midnight. Happy New Year!"

"Happy New Year, indeed." I kissed him deeply. "Better make a wish."

"I already did." He kissed me back, sweet and light, the opposite of the intense fuck, but the same emotions running through us both.

"Need you," I murmured. "Always gonna need you. Right here. In my bed. In my life."

"I'm here." He kissed my damp cheeks. "This New Year's. Next New Year's. I'm here. Promise."

"Next year?" I inhaled sharply, finally allowing myself to truly believe Zeb was here with me, not leaving, and that we would make this thing work.

"Next year." He made the words sound like a solemn promise. "For the first time in my life, I'm truly looking forward to another holiday season. I can't wait to spend next Christmas with you and the one after that."

"Deal." I kissed each of his eyelids, his nose, the curve of his upper lip, his fuzzy chin. "All my Christmases are yours, Zebediah Seasons."

Thirty-Four

ZEB

ONE YEAR LATER: THE DAY BEFORE THANKSGIVING

"Over the river and through the woods..." Atlas sang along with the cheesy holiday classic playing on the car stereo, seemingly uncaring that we were caught in a holiday traffic snarl of epic proportions.

"Is it possible to hate Delaware?" I stared out at the same line of interstate traffic we'd been in for what felt like hours. "Because I might hate Delaware."

"What's to hate?" Atlas drummed his fingers against the steering wheel of the small hybrid SUV we'd piled mileage on over the last year of repeatedly driving through the many, many small towns of Delaware. We'd done the five-hour drive between Kringle's Crossing and Virginia Beach in four hours and change with amazing traffic luck and in a seven-hour slog with the worst. The day before Thanksgiving threatened to beat that record as everyone along the Eastern Seaboard raced to make it home for the holiday weekend before the predicted snowy weather hit.

We'd done the drive so much, both together and alone, that we'd made a game of finding offbeat places to stop. "It's green, quaint, and far better than the parking lot of I-95, especially today."

"Says the dude who hasn't found a clam shack or chowder house to hate yet." I laughed. Atlas, ever the world traveler, was the far more adventurous eater on these frequent road trips. I'd learned that the weirder the diner or pizzeria name, the more likely he was to want to stop. "And we're past the pizza place I liked in Millsboro."

"Ah. You're hangry and missing that ham stromboli." Atlas's good humor never wavered. Anyone watching us would never have guessed he'd worked a long swing shift in a month filled with far more days on duty than off. He'd crashed for a brief sleep with me after coming home to our little rental in the middle of the night, but he'd been up and loading the car even before I showered. "Luckily, I packed snacks."

"You did?" We were so into our road food game that we usually didn't bother with more than our water bottles.

"There's something behind you." Traffic continued to creep along at such a pace that Atlas could easily swivel his head and point to the floor of the backseat where a legit old-fashioned wooden picnic basket sat complete with red fabric napkin and double folding handle.

"Since when do we own a picnic basket?" A delighted sound escaped my chest. Maybe I wasn't so grumpy after all. "It looks just like my ornament."

"Must be a coincidence." Raising his eyebrows, he grinned at me. He usually let me do most of the driving, so his insistence on being the one to both load up and drive this morning made more sense now that he'd revealed his surprise.

"Nothing is a coincidence for a planner like you." I waved a finger at him before hauling the small basket into my lap in the passenger seat. I carefully opened the wooden top to reveal a familiar green bottle. "Champagne? Same brand as the Zimmerman rehearsal dinner?"

"That's for later. And Gabe says the Zimmermans are back on the schedule with a baby shower next month." Atlas glanced over at me, eyes shiftier than usual. He was up to something, and not simply champagne for tonight at my old apartment. We were back and forth so much that it had made sense to keep the apartment as a base of operations for us. Down the road, someday, we'd buy a house in Kringle's Crossing, but for now, the part-time apartment served us well. Atlas pointed at the basket. "Keep looking."

"Cookies!" I revealed a cellophane package of what looked to be the first iced sugar cookies of the holiday season. But then my hand landed on a much smaller box. A *velvet* box. "Whoa, what's this? "

"Might want to open that before we hit Pennsylvania."

"Is it a ring?" I wasn't sure whether I was closer to passing out or hurling or possibly both simultaneously. Definitely lightheaded, maybe a little feverish.

"It's not dynamite." Atlas made a noise that managed to be both frustrated and nervous. "Open it, Zeb."

I cracked the little box open and, as expected, revealed a chunky but simple masculine ring. Platinum. Titanium. I wasn't up on my metals, but it was shiny with beveled edges. Inside, an inscription lurked, and I squinted to read it.

Always my favorite Season.

"Oh my *God*." I had uncovered any number of diabolical twists in games over the years, always guessed the murder suspects first in TV shows, and yet was entirely unprepared to deal with this surprise. "Is this because Gabe joked that you better make an honest dude of me?"

After getting over the initial shock of Atlas and me being a couple, Gabe had rallied admirably, rising to our new partnership to bring Seasons forward into the future together and generally making a pest of himself suggesting real estate options and honeymoon spots. Paige and Aunt Lucy were no better with their constant hints that we needed to go ahead and get engaged already.

"Since when do I listen to Gabe?" Atlas scoffed as traffic inched forward. Outside, Delaware was cold and flat, but in here, things were definitely heating up. "It's the start of my favorite season. Our season. And I want to make it official so the whole time we're serving Thanksgiving, you can look at your ring and know I'm gonna marry you for New Year's."

"You're gonna what?" I croaked, blinking rapidly. Yup. Still in Delaware. Not dreaming, but stuck in the world's most bizarre proposal. "Shouldn't you ask me first?"

"You like me bossy, and you know it." Atlas's laugh had a pronounced nervous edge now. "Fine, *may* I marry you for New Year's?"

"Like this New Year's?" I twirled the ring in my palm, both dying to try it on and also simply dying, full stop. That he wanted a future was no surprise. We both did. We talked all the time about our lives four years from now. We'd even lain in bed more than a few nights, daydreaming over ideal celebrations. But *now?* That was the shocker.

"No time like the present. I already asked for the leave.

What is it you always say in your gameplay videos? Go big or go home."

"I like our home." My voice came out thin and dazed. We had a little rental in Virginia Beach that my gamer friend had hooked us up with. Cute. Close to base. Perfect starter house.

"Zeb." Atlas softened his tone. "Do you not want to get married? Too much? Too soon?"

"Too perfect," I whispered. "It's too perfect. I'm not sure I deserve this."

"I am." Atlas firmed his voice right back up. "You deserve all the happiness. We both do. The final business partnership papers are done. I'm ready to become a Seasons."

"You're going to take my name?" We'd talked about so very much, but not that.

"With your permission." A ruddy flush spread from Atlas's neck to his forehead. "But Atlas Orion Seasons has a great sound to it."

"It does." I nodded, not even trying to hide how much I loved the idea. "And you're family now, even without a name change. But…damn, I want that. Atlas Orion Seasons."

"See? You've spent all year convincing me I deserve a home, a family, love, and commitment, and I believe you. And us. I believe in us. We deserve this, Zeb."

"We do." I waited until he glanced over at me again. "Yes, yes, I'll marry you for New Year's."

"Good." Atlas exhaled like he'd held his breath for a fifty-yard swim. "God, I love you. Thank you for saying yes to my wild scheme."

"You were worried I might turn you down?" I tilted my head, examining him closer. Yep. In addition to the blush, he kept darting his eyes around, and his hands continued their nervous drumming. "Seriously?"

"Maybe a little worried I might be drinking champagne alone tonight."

"Like I'd let you drink alone." Traffic continued to plod forward, so I risked a quick kiss on his cheek. "And why the heck did we agree to work tomorrow? We better not show up with hangovers."

Atlas chuckled, his laugh much looser now that I'd agreed. "Nix will kill us if we're not there to taste the cranberry sauce."

"Taste." I held up my index finger. "No one's wearing it this year."

"I wouldn't mind." Atlas shrugged. "Look what it got me."

"Me. It got you me." I went ahead and slid the ring on. It fit perfectly because, of course, it did.

"Worth it. Totally worth every red berry." We both laughed before he pointed at the highway in front of us. "Hey, look, traffic is moving again."

"We're practically almost home." I grinned and looked down at my ring. It was heavy and cool, and I already loved the weight of it on my finger.

"I already am." Atlas's voice was so serious I glanced up. "My home is with you."

"Same." If the past year of long drives and long waits and learning to be a couple had shown me anything, it was that home was far less about Kringle's Crossing than I'd thought and far more about how I felt in Atlas's embrace. "I'm not sure who's gonna freak more, my fans or Aunt Lucy and Paige. They've all got holiday wedding ideas for days."

"I'm sure." Atlas took my hand, thumb tracing over the ring. "I'm ready for it."

"Good." I grinned as traffic zipped along. "It's our season after all."

Atlas grinned back even wider, eyes crinkling, so much love in his gaze that goosebumps popped up on my arms. "It's always our season."

Thirty-Five

ATLAS

The snowy solo drive to Kringle's Crossing on Christmas morning dragged on and on with none of the excitement of my Thanksgiving proposal. But it was all worth it when Gabe opened the side door of his house to let me in. Same house I'd visited hundreds of times as a teen and the same warm sensation in my chest, a feeling of rightness. *Homecoming.*

"Zeb doesn't know you're coming," Gabe whispered as he ushered me into their mudroom. The aroma of cinnamon rolls wafted in from the nearby kitchen, and happy voices sounded from beyond that, likely the living room. Gabe was in Christmas pajamas and big poofy slippers that matched the plaid print on his pants. The shirt spelled out *Papa Bear,* and I had a strong feeling Paige had been the one to pick his attire.

"Hope not." I quietly stamped my feet before removing my boots. I'd returned home long enough to shower, pull on jeans and a heavy sweater, and hit the road to Kringle's Crossing. Zeb had already been here much of the month, helping with the holiday rush, while I'd pulled a lot of long hours and two overseas trips. It had been a long month, little of it together, but it would all be worth it with my upcoming leave for the wedding and honeymoon. "He thinks my leave starts the thirtieth."

"And he for sure doesn't know about your traveling companion." Gabe gestured at my surprise for Zeb. Thank goodness my present was proving to be quiet and calm, doing little more than an enthusiastic tail wag and canine grin for Gabe while hanging back by my side. I'd bought him a Christmas-themed leash and collar adorned with snowflakes, and once I'd removed my outerwear, I knelt to add a big silver bow to his collar.

"Good dog," I whispered before standing back up. Not wanting the sound of the collar or nails on the hardwood floors to give the surprise away, I lifted him into my arms to follow Gabe into the main part of the house. The original Seasons home was a colonial farmhouse that had been updated, added onto, and renovated over the years.

"Now, to find your husband-to-be," Gabe said quietly as we passed through the friendly white kitchen with a big butcher block island and double farmhouse sink. He paused by the archway to the living room and gestured for me to take a peek.

The comfortable room with familiar maple pieces and homey colors was dominated by the large Christmas tree in the corner. A trash bag next to the tree held the evidence of the earlier festivities, and Aunt Lucy and Paige were slumped on opposite ends of the large couch, both looking exhausted in pajamas that matched Gabe's. However, my attention went straight to the floor in front of the couch.

The twins had taken their first steps over Thanksgiving weekend, and now the brand-new one-year-olds toddled around Zeb, who was sprawled on the rug, playing some sort of game where the babies raced around, over, and on him. The twins, with their wispy red hair, were in plaid sleepers while Zeb had an "Uncle Bear" shirt that matched Gabe's. Zeb had both babies giggling, and I couldn't help my happy sigh.

"Okay, he can have the Uncle of the Year title," I whispered to Gabe. "This year."

"It's not a competition." Gabe laughed a little too loud, and Zeb's head whirled around.

"Atlas!" He struggled to sit up, and his wide grin made the long drive, the favors I'd had to pull to get the time off, and every other sacrifice of the past year worth it. He was always so happy to see me, whether it had been fifteen minutes or two weeks, and I loved how full his joy made my heart. "You came."

"Of course I did." I chuckled as he rushed over to me, babies fast on his heels. They were walking so much more steadily now than a few weeks ago.

"Doggie!" Plum had been the first to talk, and her itty-bitty pigtails bounced as she pointed at my arms.

"And you brought a dog?" Zeb's eyes were even wider than the twins.

"Eh." I faked indifference. "We were short a ring bearer for the wedding."

"Hey there." Zeb bent slightly to take the dog from me and pet his head. "Sounds like Atlas is putting you to work already." Looking up at me, he asked, "Does he have a name?"

"The rescue shelter called him Snowy." I'd wanted the medium-sized dog for Zeb even before I'd seen the name, but it fit the dog and us perfectly. He was a mix of some sort with an Australian Shepherd face, an unusually pale coat, and the longer limbs of a golden retriever. "He's about to turn one. Rescue thinks he might even have a Christmas birthday. His first family got deployed overseas and worked with the rescue to find a new placement."

"He's perfect." Zeb glowed like the star on the top of the tree, eyes twinkling as he petted Snowy. He set the dog down so he could give me a tight hug. "Just like you."

"Awww." Paige left the couch to come admire the dog. "Welcome to the family, Snowy Seasons."

"I did promise you a home and dogs." My face heated from all the attention, but when Zeb rested his head on my shoulder, there was nowhere in the world I'd rather be.

"You did." Zeb gazed up at me with so much love and adoration it was a wonder my heart could hold it all.

"Hey, one of the neighbors put up a For Sale sign last week," Gabe added cheerfully. "Snowy's going to need a yard. Just saying."

"Let's worry about getting through the wedding first." Zeb laughed as he held up his hands before bending to pet the dog. The ring I'd given him as part of the Thanksgiving proposal caught the tree lights. Zeb hadn't removed it since he'd put it on, which I loved. "I still can't believe I—*we*—are getting married for New Year's."

Pine toddled closer and held up his arms, so I scooped him up. He patted my chin approvingly. "Unca."

"That's right!" Paige kissed the baby on the top of his head. "That's your Uncle Atlas."

"Welcome to the family, Atlas Orion Seasons." Zeb stood back up and kissed me softly. "This might be my favorite Christmas yet."

"Just wait till next year." I kissed him back. Last Christmas had been the best, then this year better, and I could already picture next year, packing Snowy up for the trek to Kringle's Crossing, adding to Zeb's ornament collection, pulling into that house Gabe mentioned, For Sale sign long gone, our own tree in the window, champagne chilling in the fridge… Yep. My favorite season would grow more and more magical with each passing year, and I couldn't wait to see it all.

❋

Dear readers,

If *Catered All the Way* left you in a holiday mood, I have several holiday stories in my backlist you may enjoy. And… I have a brand-new holiday romance for the 2024 holiday season. **Deck the Palms** stars two middle school teachers in over their heads in an opposites-attract, fish-out-of-water romance set in Hawaii. Turn the page for a sneak peek of Deck the Palms or preorder if here: https://readerlinks.com/l/4364998

Love,
Annabeth

Sneak Peek of Deck the Palms

NOLAN

Welcome to November, ohana!

It was lovely to see so many of our middle school family members at our Autumn Festival. Now, the countdown begins for our annual Lights Festival. Mrs. Crenshaw is on a medical leave of absence, but never fear! Our holiday extravaganza is in excellent hands...

I stared down at the colorful newsletter distributed to students during last period and sent to parents via email. As someone who'd enjoyed a rocky relationship with reviewers, I tried to believe any press was good press. However, Principal Alana was testing that belief by way overselling my talents for a job I'd only learned about twenty minutes prior.

"Are you sure you want a substitute in charge of something so important?" I asked Principal Alana. She had arrived at the choir room shortly after the final bell sounded, undoubtedly to prevent my escape with the students and ensure my attendance at the holiday festival planning meeting.

"First, you're not just a sub. You're a Broadway star." The principal was barely over five feet with long dark hair piled on her head. Many of the middle schoolers were bigger, and indeed, she didn't look much older than the eighth graders. However, the principal had a voice worthy of commanding a fleet. "You're exactly the shakeup this festival needs after years of the same script."

"Star might be pushing it," I said demurely. Sure, my resume was full of production credits, and if we counted Off-Off-Broadway, a few leading roles, but no one in New York would ever mistake me for a *star*. Perhaps things were different in Hawaii.

"Second, I'll be honest, we don't have a ton of other options." Principal Alana continued her forthright attack on my resistance. Unlike the cushy New York private high schools where I encountered stiff competition for my substitute teaching and voice lessons gigs, I'd apparently been the only applicant for the role of substitute choir director and drama teacher at this public arts magnet middle school. It was a sobering thought.

Impervious to my glum thoughts, Principal Alana plowed ahead. "Merry Winters will help, of course, but Merry lacks your flare. However, you can count on the industrial arts students to deliver whatever decorating vision the two of you arrive at."

Merry Winters. I immediately visualized the industrial arts teacher as a kind, gray-haired British hippy lady. Probably ever so slightly butch, what with the woodworking classes, but churning out domestic projects like cutting boards and candlestick holders. Good at set construction, but seeking the guidance of a plucky Broadway *star* for this holiday festival.

And yes, I was exactly vain enough to love that vision.

"Lucky for you, I'm a praise wh—junkie, and all that ego stroking worked." I winked at Principal Alana, narrowly avoiding calling myself a praise whore in front of my boss for the next two months. "Lead the way to this meeting."

"How was the first day of classes?" she asked as we navigated the wide hallway lined with lockers, artwork, rules and reminders, and varied club and activity announcements.

"Fine. Loving it here."

I delivered my lines crisply, with no hint of deceit. In reality, though, public middle school was way different from Upper Eastside high schools. No celebrity kids, no bodyguards lurking at the back of classrooms, no designer bags or gourmet lunch options, and definitely no ten-to-one student-to-teacher ratio to brag to the alums about. Instead, I'd had six periods of thirty to forty loud, rowdy tweens in barely controlled pandemonium. In fact, I'd narrowly avoided being locked out of my classroom by a pair of twin pranksters during first period. "Such spirited students."

"Wonderful. Did Dory leave you good notes?"

"Oh yes." More lies. Dory Crenshaw's notes for a substitute included video recommendations out of the 1950s, suggestions for classes no longer offered, information pertinent to the school's prior building, and very few real resources for the next two months. Naturally, the woman couldn't have predicted emergency hip surgery following a fall doing the Halloween Hula at the school event, but Dory sure could have left more help.

"Feel free to put your own spin on the classes," Principal Alana chirped. "I'm excited for some new material."

From what I understood, Dory Crenshaw had been

around since the arts-focused middle school achieved charter status in the nineties. Principal Alana was an alumnus of one of those early classes who'd shot up the teaching ranks to become principal of her old school. I liked her fresh ideas and enthusiasm because Dory's musical selections desperately needed to leave the stand-still-and-sing generation behind.

However, not everyone shared Principal Alana's desire to bring in new ideas.

"What do you mean we're not doing *Holly Holliday's Holiday Surprise?*" Belinda Masters had taught math longer than I'd been alive, and from her stony expression, she also hadn't smiled in nearly that long. "Parents look forward to that every year."

"Emphasis on *every* year, Belinda." Principal Alana released a long-suffering sigh. "Dory created that script thirty years ago, and it's barely been updated."

"That's the charm." Belinda gave a haughty sniff. With her long gray braid and pressed khaki shorts, she looked ready to lead an excursion for an Oahu bird-watching club, not unruly middle schoolers needing long-division help. "And what's this I hear about food trucks?"

"The festival needs to grow." The principal spread her palms wide. "We need the festival to be a big fundraiser for us this year. With budget cuts, we need the Lights Festival to fund spring field trips and cultural speakers. A fresh production, new sets, and, yes, new food options mean more tickets sold. The kids are counting on us."

"Trying something new isn't a terrible idea." Ken Kekoa was a round, affable fellow around fifty who gave off lounge singer vibes, but he was actually a well-regarded art teacher whom my nieces adored.

"Thank you, Ken. I appreciate the open mind." Principal Alana graced him with a wide smile, revealing her perfectly straight teeth. "I know Nolan and Merry—"

"Sorry, I'm late." A dude who had possibly wandered in from the nearest beach rushed into the room to take the open chair next to Principal Alana. Sandy-blond hair a good year past a trim, scruffy stubble, faded surfer board shorts, and a paint-stained T-shirt added to his haphazard vibe. "Did I hear my name?"

"You did." Principal Alana beamed while I inwardly groaned. Like any good actor, though, I schooled my expression as she made introductions. "Merrick Winters, meet Nolan Bell. He'll be in charge of this year's holiday production for the Lights Festival. You'll still handle all the lights and sets, of course."

"Of course." Merrick "Merry" Winters was neither British nor elderly nor a lady. And with a voice drier than week-old sand in a bucket, he clearly wasn't thrilled about working with me.

"Like I was telling Ken, we'll all need to work together." Principal Alana either hadn't picked up on Merry's hostile glare or had decided to plunge ahead in her usual fearless style. She smiled encouragingly at Merry. "I know you and Nolan will appreciate the help from the students, and you'll be the perfect right-hand man for Nolan in coordinating everything."

"Uh-huh." Merry sounded far from convinced as he leaned back in his ancient plastic chair, which let out an ominous creak.

"Just tell me what you need painted." Ken motioned at both Merry and me. "But I'm going to leave the festival details to you both. I've got to run to my second job."

"Ken works evenings as a host at a popular resort restaurant," Principal Alana explained. "Budget cuts state-wide and rising housing prices mean more and more of us working second and third jobs. They've got two in college and one in high school. It's hard to make it as a two-teacher family these days."

"Or as a struggling actor." My voice was bright, but Merry remained anything but as he glowered at me.

"I'm sure. You're the Bell sisters' uncle from New York?" His brown eyes peered sharply into mine. "The famous Broadway dude?"

"You've heard about me?" I couldn't help preening. And clearly, I'd oversold the whole *star* thing to more than Principal Alana.

"Yep." Merry's tight nod deflated what was left of my ego. "You're the fun uncle. What did they call you? The Funcle?"

Merry made it sound like a rash in a personal area rather than a cute inside joke between me and my favorite sister-in-law.

"I *am* the fun uncle. And the Guncle." I adopted a proudly defiant tone. Might as well toss the gay uncle part out there right now. "And the little brother who can't say no when his big, bad lieutenant colonel bro asks for a favor."

As much as I liked being an uncle and adored my two nieces and new nephew, I was only in Hawaii because Craig had summoned me. And for all we were total opposites as adults, my heart still remembered him as the big brother who'd scared away all the monsters under my bed and defended me from school bullies.

"Bet you can't wait to get back to Manhattan." There was a challenge in Merry's tone that I had to work to not take personally.

"I sublet my studio through the end of the year. I'm

CATERED ALL THE WAY

kind of stuck, but I'm not complaining." More lies. I'd done nothing but complain in texts to my theater friends about the humidity, the sand in strange places, the lack of a social life, the unreliability of the public transit options, and more. But for Merry, I smiled serenely. "I'm happy to help with Craig and Cara's new baby and the girls."

"How is the baby?" Principal Alana jumped in before Merry could continue whatever this cross-examination was. "I heard Cara delivered him early."

"Yes, that's a big part of why Craig sent for me." For all my excellent imagination, I didn't harbor many illusions. Craig was deployed, leading some army mission, and if he'd had any chance of making it home before his wife had their surprise third baby, he wouldn't have called on his flighty younger brother for help. "The baby came at thirty-four weeks in a dramatic fashion. Takes after his uncle." Principal Alana laughed. Merry didn't. Undeterred, I continued, "Noah Craig is out of the NICU now and home. He's still teeny, but he's doing great."

"Wonderful. Love the name," the principal enthused. It wasn't exactly the same as having a namesake, and everyone kept calling Noah Craig Baby, but I was awfully proud of the little guy nonetheless. "And I know you will make the whole family proud of you with this task for the school as well."

Way to lay the pressure on a little more. I grimaced, trying to figure out how to tell her to lower her expectations. Luckily, the ill-tempered Belinda saved me from a reply, shuffling her papers and various tote bags on her way out the door.

"I have to head out as well. At least *try* to have some of the elements our Anuenue community has come to expect." Belinda's glare was almost as poisonous as Merry's. The school was named after the Hawaiian word for rainbow, but there was little sunny about my reception thus far.

"Sorry. Belinda's...*passionate* about our history. I'm sure whatever you come up with will be perfect." Principal Alana managed to never waver from her chipper tone as she stood up from the table. "And with that, I'm going to leave you and Merry to get to know each other and devise a plan while I make some phone calls."

"More disciplinary issues?" Merry groaned. "Please tell me I'm not on the naughty list."

"Not this time." She laughed lightly. "Legend and Ryder managed to survive the entire day."

"Legend and Ryder are yours?" I blinked. Those were the identical twin pranksters from first period. I knew I should have sent them to the office, but I hadn't wanted to make a fuss fifteen minutes into my new job. "You're a dad?"

Merry seemed way too young and carefree to be a dad, but he nodded. "Yep. I trust they weren't too much trouble."

"Perfect angels," I lied through my best smile. *Never let the audience see you sweat.* And precisely how I would put together an entire holiday festival in six weeks with Merry, who seemed to hate me on sight, remained to be seen.

❄

Curious to know what happens next with Nolan, Merry, and the Lights Festival performance? Preorder *Deck the Palms* here: https://readerlinks.com/l/4364998. Available December 4, 2024!

Also By Annabeth Albert

Amazon Author Page
Many titles also in audio and available from other retailers!

Stand-Alone Holiday Titles :

- Better Not Pout
- Mr. Right Now
- The Geek Who Saved Christmas
- Catered All the Way
- Deck the Palms

Mount Hope Series

- Up All Night
- Off the Clock
- On the Edge
- Over and Above

Safe Harbor Series

ALSO BY ANNABETH ALBERT

- Bring Me Home
- Make Me Stay
- Find Me Worthy

A-List Security Series

- Tough Luck
- Hard Job
- Bad Deal
- Hard Job

Rainbow Cove Series

- Trust with a Chaser
- Tender with a Twist
- Lumber Jacked
- Hope on the Rocks

#Gaymers Series

- Status Update
- Beta Test
- Connection Error

Out of Uniform Series

- Off Base
- At Attention
- On Point
- Wheels Up
- Squared Away
- Tight Quarters
- Rough Terrain

ALSO BY ANNABETH ALBERT

Frozen Hearts Series

- Arctic Sun
- Arctic Wild
- Arctic Heat

Hotshots Series

- Burn Zone
- High Heat
- Feel the Fire
- Up in Smoke

Shore Leave Series

- Sailor Proof
- Sink or Swim

Perfect Harmony Series

- Treble Maker
- Love Me Tenor
- All Note Long

Portland Heat Series

- Served Hot
- Baked Fresh
- Delivered Fast
- Knit Tight
- Wrapped Together
- Danced Close

ALSO BY ANNABETH ALBERT

True Colors Series

- Conventionally Yours
- Out of Character

Other Stand-Alone Titles

- Resilient Heart
- Winning Bracket
- Save the Date
- Level Up
- Sergeant Delicious
- Cup of Joe
- Featherbed

About Annabeth Albert

Annabeth Albert grew up sneaking romance novels under the bed covers. Now, she devours all subgenres of romance out in the open—no flashlights required! When she's not adding to her keeper shelf, she's a multi-published Pacific Northwest romance writer.

Emotionally complex, sexy, and funny stories are her favorites both to read and to write. Fans of quirky, Oregon-set books as well as those who enjoy heroes in uniform will want to check out her many fan-favorite and critically acclaimed series. Many titles are also in audio! Her fan group Annabeth's Angels on Facebook is the best place for bonus content and more! Website: www.annabethal bert.com

Contact & Media Info:

- facebook.com/annabethalbert
- x.com/AnnabethAlbert
- instagram.com/annabeth_albert
- amazon.com/Annabeth/e/B00LYFFAZK
- bookbub.com/authors/annabeth-albert

Acknowledgments

Like so many of my books, CATERED ALL THE WAY centers around found family. Atlas needs a family and a place to call home, and he finds one with the Seasons. I dedicated this book to Abbie Nicole because kinship means so much more than blood. I am blessed with so many friends who are siblings of my heart—Katie, Kayce, Wendy, Rae, Edie, and everyone else who makes my world so much richer.

My therapist likely won't see this, but as I wouldn't have gotten a draft without the best therapist in the world, I would be remiss not to thank the power of good mental health help. If you too are struggling in this crazy world, know the value of seeking and getting help. It's worth it. My life is immeasurably enriched because of readers like you and the support from the romancelandia community. Never doubt that your purchases, borrows, and support make a huge difference in the lives of authors, now more than ever. I'm grateful for each and every one of you. If you loved this book, please tell a friend!

A huge thank you as well to Lori at Jan's Paperbacks. She makes providing signed copies to my readers so painless, and she's an amazing beacon in the romance community to boot! Her tireless advocacy for romance, queer fiction, and small businesses inspires me.

Lauren Dombrowski and Reese Dante made my cover dreams come true. Lauren's illustration is particularly perfect for this book, and I'm honored to have their work on my cover. Alexander Cendese is on the microphone for this audio and deserves a huge thank you for short-notice availability and awesome work!

I couldn't have finished this book without my writing sprint buddies, my author friends, my beloved readers, my kids, real life friends, and the rest of the cheering squad pushing me on.